TEXAS AND THE WAR

Blue arrived at the Miles ranch a week later, tired, hungry, and thirsty.

"Littleton Blue?" Mort Miles asked, when Litt introduced himself, "of course we know who you are. Fought right alongside Ben. He mentioned your name in one of his letters, said he probably owed you for saving his life."

"Yes, sir," Blue said, "that's me. Is Ben around?"

"I hate being the one to tell you this, son," Mort said, taking charge of Blue's animals and leading them toward the watering trough, "but Ben didn't make it. We got word right before Christmas that he was killed somewhere around Petersburg." Litt stood very still, staring at the ground as the news soaked in, visions of the reckless young soldier dancing before his eyes. Reckless to the point of being foolish, some had said.

Other books by **Doug Bowman**
from Tom Doherty Associates

Gannon
Sam Curtain

THE
THREE LIVES
OF LITTLETON BLUE

DOUG BOWMAN

A TOM DOHERTY ASSOCIATES BOOK
NEW YORK

This is a work of fiction. All the characters and events portrayed in this book are fictitious, and any resemblance to real people or events is purely coincidental.

THE THREE LIVES OF LITTLETON BLUE

Copyright © 1996 by Doug Bowman

Cover art by Tim Newsom

A Forge Book
Published by Tom Doherty Associates, Inc.
175 Fifth Avenue
New York, NY 10010

Forge ® is a registered trademark of Tom Doherty Associates, Inc.

ISBN: 0-812-53454-9

First edition: October 1996

Printed in the United States of America

0   9   8   7   6   5   4   3   2   1

In memory of my departed siblings: Clara, Charles, Buddy, Wayne, and Phil.

1

L ord, we're a-givin' ya back the bidy o' this pore soul," the old preacher was saying, as he stood over the last of the newly occupied graves. "They say his name wuz Littleton Blue. Prob'ly never done a wrong thang in his life, prob'ly jist a God-fearin' Southern boy that done his part."

"Amen!" several members of the congregation shouted in unison.

"Now, Lord," the preacher continued, "I ain't a-sayin' that he never kilt nobody. What I am a-sayin' is that they wuz all on th' other side, an' we all know that shootin' Yankees don't count ag'inst a man. Says so right here in th' Book, somewhur." He held his Bible aloft, riffling its pages with his thumb.

"Amen!" the congregation repeated.

The grave was filled in and patted down by young boys with shovels, and the people returned to their respective homes. Thus the little churchyard in western Virginia became the final resting place for six Confederate soldiers who were among the last few men killed in the American Civil War. The date was April 8, 1865, and tomorrow General Lee would surrender his ragged army to General Grant.

Once he had been forced to abandon both Petersburg and Richmond, Lee had retreated westward, hoping to join with the Confederate troops of Joseph Johnston in North Carolina. He found that his way was blocked by Union forces, however, and after fighting several running battles, the decision was made to surrender.

Two members of Sage Hill Church had found the bodies of the six soldiers, left where they fell by a fast-moving company of Confederates who were running for their very lives. The decision was quickly made to bury the fallen men in the church cemetery the following morning.

The funeral of Littleton Blue was many years premature, however, for though he had received a decent burial, a grave covered with flowers and a spoken eulogy of sorts, he was not in that hole. He was at this very moment lying behind a log thirty miles to the east, keeping his head down and waiting for confirmation that Lee had surrendered. Then, and only then, could he return unmolested to his South Carolina home.

The true name of the soldier who had been buried in Blue's stead would probably never be known. The luckless young man had been identified only by a letter that he carried in his pocket. The letter had been lost by Littleton Blue several days earlier.

Upon General Lee's surrender, General Grant had ordered General Sheridan to see that the starving Confederates received an abundance of food, and they had indeed eaten well for the past three days. Today was April 12, and the time had come to surrender weapons.

All morning long the ragged Southern divisions came into the field. Before the watchful eyes of Union officers, each Rebel soldier affixed his bayonet, then stepped forward and laid his rifle on the huge stack, followed by his cartridge box. Then, with much anguish, and some men crying unabashedly, the Confederate flags, all battle-worn and some bloodstained, were carefully folded and laid down. The Army of Northern Virginia was no more, and indeed the Confederate States of America would soon cease to exist.

Grant allowed the Confederate officers to retain their sidearms, as well as their private baggage. When informed by General Lee that, unlike the Union soldiers, the men of the Southern army owned the horses and mules they rode, Grant acquiesced further. He stated that he had not known that the soldiers of the South rode their own animals. Then, either out of compassion or because he already had his eye on the White House, Grant made another decision: Any Southern soldier now in possession of an animal could keep it, for it would be needed for spring planting.

Though Littleton Blue was unarmed when he headed south, he would not be for long. General Lee's impending surrender had become common knowledge along the line several days prior to the actual happening, and many of the Southern soldiers had begun to stash things against the day when they would be left with only the shirts on their backs. Littleton

Blue was among them. During the final days of fighting he had hidden the rifle and cartridge box of a fallen comrade in a hollow log, knowing that his own weapon would be taken from him when the surrender became final.

Today, not far from the little churchyard that had supposedly become his final resting place, he retrieved the rifle and cartridge box, then rode south on a twenty-year-old mare named Nellie.

At six-foot-four and a hundred thirty-five pounds, the young man was a mere shadow of his former self, and could count on his fingers the times when he had actually sat down to a decent meal during the past year. He had lived mostly on hardtack and parched corn, usually eaten on the run, while his weight dwindled by more than seventy pounds.

Nellie had fared no better, losing at least two hundred pounds during the campaign. Always on the move, the horses were seldom allowed to graze all day or all night, and on occasions when good grass could be found, it could rarely be held for long. Many was the time when Nellie had fought the bit and Blue literally had to whip her away from her grazing. Today, on his way south to Orangeburg, he set a slow and deliberate pace, allowing the faithful animal to graze as much as she wanted. He would also eat well himself, for he had stolen a sack of food from the Yankees.

On the first night of his journey he camped on the north bank of Sandy Creek, where it emptied into the Banister River. He picketed Nellie on good grazing, then built a small fire. He had no cooking utensils, but had retained his drinking cup and spoon, as well as his folding knife. When the fire began to die, he laid three potatoes on the gray coals, covering them with hot ashes. Supper would be ready in half an hour.

Later, lying on his bed of leaves, he was thinking of home, and expecting the worst. He knew from word of mouth, as well as from the few newspapers he had read, that Sherman's march through South Carolina had been devastating. The city of Columbia had been reduced to ashes, and Blue had no reason to believe that the small town of Orangeburg, which lay directly in Sherman's path, had not suffered a similar fate.

On one of the propaganda sheets that were systematically passed up and down the Southern lines, Blue had read that not one male had been left alive in Sherman's wake, and that all females had been beaten and raped. He could only hope that Uncle Charley and Aunt Effie had been spared, and that his sister, Roberta, who was one year younger than himself, had not been molested.

Littleton and Roberta had been brought into the world by Mary and Walter Blue, who had dumped the children on Mary's brother, Charley Mangrum, at the respective ages of six and five. The couple then sailed for Germany, never to be heard from again. Charley and Effie Mangrum raised the children on their small farm and saw that they received an education.

Though the children had wanted many things that they never got, Uncle Charley had seen to their physical needs in an adequate fashion, working from daylight till dark as he scratched a living from the thirty acres left to him by his father. And he had done it all while dragging about on a wooden leg that he had made himself. Many were the times that the children had watched Aunt Effie bathe his blistered, bleeding stump with liniments and salves, brought on by his sometimes futile effort to keep up with the fast-walking plow horse. Eventually, Uncle Charley had partially remedied the situation by trading the horse for an older, slow-walking mule.

Young Littleton stood half a head taller than other boys his age, and established himself early on as one not to be trifled with. All of the would-be school bullies quickly learned that picking on Littleton Blue or his sister was a sure way to get clobbered. Though Roberta had never fought anyone in her life, she usually stayed close to her brother when other children were around, for she knew that he would be quick to defend her.

Roberta had just turned sixteen when Littleton rode away to join the Army of Virginia, and he had heard her described by more than one person as the most beautiful girl in the county. He supposed it might be so, for with her well-turned figure, long, wavy hair the color of corn silks, and copper-colored eyes as big as quarters, she was a creature that even a brother could find fascinating.

Littleton had often been told that he was the spit and image of his father, a man he remembered only vaguely. With dark, curly hair and dark complexion, a straight, well-shaped nose, and wide, firm mouth, young Blue's face looked as though it might have been chiseled from stone. Handsome though his face was, it might have gone unnoticed by some except for the eyes. Seated beneath heavy brows, his eyes were the clearest of azure blue, seeming to have a life of their own as they darted about. The eyes went unnoticed by no one, especially the opposite sex.

Like his father, Littleton was broad at the shoulder and narrow at the hip, with long, muscular arms and legs. He had stood six feet tall on his fifteenth birthday, and was still growing to this very day. He would be twenty years old at the end of next week, and was hoping to celebrate his birthday at home. As his campfire died on its own, he pulled some more leaves under his body and was asleep quickly.

It was now the first week in May, and Blue's trip south had taken longer than he had anticipated. Nellie had pulled up lame, and there was no course but to wait for her leg to heal. He had turned twenty years old in a dry creek bed in North Carolina, having a baked potato and half of a possum for his birthday dinner.

Today, sitting astride Nellie and gazing at the ruins that had once been the beautiful city of Columbia, the full realization of what it was like to be conquered both physically and mentally came home to him. Few buildings were left standing, and Blue could see none that were undamaged. A few of the fires had been put out even as the Union soldiers were leaving town, and the occupants had patched up their homes to livable status again. Others lived anywhere they could among the ruins, or out in open fields.

Recognizing Blue as a returning Confederate soldier, most folks spoke to him with reverence, and some of the older women cried as they asked the Lord to bless him. Seeing the dilapidated condition of his footwear, one woman offered him a pair of new shoes that had belonged to her now-dead husband. After being told that the shoes were size twelve, he happily accepted them, discarding his worn-out footwear before her very eyes.

Another woman who stood nearby produced a denim shirt, and yet another handed him a new pair of overalls. There would be no problem with a fit on the overalls, any discrepancy in length could be adjusted with the galluses. After accepting a dipper of cold water, he spoke to one of the women.

"Any word on how it went over at Orangeburg?"

"The same way it went right here," she answered. "Went up in smoke." Nodding, he reined Nellie south and kicked her to a trot. He soon turned slightly west, away from the path that had been taken by Sherman's sixty-two thousand troops. The mare would need some grass on the two-day ride home, and there was none to be had anywhere near the road. Every living thing within a mile-wide swath had been eaten or trampled, and the earth scarred to a point that it would be several years in renewing itself. He rode till sundown, then camped near good grass on the North Fork of the Edisto River.

Nellie quickened her step the following afternoon, and Littleton wondered if, considering all that she had been through, she actually realized that she was on familiar terrain. His question was answered a few minutes later. Of her own free will, the mare broke into a fast trot. No doubt about it, Nellie knew that she was finally home again.

Blue sat at the edge of the clearing for quite some time, staring at the place that he had called home for most of his life. The unpainted, clapboard house was still standing. The barn and crib were also still in place, though it looked as though someone had torched the chicken house and pigpen. As he rode forward he could see Aunt Effie standing in the yard, one hand shading her eyes from the sun as she stared at the approaching rider.

"Is that you, Litt?" she yelled when he was forty feet away. He dismounted and ran the rest of the way.

"It sure is, Aunt Effie," he said, wrapping his long arms around her frail body.

"Lordy be," she said softly, tears running down her bony cheeks. "I didn't have no way of knowing if you made it or not. Lordy, this is a good day." He continued to hold her for a long time, then led her to the edge of the porch, where they sat down.

"Uncle Charley and Roberta all right?" he asked.

"Charley's dead, Litt, Yankees killed him right out there at the pigpen. He's buried out behind what used to be the cabbage patch." The lady looked away quickly, as if trying to hide the pain in her eyes.

Staring between his knees at the ground, Blue spoke softly. "Why in the world would they kill Uncle Charley? That man wouldn't have hurt a fly."

"Oh, yes, he would, too," she said quickly. "Fought 'em tooth and nail when they commenced to butcher our hogs. One of the sons of bitches hit him in the face with a rifle butt and broke his neck, then went right on butchering the hogs. They killed the milch cow too, then caught up all the chickens and burned the chicken house. Tore down the pigpen and used the planks for their cooking fires. They camped right out yonder in that field for three days and nights."

"Where's Roberta?" he asked. "She all right?" His question was ignored. The lady stretched her arms above her head and let out a deep sigh, then changed the subject.

"I thought that I recognized Nellie right away coming down that road a while ago, but I wasn't sure about you; you've fell off so much since you left. I tell you—"

"Where's Roberta, Aunt Effie?" he interrupted. She moved directly in front of him, looking him straight in the eye.

"I can tell you all about Roberta," she said, "but

knowing how close the two of you were, I ain't for certain that you're ready to listen to it."

"Tell me anyway," he said.

"Your sister took up with the Yankees," she said, continuing to hold his eye, "just like a common whore." Something inside him wanted to refute what he was being told, but he knew his aunt well enough to know that he was being served the plain, unembellished truth.

"I tell you, Litt, you should have seen her shaking her ass and flirting with 'em, riding around in that field on their horses and laughing like a kid with a new toy.

"She laid up with 'em for two straight nights out there in that ditch, probably cooking our very own chickens for the sons of bitches. In a way I'm glad your uncle Charley wasn't around to see it, 'cause it just might have killed him anyway.

"I mean, they didn't drag her down there, neither, Litt, she went on her own. I stood right there at that window and watched her doing things for 'em all day, kissing on 'em and such. Lord only knows what all she did for 'em at night. And she was liking it, Litt, you could tell by just looking at her.

"That last day she came up here to the house on the arm of a damn Yankee lieutenant to get the rest of her clothes. Didn't say a damn word to me, not that it would have done her any good. They left here riding double on a high-stepping roan, and she never looked back."

Rising to his feet, Litt began to walk around the yard. He was thinking of all the good times they had shared growing up on the farm. Roberta had been his friend, his buddy, and they had kept few secrets from each other. The newfound knowledge that his beautiful, honey-haired sister had been sleeping with Union soldiers even as he had been fighting them in Virginia, was indeed a bitter pill to swallow.

"Guess you're sorry now that you pulled her out of the deep end of that swimming hole," Effie said over her shoulder. "Remember that day when she was going down for the third time? Ain't you sorry?"

"No," he answered, continuing to walk around. He held no ill will in his heart for his sister, but he never wanted to see her again. Roberta had made her bed.

He unsaddled Nellie and picketed her on good grass a hundred yards from the house. There was no pasture as such, for the Yankees had used the posts and rails for their fires. The barn had also been ransacked for anything that would burn. Every feeding trough and grain bin had been carted away, and dozens of loose boards had been ripped from the building. As he stood in the doorway taking in the scene, Litt wanted to believe that Roberta had been the prime reason the barn, and indeed the house, had been left standing. He said as much to his aunt when he returned to the house.

"I don't give a damn if she did ask 'em not to burn us plumb out," Effie said loudly. "That don't in no way excuse her other actions. I mean, you should have seen her strutting around, hanging onto that damn Yankee. Like she was afraid he was gonna get away or something."

"I'm glad I didn't see it, Aunt Effie," he said, heading for the back room to try on the new clothing given him by the women of Columbia. When he emerged from the room he had discarded his Confederate clothing once and for all. Finding that the shirt was several inches too short in the sleeves, he had used his folding knife to turn it into a short-sleeved shirt. The overalls would fit well enough once he regained enough weight to fill out the seat. The thought reminded him that he was hungry.

"Have you got any food, Aunt Effie?" he asked.

"Ain't got no whole bunch of choices," she said, rising from the table. "Got plenty of turnips and cornbread, ain't never heard of nobody starving on that."

The food was served an hour later, along with cool water from the well. It was a meal that, many times over the past three years, Litt had thought he would never live to eat. He enjoyed it thoroughly, and ate everything but the pot.

"What are you gonna do now, Aunt Effie?" he asked when they had resettled on the front porch.

"Gonna go up to Ridge Spring and live with Caleb," she said. "They didn't get hit near as hard as we did. He was down here two months ago; fact is, he's the one that brought me that cornmeal. He tried to get me to go back with him then, but I'd already heard that the war was about over. I told him I'd stay around here to see if you made it back. I really didn't expect you, Litt, if you want to know the truth of it. The Yankees told us that every Southerner who rode off to Virginia had been killed."

"They just wanted to inflict some more pain on you, Aunt Effie," he said. "They especially hated the people of South Carolina, because they think we started the war." He walked into the field, pulled the pin on Nellie's picket rope and moved her to new grass. Then, rejoining his aunt on the porch, he spoke softly.

"When do you plan to move up to Uncle Caleb's place?"

"Why, guess I'll be leaving tomorrow. Ain't no use in putting it off. You can have what's left of this damn place if you want it, and I'll put that in writing."

"Don't want it, Aunt Effie," he said, staring down the red clay hillside. "I served in the army with several boys from Texas, and the things they told me . . . well, I've just got to go and see it for myself." She clapped her hands together several times in a feeble effort at applause.

"Probably the best damn decision you ever made, Litt. A young man like you, who ain't afraid of hard work, should do mighty well out there." He walked up and down the porch for a few minutes, then spoke again, saying, "All right, then, it's settled. Tomorrow morning I'll put you on Nellie and take you up to Ridge Spring. You'll have to rig yourself up some way of sleeping on the ground, 'cause it'll take two days to make it."

"I know," she said. "I'll be ready."

As Litt had predicted, the trip to Ridge Spring took two days. Though frail and getting on in years, Aunt Effie was tough, and did not complain once. Litt, however, arrived with several blisters on his feet from breaking in the new shoes. A few times he had stopped and drained the blisters with his knife, bathing his feet in the cold water of fast-moving streams. Otherwise, there was no help for it, for Nellie was not yet strong enough to carry double for sixty miles.

Caleb Moore was Aunt Effie's oldest brother, and though not actually related to Littleton Blue, he had always treated the youngster as blood kin, and had been addressed as "Uncle" Caleb right from the start. Tonight the old man was hugging Litt like a long-lost son, his gray eyes growing misty.

"We've missed you and prayed for you, son," he was saying in a raspy voice, "and it's so good to have you back. I know you've been to what must have seemed like the bottomest pits of hell, but you're back now. Most of the boys we knew around here didn't make it." Caleb directed one of his farm hands to care for Nellie, shaking his head at her emaciated condition. Then he invited the tired travelers to supper, for the table was already set.

"That's the best eating I've had since the last time I was here, Aunt Hilda," Litt said to Caleb's wife when he had finished his meal.

"You ain't done, yet," she said, placing a quarter of an apple pie before him. "We've got to put some meat back on them bones." Saying no more, Litt ate the pie.

Later, they sat on the porch talking till late in the night, their conversation at times being almost drowned out by crickets, tree frogs, and whippoorwills. When it became obvious that Litt did not like talking about the war, the questions ceased. When told by his sister that Litt was about to head for Texas, Caleb had much to say.

"Of course, I don't know exactly how it really is out there," he said, rocking back and forth in his cane-bottom chair, " 'cause I ain't been. But from what I've heard, I'd say you're doing the right thing.

"I believe they've got a lot of the Indian problems cleared up, and I hear you can buy good land awful cheap. I had a fellow tell me once that it was there just for the taking if a man really wanted to put down some roots.

"Of course, that old mare of yours ain't in no shape to go nowhere; miracle she got you here. It'll take at least six months of loafing and grazing to straighten her out, and she ought to be retired, like any other old war veteran.

"Just leave her in the pasture, and I'll let you take

Ike and a pack mule. Ike's a good solid eight-year-old, and he'll take you out there at a fast trot and be no worse for the wear."

"I don't know of any reason why I'd need a pack mule, Uncle Caleb," Litt said. "I don't have anything to pack."

"You will have," Caleb said. "Now, you just keep listening. I intend to see that you've got everything you need. The Yankees didn't clean us out like they did a lot of other people. Of course, that's only because they didn't find us. If they had, we'd probably be sitting here hungry right now."

Uncle Caleb had freed his six slaves quite some time ago, and four of them had gone north. Two had remained, however, agreeing to work as hired hands for room and board and whatever other compensation Caleb could afford to pay them. Both of the ex-slaves were getting on in years, and would have found beginning a new life of independence a difficult road to travel. They seemed happy with their new hired-hand status, and they sang and laughed a lot.

Litt spent the next several days putting together the things he would need for his journey, as well as working himself into the correct frame of mind. Uncle Caleb had been true to his word. In addition to supplying everything Litt would need for the trail, the old man had given him a leather pouch containing enough gold to cover his expenses and to provide a small stake when he reached his destination.

Litt had given much thought to the planning of his route. Remembering that his Texas friends had told him to beware of Mississippi's lowlands and that the marshes of Louisiana were always difficult and sometimes impossible to cross, he chose a more northerly route, through Arkansas.

Then, on the thirtieth day of May, he boarded Ike and took up the slack in the pack mule's lead rope. After saying his good-byes to the Moores and Aunt Effie, he pointed the horse west, waving for a final time as he rode out of sight.

Though Littleton Blue would never know it, on this very day his name was being engraved on a tombstone in western Virginia.

2

It was now the middle of July, and Blue had reached the Ouachita River in southern Arkansas. Though the time of day was only a little past noon, he decided to camp on the east bank of the river. He had been on the move since well before daybreak, and his animals needed to rest and graze for the remainder of the day and night.

Because he had not yet selected a campsite, he simply unburdened his pack mule and tied it to a tree limb. He would seek out the proper location for his campfire later. Then he rode downriver in search of game, for he was very hungry. He did not care to devote the time involved in boiling a pot of beans, broiled meat was both tastier and quicker.

Half an hour later, he shot a small fawn and laid the

carcass across his saddle. Then, rethinking the situation, he dropped the deer to the ground and dismounted. He would butcher it on the spot, build a fire, and satisfy his hunger. No use worrying about the mule, he would get it after he had eaten, then camp right here. Anyway, he had both salt and pepper in his saddlebag. Scrounging around for dead wood, he soon had a fire going. He would allow the flames to burn down while he dressed out the fawn, then broil his meat over the gray coals.

An hour later he sat beside the dying fire, sipping cool water from the river and wolfing down large chunks of tender venison. He had hung the remainder of the carcass in the fork of a small tree, for his supper would be more of the same. When he had eaten his fill, he mounted his horse and rode upriver to retrieve his pack mule.

Just short of the clearing, he stopped the horse suddenly, staring straight ahead. He sat very still for a long time, his ears listening for the slightest sound. The mule was nowhere to be seen. He knew immediately that someone had taken the animal, for he was certain that he had tied a knot that would not slip. Besides, the mule's pack that had been left beside the tree was also missing.

After a while, gun in hand, Blue eased his horse forward. The tracks told the story: Two men had fitted the pack to the mule's back and led the animal upriver. It appeared that both men were afoot and the mule had been led away at a trot.

Blue was back in the saddle quickly. He first thought about circling the men and waiting for them a few miles up the river. He discarded the idea, however, for there was a strong chance that the men would eventually cast the pack aside, mount the mule double, and ford the river. His only choice was to follow the tracks, ever mindful of a possible ambush.

He followed the trail with no difficulty, for he was an excellent tracker with much experience, most of it gained while tracking animals much smaller than a mule or a man. As he neared a hilltop half a dozen miles upriver, he received another surprise: The men had slowed their pace considerably, even sitting down and eating two small cans of tomatoes from the pack. The empty cans had been discarded beside the trail.

Sometimes passing through thickets so dense that he had to dismount and lead his horse, Blue continued to move north, losing the trail a few times, but never for long. The shod hoofprints of the mule were easy enough to follow most of the time.

It was now sunset, and he knew that he was not going to overtake the men this day. He selected a small spring as a campsite. When he had watered, unsaddled, and picketed Ike on good grass, he set about making himself a bed of leaves. He could only hope that the men he was trailing would do the same, for if they continued to move throughout the night they would probably be lost to him forever.

He had been lying on the bed for close to an hour waiting for the sleep that would not come, when he thought he saw a flicker of light to the north. He continued to stare in the same direction for a long time, but saw nothing else. Then, there it was again. The flicker soon turned into a steady glimmer that was undoubtedly a campfire. Somewhere near the top of the hill, Blue decided, gauging the distance to be about two miles. He had now slipped on his boots, and stood staring at the glimmer that had now escalated to an open flame.

He knew that he was going to investigate the fire,

although he supposed that it had been built by someone who was just passing through. Nobody who was
leading an animal that had been stolen only a few
hours ago would build a fire . . . would they? Remembering that they had casually sat down and eaten two
cans of his tomatoes, he decided that they just might.

He left Ike on his picket, for though he was a good,
strong horse, he was overly clumsy. Blue would do his
stalking on foot. Taking one last look at the fire, and
trying to figure the lay of the land in between, he
moved off into the night. He covered the first mile at a
fast trot, for he was thinking that the men might only
make coffee or heat up something, then extinguish the
fire.

An hour later, after having waded two creeks, he
stood behind a giant oak, less than a hundred yards
from the fire. He had stumbled over a log, bruising his
knee badly, as well as suffering numerous lacerations
on his face and arms from collisions with unseen
branches and briars. He stood very quietly, straining
his ears. He could hear the men talking, but could not
make out what they were saying. Then, bending at the
waist, he crept forward, taking one step and waiting
two. Using a degree of stealth that had filled his pot
many times as a youngster in South Carolina, he was
soon behind a clump of bushes, no more than forty
feet from the camp.

Two bearded men lay on their elbows before the
fire, sipping coffee from tin cups. A rifle lay on the
ground beside each man. Blue's yellow mule was tied
to a sapling no more than twenty feet away. He stared
at the thieves disgustedly, as one man moved to the
fire and refilled his cup. Then, reseating himself, the
man said with a smirk,

"I'd shore like ta seen th' look on 'at joker's face when he found out he didn't have no mule."

"Yeah," the other answered, laughing loudly. "Me, too." Blue waited no longer.

"Well, here's the face," he said, stepping into the firelight. "Take a quick look, 'cause that's all you're gonna get." Not waiting to see if they would go for their rifles, he fired twice, killing each man instantly. They fell in a heap, eyes staring at the sky glassily. Blue had seen the same picture many times during the recent war. He had felt no empathy then, nor did he now. The sons of bitches had stolen his mule and eaten his tomatoes, and had paid the going price.

Blue touched neither the men nor their belongings. After refitting his pack to the back of the mule, he kicked dirt over the fire and led the animal down the hillside. An hour later, he picketed the mule alongside his saddle horse and returned to the bed of leaves he had fashioned earlier.

He slept till long after sunup, for he had been very tired. When he had pulled on his boots and moved to a standing position, his eyes were drawn to the many buzzards that were already flying above the hilltop, circling ever lower with each pass. The scavengers' early-morning search for breakfast had been rewarded.

He forded the Ouachita an hour later and traveled in a southwesterly direction, for he was several miles north of his intended route. The remainder of the fawn he had shot yesterday would be left in the fork of the tree for any animal who could climb and get it. Blue would have been reluctant to eat the meat anyway, for the afternoon and night had been extremely hot.

After a few hours he pointed his horse due west, knowing it would lead him straight to Texas. When he reached a small spring, he put his animals on good grass and built a fire. When he had sliced several potatoes into small chunks and dumped in a can of tomatoes, he placed both the skillet and the coffeepot on the gray coals. Then he sat back to wait, recalling in his mind some of the conversations of the Texans he had served with.

"If you happen to live over all this shit, you ought to come to Texas, Blue," Corporal Ben Miles had said. "I can put you on to a good job. The work ain't hard, and you can eat beefsteak three times a day if you want to." Blue had questioned Miles several times about Texas during the summer of '64.

"Hell, yes, I can help you," Miles had said. "You just get yourself out there, I'll take care of the rest. My family owns more'n ten thousand acres, and we can always use another hand. Just head due west out of southern Arkansas, and you'll be right in line with our ranch, thirty miles east of Dallas. Just ask anybody you see for directions to the Mort Miles spread, everybody knows Papa."

Blue intended to do exactly that. Judging from his own reckoning, and by studying the crude map he carried, he believed that he was no more than a week's ride from the ranch at this very moment. Pulling his food from the fire and filling his cup with coffee, he began to eat directly from the skillet, still thinking of Corporal Miles. It was going to be good seeing Ben again, for the man had not only been a good friend, but a gutsy warrior who commanded the respect of his superiors and comrades alike. Blue had lost track of the man shortly before the war ended, for he had been transferred to another company. Yes, indeed, Litt, was thinking, it was going to be good sitting in the shade with his friend once again, rehashing hard-fought battles and perhaps sipping some kind of strong drink.

He allowed his animals to graze throughout the hottest period of the day, then pointed Ike toward the western horizon. He spent the night on Caney Creek, and the following afternoon reached the Red River. Sitting on the east bank he could easily see how the river had come by its name, for it was indeed, red. Picketing his animals, he began to look around for firewood. He intended to make an early camp, for he needed time to cook a two-day supply of beans before dark.

He made his bed under the canopy of a willow, whose dense, low-hanging limbs and pendant branchlets completely obscured his view of the starlit sky. His roost was also well-hidden from the eyes of any human who might happen by. He lay awake for a long while, trying to imagine what the next few years of his life were going to be like. Uncle Caleb had given him a good stake, of which Litt still possessed more than three hundred dollars. Caleb had also furnished him with weapons that were almost new, obtained from God only knew where.

The rifle was a .44-caliber, twelve-shot Henry, manufactured in 1860 and considered by many to be the best all-around rifle ever made by anyone. The weapon was appreciated for its accuracy, weighed just a little over nine pounds, and fired a copper-cased cartridge that rainy weather did not affect.

The handgun was a Colt six-shot army revolver that was also manufactured in 1860, and it too fired .44-caliber ammunition. The principal revolver of the war, over one hundred thousand had been furnished to the federal government during the first two years of the conflict, many of which fell into Southern hands.

Blue had no doubt that he was now wearing a former Yankee weapon on his hip. He had neglected to ask Uncle Caleb how he had come by the weapons. The old man simply had "getting places," and had the money to pay for his merchandise.

After a good night's sleep and a hearty breakfast, Blue forded the river and continued west at a leisurely pace. He saw no reason to hurry, for he had no appointments and no commitments. Besides, he must be careful not to overwork his animals, for the weather was very humid and extremely hot. Though he had seen what seemed like a multitude of animals die from gunfire during the war, he had also seen a sizable number fall over dead from simple exhaustion and overheating. Litt had long held a strong compassion for dumb animals. All a caring man had to do was keep an eye on his horse, for the beast would invariably display numerous signs of weariness long before it reached its limit of endurance. A horse that was properly taken care of, would in turn take care of its master. This Litt knew from firsthand experience.

He crossed the Sulphur River in the afternoon, and spent his first night in Texas camped beside a small stream. He built no fire tonight, for dead wood was not immediately available. He needed no fire anyway, for he was tired enough that he preferred eating yesterday's cold beans for his supper.

After eating, he sat with his back against a tree for a long time, watching the lightning bugs flitting to and fro. As the insects darted about with their tails blinking, he was reminded of the summer he was ten years old, when he, along with his distant cousins, chased the bugs down and put them inside jars with perforated lids. That was the summer that Litt had been allowed to spend two weeks on his cousin's farm, located twenty miles from his own home.

Cousin Leonard. Leonard Rafus was a skinny, fifty-year-old man with no book learning. Married to the former Maybelle Jones, who was the same age and possessed the same degree of formal education, the couple had six children ranging in age from ten to twenty-five years. None of the three oldest, all girls, had ever married. The prime reason was a lack of suitors, for it was believed by all and openly stated by many, that Leonard Rafus and his entire family were crazy. Young Blue had even heard the same opinion spoken in his own home.

Seemingly oblivious to the outside world, the Rafus family eked out a living on their two-hundred-acre cotton farm. Living in near isolation, none of the children had ever attended public school. Cousin Leonard contended that there was nothing in those schoolhouses that a child needed to learn. They had never yet taught a boy how to plow a straighter row, nor a girl how to make a better biscuit.

Though they had on occasion visited with Charley and Effie Mangrum, and the children had played with Litt and Roberta, Maybelle Rafus and her brood were seldom seen by anyone who did not visit them at their own farm. Leonard himself, however, could often be seen traveling around the area, for it was sometimes necessary that he conduct business with "outsiders."

Scorning every type of organized religion, Leonard Rafus firmly believed that he and he alone understood the meaning of life, and the sole reason for man's existence.

"I figgered it all out my own self," Litt had heard Leonard say to Uncle Charley, "then th' Lord give me a sign. Now, I ain't gonna say what ʋat sign wuz, 'cause 'at'd be like my tryin' ta take over th' Lord's job." Uncle Charley had remained silent, while Litt had scooted closer to hear more.

"Ya wanna know why a man's put on this earth, Charley?" When Uncle Charley did not answer, Leonard continued. "I'll tell ya why a man's put on this earth. A man's put on this earth ta take care o' his own, an' ta keep his nose out'n th' the Lord's bizness. 'Course, a man's s'posed ta fight sin, always s'posed ta fight sin. Sin's ever'whur, ya know, eeb'm in th' air ya breathe. 'At's why a feller ort not ta never breathe through his mouth.

"Feller ort ta always breathe through his nose. Ya nose has got a whole lotta little hairs in it, ya see, an' 'at's what strains out th' sin an' turns it back. Ain't nowhur fer it ta go but right back whur it come frum, maybe ta git sucked down somebidy else's throat. 'At's th' way th' big devil works, Charley, he's got jillions o' little devils jist a-floatin' aroun' in th' air a-waitin' ta git in somebidy, an' they all imbizable." When Charley raised his eyes questioningly, Leonard added, "When sump'm's imbizable, 'at means ya cain't see it." Resisting the urge to smile, Charley nodded, and cast his eyes elsewhere.

That was the day Litt begged that he be allowed to go home with the Rafus family and visit for several days. Aunt Effie had balked at the idea, but had been overruled by Uncle Charley, who said it would be "educational" for the boy.

Now, sitting under a cottonwood in east Texas, Litt was thinking that his visit to the Rafus farm had been an education of sorts. He well remembered that first Sunday, when Cousin Leonard walked from the barn.

"Build th' fahr up hot, Maybelle," he said. "I jist sold 'at one-eyed mule, an' I got some money 'at needs a-cookin'." Wide-eyed and innocent, Litt immediately had a question.

"Cook money?" he asked.

"Shore, ya got ta cook money," Cousin Leonard explained. "It's the root o' all evil, an' th' onliest way ta git th' devils an' demons out'n it is ta cook 'em out. Demons cain't stan' heat. Ya cain't drownd 'em neither with jist plain ol' water, it's got ta be hot. Boilin' hot.

"Ya see, ever' time money changes han's, all th' devils 'at other person had goes right along with it. Like fleas a-jumpin' off'n a dog's back, only worse. Ya cain't see th' little devils, ya know, on account o' 'em bein' imbizable.

"They live inside o' people, son, frum th' heart ta th' fanger tips, jist a-waitin' ta jump off an' infeck somebidy else. They git on 'at money right off, 'cause they know it's gonna keep changin' han's. Ya got ta boil it fer ten minutes, son, takes 'at long ta clean th' sin out'n it." Then, turning toward his wife, Leonard asked, "Is 'at water hot a-nuff yet, Maybelle?"

"It's a-boilin'," she said. "If ya teched 'at money ya better wash ya han's good."

"Never teched it a-tall," Leonard said, holding out a small cloth bag with drawstrings at the top. "I made 'im drop it straight inta this 'backer sack." Leonard then walked to the stove and dropped the coins into the boiling water.

"Op'm all th' doors an' raise th' winders," he said to his wife. "They gonna be a-comin' out o' here." Maybelle was quick to comply, then began to walk around the room waving a blanket back and forth through the air, chasing the devils out of the house. Leonard stood holding his hands over the steaming pot.

"I c'n jist feel 'em a-jumpin' out o' here," he said loudly. Then, speaking to his oldest daughter, he said,

"Come 'ere, Sarah, an' feel it fer yaself." The homely, overweight girl was quick to put her hands over the steam.

"Oh, yes!" she squealed, then went into some kind of convulsive dance. "I feel it! I feel it. Lordy, Lordy, Lordy! Oh, Lord, yes!" She then began to mumble something that could be understood by nobody, and danced off down the hall.

" 'At girl has shore got th' Spirit," Leonard said, nodding his head in approval. Then, speaking to his youngest daughter, he said,

"Yore turn, Willadean, come 'ere an' feel."

"I don' wanna feel," the girl said gloomily.

"Git over ta 'at stove an' do like ya wuz tol', girl," Maybelle screamed at her daughter, " 'fore ya deddy knocks ya a-windin'. Ever' one o' ya's been tol' a dozen times 'at he's had a sign." The girl moved instantly. Holding her small hands over the hot steam, she admitted that she could feel something, but she did not dance. Afterward, she ran to the porch to be alone.

When Litt's turn came, he told his cousin quite honestly that the only thing he felt was the heat.

" 'At's all right," Leonard said, "ya still young yet. When th' Spirit's had a little more time ta work on ya, ya gonna feel plenty." When the money had been properly cooked, and the tobacco sack boiled, Leonard returned the coins to the bag and laid it all up to dry.

Now, as he sat watching the moonlight bounce off the dark water Litt could remember the time spent with the Rafus family as if it had been yesterday. He recalled one night sitting on the porch, when Willadean had said,

"Ain't none o' us girls never gonna git married, ain't nobody ever sees us."

"Ya'll all git saw," Cousin Leonard had scolded, "when th' Good Lord thanks it's time fer ya ta git saw."

Litt wondered now if the invading Yankees had found the Rafus farm. If the Union soldiers came calling, it was quite possible or even probable, that each of the Rafus girls had learned what it was like to have a man, whether they wanted one or not. With that thought, Litt crawled into his bed and did not awaken till sunup.

3

B lue arrived at the Miles ranch a week later, tired, hungry, and thirsty.

"Littleton Blue?" Mort Miles asked, when Litt had introduced himself. "Of course we know who you are. Fought right alongside Ben. He mentioned your name in one of his letters, said he probably owed you for saving his life."

"Yes, sir," Blue said, "that's me. Is Ben around?"

"I hate being the one to tell you this, son," Miles said, taking charge of Blue's animals and beginning to lead them toward the watering trough, "but Ben didn't make it. We got the word right before Christmas that he was killed somewhere around Petersburg." Litt stood very still, staring at the ground as the news soaked in, visions of the reckless young soldier dancing before his eyes. Reckless to the point of being foolish, some had said.

Nevertheless, Litt could recall more than one occasion when Ben's disregard for danger had resulted in a Yankee retreat. Like the day Corporal Miles, who for some reason could not get his own rifle to fire, had openly charged a Union soldier, physically taken his weapon from him, and reversed the bayonet's thrust. Ben's bravery had been contagious, and the charging Rebels soon had the Yankees on the run.

"You can't let it get to you, son," Mort said, tugging at Blue's elbow. "Come over to the porch and get out of this hot sun." Allowing himself to be led to the porch, Litt took a seat in a cane-bottom chair.

"I'll tell you one thing," he said, "if it helps your feelings any. Ben was a good soldier, and he damn sure took the fight to 'em."

"That would have been his nature," Mort said. "Never was afraid of anything."

"I can attest to that. I think even a few of the Union soldiers knew who he was, and they respected him just like we did."

"I'm glad to hear that he did his job, son. We miss him terribly around here."

As had been his son, Mort Miles was a light-complected man with blond hair, now tinged with gray. Rangy, and thin in the middle, he stood just under six feet tall, weighing a hundred seventy pounds. Now forty years old, he had come to Texas with his father in the spring of 1846, shortly after statehood.

The Henry Miles family had endured fewer hardships than had many others, for in addition to being well supplied, they had money. Henry and his wife, Sally, along with their eighteen-year-old son, Mort, and his wife, Ellie, had quickly settled on the same property that they still called home. As Mort himself was an only child, his wife had also given birth to only one offspring, Ben.

Two-year-old Ben had called his father "Papa," and long before the young boy learned to count, he named his grandfather "Two Papas." These days, Henry Miles was seldom addressed by any other name. His wife was likewise, "Two Mamas." Neither grandparent had ever objected to the name, even when used by people outside the family. Both Henry and Sally were now sixty years old, and enjoyed excellent health. They lived in the large, much-improved house that had been the original homestead, a hundred yards west of Mort's place.

Blue met Mort's father a short time later, and was awed by his size. Two Papas was not a fat man, he was simply tall, thick, and wide. He stood at least as far from the ground as did Blue himself, and Litt gauged his weight at two hundred sixty pounds. Also light-complected, he had a shock of hair that had probably once been blond, though it was now as white as milk. With oversized feet, hands the size of small hams, and a bull neck that jutted from his collarless shirt, the man cut an imposing figure indeed. At his introduction, when Blue made an effort to rise to his feet, he was stopped cold by the big, bass voice that seemed to shake the entire porch.

"Keep your seat, son!" Two Papas commanded. "You've come a long way."

Nevertheless, Blue was on his feet quickly, shaking the big man's hand.

"Mort tells me that you knew Ben," the elder Miles said, pulling up a chair for himself.

"Same company," Blue said. "Saw him day and night for nearly a year."

"Then I suppose he told you about us, told you how to get here."

"Yes, sir. He seemed to think I could find work out here. Anyway, there ain't much left at home, South Carolina took a beating."

"So I've heard," Two Papas said. Then, rising to his feet and stretching his arms above his head with a groan, he added, "Today's our day to eat dinner with Mort and Ellie. Come along, son, let's get a good meal under your belt." Inside the house, the big man introduced Litt to the womenfolk, then led the way to the dining room.

In short order, Blue was enjoying the best meal he could remember ever having anywhere. While both women ate from small plates, the men were served on large platters, each of which contained beefsteak, baked ham, mashed potatoes and beans, banked by two large ears of corn, fresh from the garden. Coffee, milk, or tea were there for the choosing, and Litt could see at least two different kinds of pie. He immediately thought of the times he had heard Ben curse army rations, boasting of the good food he had always eaten at home. Ben had not been exaggerating. These people obviously ate this good all the time, for they had not been expecting company for dinner.

As Ellie refilled Blue's cup with steaming coffee, she spoke softly, almost at a whisper.

"Eat as much as you can, young man, it'll be good for you."

"Thank you, ma'am," he said, pushing himself away from the table. "I already have." Ellie was a tiny woman, scarcely five feet tall, and her small, brown eyes and bobbed haircut made her look even smaller. Looking at her now, Blue remembered that Ben had once jokingly said that his mother could take a bath in a water bucket.

Not so with Two Mamas. Sally Miles stood at least a foot taller, and straight as a fence post. With green eyes and graying hair that was rolled into a bun at the back of her head, she was a striking woman, with a figure that belied its age. A man would need only one glance to know that she had been a raving beauty in her younger days. As he finished his coffee and pushed the cup aside, Blue was thinking that the lady was probably capable of turning a few heads even now. He arose from the table and followed the men outside.

"Just put your animals in the barn, Litt," Two Papas said, pointing. "You'll find grain and hay easy enough. If you leave the stall doors open, they can water themselves in the corral." Nodding, Blue headed for the barn, leading Ike and the yellow mule. He stashed the mule's pack behind a grain bin, then fed each animal a generous portion of oats.

"You can sleep in the guest house," Mort said when Blue returned to the porch. "I think you'll find it comfortable enough." He pointed to a small, newly built cabin, only a short distance from the yard. Blue followed the point with his eyes, saying,

"I'm sure it's a giant step up from what I'm used to."

"Well, you just go on over there and rest yourself up for a few days, somebody'll call you when it's time to eat."

"Thank you, sir," Blue said, "I'll do that."

"The name's Mort," Miles said. "Just Mort." He then walked toward the corral, while Blue headed for the guest house. Litt acquainted himself with the furnishings of the two-room cabin, then stood in the doorway watching as Mort mounted a big strawberry roan and headed north at a gallop.

For the next several days, the routine never varied. He quickly learned that breakfast was served at daybreak, and had fallen into the habit of walking over to the porch as soon as he saw lamps burning in the house. Throughout the remainder of the day someone, usually Ellie, would call to him at mealtime.

The rest of the time he was left to his own devices. He prowled around the immediate area, investigating the bunkhouse and the farmers' cottage. He spent enough time around the barn to learn where everything was kept, and to differentiate between the animals in the corral. A big, blaze-faced chestnut with three stockings had caught his eye the first day, but so far Blue had seen no one using the animal. He supposed that the reason might well be that the chestnut was simply not as good as it looked, which was very often the case with horses. The big animal stood at least a hand taller than its companions, and was obviously full of "vinegar," as it trotted up and down the fence, occasionally stopping to poke its head over the rails and stare at the plains longingly. That the horse wanted to run was obvious; whether or not it would tolerate a passenger, Blue had no idea.

Though neither Mort nor Two Papas had ever discussed it, Litt had decided from his own observation that, in addition to himself, Mort had two men who worked at raising cattle, and three who were farmers. There was a cook shack and a full-time cook, and though the cowboys and the farmers slept in separate quarters, all ate their meals at a common table. An early-morning call by the cook brought each of the workers to their feet long before daybreak each day.

And though Mort spent most of the daylight hours in the saddle, and was probably his own foreman, he seemed to rely heavily on Bill Shelton, a red-haired man who was in his early twenties. Blue had reached this conclusion because Mort spent more time talking with the redhead than with everyone else combined. Litt had once spoken to Shelton in the yard, and had received a grunt and a vacant stare in return. Blue had expected no more, for he had already been told that Texans in general were of a suspicious nature.

Nevertheless, he determined not to speak to the man again unless spoken to. Even then he would use only as many words as was necessary. And though he knew that if he was ever hired to work on this ranch he must get along with Shelton, he would bow to no man. If the redhead ever attempted to run roughshod over him, Blue would set him straight, and quickly. Besides, even though it appeared that Mort and Bill Shelton were running the ranch, Litt believed that it was Two Papas who actually called the shots.

That belief was reinforced the following morning shortly after sunup. Blue had eaten his breakfast and watched the other men ride out to their respective jobs, when Two Papas showed up at the guest house door.

"What do you think about the two of us taking a ride this morning?" he asked.

"I think it's the right thing to do," Blue said, stepping into the yard. "I've been getting mighty restless." He followed the elder Miles to the corral, then watched as Two Papas neatly roped a buckskin and led it from the bunch.

"Six horses there," he said to Litt. "Take your pick."

"I sure like the looks of that chestnut," Blue said, bringing his saddle from the tack room.

"You and everybody else," Two Papas said, pulling the cinch tight on his buckskin. He was quiet for a long moment, then added, "Ride him if you want to, just be sure you keep a firm hand on him."

"Is he wild?" Blue asked, uncoiling his rope.

"Not exactly," Two Papas said, beginning to chuckle. "He just seems to sometimes get the idea that life would be a whole lot better in New Mexico territory, or maybe Arkansas."

Smiling, Blue laid a loop around the chestnut's neck and soon had his saddle on. He had scarcely taken his seat, when the big horse headed west at a trot. Blue first tried to rein the animal in a circle. When that failed, he tried the bit, only to have the horse take it in its teeth and quicken the pace. Blue had fought horses before, and knew that they respected nothing short of a firm hand. Wrapping the reins around his gloved hands, he jerked the horse's head so hard that the animal wound up on its haunches. Blue stepped from the saddle and put one foot on the ground as the chestnut went down, then remounted as the animal scrambled to its feet.

Once was enough, Blue was now turning the big horse in circles, using no more than the pressure of the reins against its neck. Two Papas had sat idly by, watching the action.

"First time I've seen one snatched all the way to the ground," he said. "Looks like you just might have made a believer out of him."

"Maybe so," Litt said, patting the horse's neck, "and maybe not. I expect to have to do it again. It usually takes three or four times, and you have to be quick about it. The very instant he takes it in his head to start doing his own thinking, you've got to bust him."

"Makes sense to me," Two Papas said, leading off at a canter.

When they arrived at a small, spring-fed lake a few minutes later, Blue got his first look at a sizable herd of longhorn cattle. Scattered about the area, munching on the prairie grass, and some standing in the water up to their bellies, Litt could see at least a hundred head. When he rode closer, and none of the cattle seemed to be alarmed at his presence, he commented.

"Ben told me lots of stories about wild longhorns. I was expecting these to run when they saw us."

"They will move off if you dismount," Two Papas said, "but they're not gonna run. They're too fat and lazy. Most of this bunch were born right here, and they see men on horseback every day.

"It's a different story with the older cows. They probably saw us coming, and that's why we don't see them. We drove them up from south Texas four years ago, and they're about as wild now as they were then. They don't like a man or the horse he rides, and they'll bury a horn in either at the first good opportunity."

Another short ride brought them to the farm, which consisted of a hundred acres surrounded by a five-rail fence. Two Papas explained that the farmers grew hay and corn for the most part, along with vegetables for the table and canning purposes.

"We feed the corn to the horses," he said, "and if we have any left over it's mighty easy to sell. Just guessing, I'd say that most of the corn we do sell ends up in a whiskey bottle."

"Is the lake the only source of water?" Blue asked, changing the subject.

"Two creeks on the other side of the hill," Two Papas said, "but they can't always be depended on. Five springs feeding that lake back yonder; I've seen it low a few times during droughts, but I've never seen it dry."

They rode about the ranch for the remainder of the morning, with Two Papas doing most of the talking as he pointed out one thing or another. As they released their horses back into the corral at noon, Two Papas said that he believed Blue had taught the chestnut a lesson, for the horse had not acted up again. Then, as Blue walked to the guest house, the big man followed, taking a seat on the porch.

"Guess I ought to put you with Cecil for a week or two," he said. "He'd be more tolerant of the mistakes that you're bound to make just learning. Bill Shelton is not known for being patient." Blue was silent for a moment, then spoke haltingly.

"Does that . . . mean you're gonna give me a job?"

"You've been on the payroll since you got here," Two Papas said quickly. Then, smiling and chuckling softly, he added, "Besides, I liked the way you set that horse on his ass."

"Well, I appreciate it Mister Miles, I—"

"Two Papas," Miles interrupted. "It's the only name I answer to these days."

"I'll learn as much as I can as quick as I can," Blue said, "and I thank you for the job."

"I'll tell Cecil to take you under his wing for a while," Two Papas said, getting to his feet. "He's a good man, and he knows what he's doing." As he walked away, he added over his shoulder, "You'll earn your money."

Blue met Cecil Hudson just before dark, after both had eaten their evening meal. Now thirty years old, the dark-haired Hudson had been on the ranch for four years, and had never taken a vacation. Litt had seen him several times as he came and went, but had never spoken to the man. Hudson, like Bill Shelton, had been among the drovers who brought the original herd up from south Texas. When offered permanent employment, each man had accepted. A six-footer with brown eyes, Hudson had been raised around Houston, but had never expressed a desire to return.

Blue was standing on the guest house porch, when Hudson crossed the yard with his right hand extended.

"Been seeing you around," he said, "and been wanting to meet you. My name's Cecil Hudson." Blue took the outstretched hand and returned its firm grip. Introducing himself, he pushed a chair toward the man.

"Two Papas says you and me need to work together for the next pretty good while," Hudson said. "Says you need to learn something about longhorns."

"I guess I do," Blue said, already deciding that he liked the man. " 'Cause I sure don't know much."

"The cows themselves will pretty well teach you what you have to do," Cecil said, taking the chair and seating himself. "I reckon it's my job to show you how to do it."

"Ben made it all sound so easy when we discussed it."

"Well, it is easy," Hudson said with a chuckle, "the way Ben did it. You see, whenever he got tired he just quit and came to the house. Of course, that's one of the benefits of being family."

They talked for nearly an hour, agreeing that Blue would be Hudson's near-constant companion for the foreseeable future. When Blue suggested that he himself should move into the bunkhouse to avoid any appearance of special treatment, Hudson agreed that it might be wise.

When talk turned to the recent Civil War, Blue offered little information, responding only to direct questions. He explained that even though he had fought with the Army of Northern Virginia, he had never even seen General Lee, much less spoken with the man. He had seen a man at a distance that he believed was the general, but then only after Lee's surrender.

Cecil said that the Miles family, along with himself and Bill Shelton, had been heavily involved in the war effort, though their participation had been limited to supplying the needs of the Confederacy. Only Ben had traveled east to join the actual fighting. At the first opportunity, Blue changed the subject. Describing the hellish war was impossible, a man who had not been there would simply never know.

An hour later, Blue stepped inside the bunkhouse door, his heavy pack in his hand. Cecil was busy stitching his saddlebag with rawhide, and Bill Shelton lay on his bunk reading a book.

"Well, well," the redhead said with a smirk, turning his eyes to meet those of Blue. "Did they close down the royal guest house and send you down here to see how us commoners live?" Now was the time, Blue decided quickly. He dropped his pack to the floor noisily, his deep voice reverberating around the small building.

"Look, fellow!" he said. "Let's get something straight. I didn't bring any shit into this bunkhouse, and I damn sure ain't gonna tolerate any of yours. I slept in the guest house because Mort asked me to, and I moved into this place of my own accord. Now, if you don't like that, get on your feet and say so." The redhead stared at Blue icily for a few moments, but he did not accept the challenge. Then, saying nothing more, he laid his book aside and turned his face toward the wall.

Blue threw his pack into a corner and set about rearranging the bunk he had chosen, making as much noise as possible. Hudson, who had of course heard the entire exchange, offered Blue a military salute, winking his eye as he did so. A short time later Hudson blew out the lamp, and Litt was soon sleeping soundly.

It seemed that he had barely closed his eyes, when he heard the cook rousting the workers out for breakfast. After dressing and washing the sleep from his eyes, he followed Hudson to the cook shack. Looking at the table, he could very easily see that the "commoners" ate like kings around this place. Bill Shelton, who had been up for at least an hour, was just finishing his meal when Blue sat down. Getting to his feet, the redhead pushed a small, clay bowl across the table to Litt.

"Here's some sugar," he said, "if you like your coffee that way. I know I like a spoonful in mine every morning." Then Shelton was gone through the doorway. When Blue looked questioningly at Cecil, the man shrugged his shoulders.

"Bill won't give you any more shit," he said. "He's done seen that you've got sand."

4

S ummer, then fall passed on Henry Miles'
Box M Ranch, and now a hard winter and
new year were dawning. Blue, whose
weight was now pushing two hundred pounds, had
only last week been proclaimed a "cowboy" by Cecil
Hudson. The word, having originated when young
boys were left alone to look after the cows when their
fathers or brothers went off to war, was now used
very loosely, and was the accepted term for any man
who worked with cattle. After half a year of hard
work, Blue was pleased that he had finally been called
a cowboy.

Bill Shelton had quit the ranch shortly before the fall
roundup, and had been replaced with a man who answered to the name of "Rope" Johnson. Whether he

had come by the nickname because of the size of his arms and legs was never mentioned, but he was the skinniest man Litt had seen since the war. He could also do unbelievable things with a lariat. More than once Blue had sat on his horse watching as the thirty-year-old roped and hog-tied one beef after another, never missing with his forty-foot loop. Though he stood six feet tall, and weighed no more than a hundred thirty pounds, he was smart enough not to play games that required an abundance of strength. He merely put his rope where it belonged, and let his well-trained cow pony do the heavy lifting.

Johnson was also one of the most likable men Litt had ever been around. Seemingly happy just to be alive, he had a ready smile for anyone, and sometimes a humorous joke. He talked freely of his earlier life, saying that his mother had been known as the local tramp in the small, Arkansas town in which he had been born. He had no idea who his father was, he added, and doubted that his mother did. He had been raised by his grandfather, whose surname he had taken, and had been on his own since the age of fifteen. He had been in south Texas for the past ten years, fighting longhorns for the wage of a dollar a day. Much of his prowess with a rope had been gained while working with Mexican vaqueros, considered by many to be the best ropers in the world. William "Rope" Johnson was liked and respected by all who lived at the Box M Ranch, especially Blue, who enjoyed listening to the man's tales of Indian fighting.

Litt had seen no Indians, friendly or otherwise, during his stay at the Box M, though he knew that several tribes, including the Caddo, Wichita, and Tonkawa, called east Texas home. The dreaded Apaches had by now been pushed far to the west, not so much by white men, but by their traditional enemies: the powerful, free-roaming Comanches, who for the most part rode where they pleased. Many of the sedentary tribes had supposedly become so only after being intimidated by the ferocious warriors of the plains, known worldwide for their superb horsemanship. Many white men of the early-day West had used the term "Boss Indian" when referring to the Comanche.

The nickname had been well-placed, for the proud equestrians had once ruled the Texas plains with an iron hand. As the white man continued to move west, he too learned to respect the Comanche, for he was a fierce fighter. And unlike many tribes, who fought only during the daylight hours, the Comanche was as likely to attack at midnight as at sunrise. "The fight ain't necessarily over just because the sun goes down," Two Papas had said to Litt. "You'd do well to remember that." Blue would remember.

It was near the end of February when Two Papas announced his plans to build a new ranch. He had come to the bunkhouse shortly after dark and spoken to all the hands at once.

"Of course you all know that the market for beef right now is practically nonexistent," he began, "but all that's gonna change in the near future. I'm talking about railroads, men, and you can bet your butt that they're coming.

"I predict that within the next two years, three at the most, trains will be hauling live cattle across the country. When that happens, I expect to be one of the men with cattle to sell. I believe the East will buy as many head as the West can supply, and more or less let us set our own price.

"Through a man named John Graves, I acquired a

sizable chunk of property a few years ago. It lies several miles west of San Antonio, along the Frio River, and I intend to stock it with longhorns. There must be a million of them running wild in the Big Thicket, and Rope Johnson knows how to get them out of there." Then, turning to Johnson, he said, "You'll be in charge of that part of the operation, Rope. Can you hire some experienced men in south Texas?"

Johnson nodded. "I'll use the Mexicans," he said. "They know what to do and they've got guts enough to do it."

"Good," Two Papas said, "then that's settled. We'll drive a hundred head of our own cattle down there first, then as each wild one is caught and branded it'll be thrown in with the domestic herd." Then, turning once again to Johnson, he asked, "Do you think that'll help, Rope?"

"Sure," Johnson said, "we've done it before. I'm not gonna try to tell you how to run your business, but if it was me, I'd take a lot less than a hundred head. Otherwise, they might create a problem of their own."

"My business?" Two Papas asked. "Hell, it's your business. I just told you that you're in charge, so how many head should we take?"

"Forty," Johnson answered decisively. "Take a few of the biggest and tamest bulls you've got, and hope the wild cows think they're good-looking enough to follow."

"Forty head it is," Two Papas said, "and we'll let you do the choosing."

"We'll take three-and four-year-olds, then," Johnson said, "nothing that hasn't been driven before."

That settled, Two Papas walked to the stove and helped himself to a cup of coffee. Then he turned to face Hudson and Blue, as he drank the lukewarm liquid in huge gulps.

"Cecil," he said, "I'll be needing you for spring roundup, we'll hire some local men to help you." Hudson nodded his head in agreement, and said nothing. Refilling his cup from the blackened pot, Two Papas walked around for a moment, then trained his eyes on Litt.

"Mister Blue," he said, his voice becoming softer, "I suppose you're wondering what you're gonna be doing while all this is going on." Blue, who had been very attentive, nodded.

"What you're gonna be doing," Two Papas continued, "is putting together a new ranch out on the Frio River. I mean, the ranch house, bunkhouse, outbuildings, and corrals have all got to be in place when Rope and his men deliver the herd late this summer.

"I'll give you a letter for John Graves. He's well-known in the area. Just start asking for him after you cross the Sabinal River. He'll show you where my property is, and put you in contact with the builders you'll need to hire. He has a cypress-shingle business himself, so he'll supply you with roofing material.

"I'll see that you have the wherewithal to get whatever you need, and I'd say that San Antonio might be the closest getting place. You'll need at least one wagon and a stout team for hauling logs. The builders will probably have their own tools, but you also might have to buy some." Blue assured Two Papas that he understood his mission, then the big man turned to Johnson once again.

"I guess you'll be taking great pains to make sure the cows you carry from here are not pregnant, huh?"

"Absolutely."

"Very well," Two Papas said loudly. "We begin the

operation in one month." Then he was gone from the bunkhouse.

Two weeks later Blue headed south, riding the big chestnut that he had named Sox. Though the animal had been his mount of choice throughout the summer, fall, and winter, Litt had never had to fight the horse again. The lesson on that first day had obviously turned the trick. The horse was easy to catch nowadays, and even seemed eager to carry Litt around all day.

Leading both Ike and the yellow mule, whose backs were loaded heavily with supplies and equipment, he was headed for the Frio River, by way of Waco, Austin, and San Antonio. Carrying a week's supply of grub and enough grain for several days, he was also well-armed. In addition to the Colt on his hip and the Henry on his saddle, his bedroll contained a double-barreled, sawed-off shotgun. He carried an adequate supply of ammunition for all in his saddlebag, and in his coat pockets as well.

He was also carrying more money than he had ever seen before. As instructed, he planned to deposit most of it in the bank at San Antonio and draw from it as needed. He would also deposit his own four hundred dollars, which he now carried in his pocket. He had loaded Two Papas's money on the mule, knowing that if for any reason he became separated from his animals, the mule would be easier to catch. Just before his departure, Litt had had one last conversation with Two Papas.

"Won't be more'n a month before Rope and his crew start dragging longhorns out of the Big Thicket," the old man had said. "I'm counting on you to have things ready on your end."

"It'll be done, Two Papas," Litt had said.

"Well, you just be careful. You're carrying things that a lot of men wouldn't hesitate to kill for. Be suspicious of every man you see, red or white, and don't ever show any more money than it takes to pay for whatever you're buying at the time." Two Papas started for his house, then stopped suddenly. Turning to face Litt once again, he said softly, "I've got all the confidence in the world in you, son, but if it comes down to losing the money or your life, save your hide."

"Yes, sir," Blue said, mounting for the second time. He kicked the chestnut in the ribs, knowing full well that he would defend Two Papas's property to the death. Not only had Litt never seen so much money, he had never been charged with such an important mission. Two Papas had left the location of the new ranch headquarters to Blue's own discretion, saying only that it must be as close as was practical to the Frio, on property that would remain high and dry when heavy rains caused the river to jump its banks.

The main buildings must be constructed of heavy logs, capable of withstanding an attack by any adversary. And they must be built on a location that could be defended with a minimum of strategy, a subject of which the young war veteran knew more than a little. Two Papas had taken that into consideration when assigning Blue to the project, confident that Litt would choose the most defensible site. Therefore, the old man had not even mentioned the word "defense" when giving Blue his instructions.

Litt camped on the Trinity River the first night, having traveled thirty miles. Placing his bedroll in a thick stand of small trees, he tied his animals only a few feet away. He fed each a hefty portion of grain, for they would not be allowed the luxury of grazing all night. He would keep them close, for he knew that thieves and robbers abounded. Besides, anyone seeing his picketed animals would have no problems locating the bed of their master.

He would build no fire at night on this trip, he simply could not afford to take the chance. However, if he was in the right location he might have one for early-morning coffee. When darkness settled in, Blue placed the mule's pack at his own head, then crawled into his bed, his shotgun close at hand.

Sleep was slow to come, for Litt had much on his mind. Two Papas had known him for only nine months, he was thinking, yet the old man had put him in full charge of a major operation, and trusted him with a small fortune in cash. The trust had been well-placed, however, for Two Papas, a shrewd judge of character, had decided early on that Littleton Blue was an honest man.

Blue slept fitfully, and some time during the night he added another blanket to his covering. Even so, he awoke at daybreak shivering. Winter had not yet given up its hold on the area, and the March wind blew day and night. The next time he made his bed he would place his bedroll on his folded tarp. He had learned during the war that, on cold nights, what a man was sleeping under was less important than what he was sleeping on.

He fed and rigged his animals, then forded the Trinity and rode south. He ate his breakfast of cold beef and biscuits in the saddle, washing it down with water from his canteen. Then he turned to some of the hard candy that had been made by Two Mamas, allowing it to melt in his mouth as he rode.

Two weeks later, Blue deposited Two Papas's three thousand dollars in the bank at San Antonio, opening an account that only he himself could draw against. Then he deposited most of his own money in a personal account. Relieved that he no longer had to guard the money twenty-four hours a day, he carried his animals to the livery stable. He would spend the remainder of the day and night in town, relaxing. He was soon walking the streets and enjoying the scenery.

San Antonio was the most beautiful place he had ever seen. Located on the San Antonio River at the southern edge of the Texas Hill Country, the town's Spanish beginnings predated the founding of the United States by more than half a century. Though many of its inhabitants were of Mexican descent, and erected their own adobe buildings, the most prominent settlers of the nineteenth century were the German builders and businessmen. Evidence of the master builders could be seen in any direction.

Litt registered at a hotel near the livery stable, then bought a haircut, shave, and bath at a barber shop next door. He changed into clean clothing at the hotel, then crossed the street to a restaurant, where he ordered beefsteak and potatoes. The food was excellent. He spent more than an hour at the table, leisurely eating his first good meal in almost two weeks.

A few minutes later he stepped inside a saloon, a few doors down from the restaurant. He stood just inside the door for a few moments, waiting for his eyes to adjust to the dim lighting. Then he walked to the far end of the bar, took a stool, and ordered a beer. The room was long and narrow, with stools on three sides of the thirty-foot bar. The building was old, but clean. A piano rested on a riser at the rear of the establishment, in front of which was a small, hardwood dance floor. Closer to the center of the room was a potbellied stove, and Blue could feel its heat. He was soon uncomfortably warm, and shed his coat.

The bartender noticed. "I guess it is getting a little warm in here," he said, walking to the stove and fiddling with its damper. Blue nodded, and sipped at his beer.

Though the bartender was obviously a Mexican, he spoke English very well. "Haven't seen you before," he said, as he returned to the bar. "You new in the area?"

"Been in town a few hours," Blue said. "Headed for the Sabinal River."

"Well, a good day's ride west will put you right on its bank," the barkeep said, then moved up the bar to serve some new customers. When he returned, he refilled Litt's beer mug, then offered his hand. "My name's Pedro Alvarez, Mister—"

"Blue." Litt said, shaking the man's hand. When he tried to pay for his beer, the money was refused.

"It's our custom here at Tom's Place," Pedro said, waving the money away. "Each new customer gets a free beer."

Blue sipped at his beer. "Do you happen to know a man named John Graves?"

"No, no, Mister Blue," Pedro said, wiping at a wet spot on the bar. "He is rich, and I am just a bartender."

Blue stared at his beer for a moment. "Are you saying he acts like he's too good to know a bartender?"

"I've never had any reason to talk to the man, so I wouldn't know what he thinks. On the few occasions that he's been in here, he just sits in the office and drinks with Tom. He did give me half a dollar once, when I carried a bottle of whiskey in there to them."

"Has he been in lately?" Blue asked.

"No. The last time was right before Christmas. I remember because I had to go out in the rain to load a case of whiskey on one of his wagons."

Blue spent another half hour in the saloon, during which time the bartender gave him directions to John Graves's ranch. The Mexican had never been there, he said, but nevertheless knew the way.

Back on the street, Litt strolled around till he found a dry-goods store, where he bought two pairs of Levi's and two shirts. Then he hired a cobbler to half-sole his boots. At the Shebang, he bought a month's supply of food and two sacks of shelled corn, telling the merchant that he would pick up the goods on his way out of town tomorrow morning.

At sunset, he ate another meal at the restaurant, washing it down with steaming coffee. A few minutes later, he returned to the hotel and retired for the night. The soft bed put him to sleep quickly.

5

lue reached the Sabinal River at noon, two days later. When his animals had slaked their thirst, he picketed them on the east bank, then built a fire for making coffee. Half an hour later he was washing down cold ham and biscuits with the steaming liquid. He was barely halfway through his meal, when a man rode out of the trees from the north. Aboard a big piebald, the man looked neither left nor right, but headed straight for Blue's campfire.

He halted his horse twenty feet away, and sat quietly for a moment. Though not a tall man, he had a well-fed look, and Litt guessed his weight to be two hundred pounds. With light brown hair and a ruddy complexion that was sprinkled with freckles, he appeared to be about thirty years old.

"Howdy," he said finally. "Ain't seen you around here before."

Blue got to his feet slowly, dashing his coffee grounds into the bushes. "Good reason for that," he said. "I ain't been here before."

The man continued to eye Blue. "You just passing through?"

"No, I don't guess you could say that," Litt answered quickly. "According to what I've been told, I'm just about where I want to be. I'm looking for a man named John Graves. Know where I can find him?"

The man nodded. "Sure do," he said. "John Graves is my pa. Folks call me Rusty."

"Well, get down, Rusty, and have a cup of coffee. You got your own cup?"

The man nodded, then dismounted and took a tin cup from his saddlebag.

Blue filled the cup, then placed the pot on a rock near the fire. "My name's Littleton Blue," he said, offering a handshake. "Most people call me Litt." The men shook hands, and Rusty squatted on his haunches.

"You got business with Pa?" he asked.

"Yes, I do," Blue said, pushing the coffeepot back onto the fire. "I represent a man named Henry Miles, back in east Texas."

"Henry Miles!" Rusty repeated. "Lord, I must have heard that name a thousand times. Him and Pa freighted together during the war, and Pa speaks highly of him. Miles bought up a whole bunch of land north of us, halfway to Frio Canyon. I believe his property reaches as far west as the Frio River. He might even own some on the west side of the river, for all I know."

"I believe he does," Blue said.

After eating cold biscuits and ham with his coffee, Rusty offered to lead Blue to the ranch. "The house is about eight miles northwest," he said. "On the other side of the river."

Two hours later, they rode up a hill to an extensive stretch of elevated and comparatively level land; a mesa. The flat tableland descended sharply to the surrounding plain, a mile or so to the west. In the middle of the plateau stood the Graves ranch house. At the edge of the yard was a large bunkhouse, with the barn and corrals farther down the slope.

Blue was surprised. As they rode closer, he said, "I had no idea that the house was made of bricks."

"Among other things, Pa is a mason. He taught me to lay bricks at an early age. We bricked the house right after the war was over."

They rode straight to the barn. Insisting that Litt unburden his animals and stable them, Rusty fed grain and hay to all three. A few minutes later, Blue was standing in the yard shaking hands with John Graves.

"So you're here to turn Henry Miles's property into a ranch, huh?" Graves asked when Rusty had introduced the men.

"Yes, sir. He's got men dragging longhorns out of the Big Thicket right now. Two Papas himself will be out here sometime in the fall."

Graves raised an eyebrow. "Two Papas?"

"Mister Miles's grandson named him that," Blue answered, "and that's what he wants to be called nowadays."

"Oh," Graves grunted. He was not a big man. Standing less than six feet tall, he weighed no more than a hundred fifty pounds. Nevertheless, he looked plenty solid, and no doubt still possessed some of the vigor of his youth. Appearing to be well past fifty, he had thinning, sandy hair that was tinged with gray, green eyes, a ruddy complexion, and the same freckles that had been passed on to his son. Standing several inches taller than Graves, Blue could see a large bald spot on top of the man's hatless head.

"Two Papas says there's gonna be a big market for longhorns before too long," Litt said.

"Two Papas is right," Graves said, motioning Blue toward the porch. "He owns some of the best grass in Texas, and it's time he did something with it."

They seated themselves on the porch, where a Mexican cook soon served them coffee. Graves was anxious to know all about Two Papas and his east-Texas ranch, and Blue answered all of his questions. When Graves had read the letter written by Miles, he was quiet for a while.

"I'll get some material from San Antonio and lay out the house," he said finally. "Then Rusty will brick it."

"Two Papas didn't say anything about brick," Blue said.

"That's because he didn't know he could get them. Trust me, son. He'll want the brick."

"Yes, sir."

"Henry's letter says that you'll make the decision on where to put the buildings," Graves said. "Tomorrow morning I'll start showing you the corners of his property. You can take as much time as you need to decide."

After a good night's sleep and a hearty breakfast the following morning, the two men rode northwest at a brisk walk, gaining elevation steadily. An early spring had brought an abundance of grass, and Graves's long-horns were scattered widely, munching on the tender green shoots. They paid the riders no mind as they passed.

Three hours later, they climbed a steep rise and stopped at the top of the hill. Graves pointed to a cedar post, around which was tied a faded strip of red cloth. "That's Henry's northeast corner. Look your surroundings over and get this place firmly in your mind, then we'll cross the river. We should make the northwest corner by noon. We'll fire up some coffee and eat our sausage and biscuits there."

Litt would have no problem returning to the location, for he had been very observant, and scribbled landmarks on a piece of brown paper. He made one last entry, then nodded that he was ready to go.

They crossed the Frio two hours later, and, at noon, built a fire beside the northwest marker. As they ate their biscuits and sipped the coffee, Graves pointed to a tall oak nearby. "I chiseled my initials on that tree the first year I was in these parts. See 'em up there?"

Blue nodded. He could read the letters clearly. He also knew that Graves had been in the area for a long time, for the initials were well out of a man's reach—perhaps fifteen feet from the ground.

"I came to Texas in 1847," Graves said. "Me and the wife moved to this county in '52, pretty close to where we live now." Graves said that he had established a cypress-shingle business in Frio Canyon, where there was an abundance of cypress timber. Though he no longer owned the business, he had a stack of shingles under a shed that would be more than enough to roof every building Two Papas might want.

Graves and Miles had served together in the Con-federacy as freighters during the Civil War, and developed a strong friendship. It was on the advice of Graves that Two Papas had bought eight sections of land in Uvalde County in 1862. After the War, with land prices taking a downward plunge, he purchased five additional sections. He now owned thirteen square miles of prime grassland, with ample shade and a year-round source of water.

"This is the prettiest country I've ever seen," Blue said, when they had finished eating. "Don't see how a cow could hope to find anything better."

"They stay put pretty well. They've got everything they need right under their noses, and you can just about count on a calf from every healthy cow."

"Do you have any trouble with cats?"

"Sometimes. They'll come off of the mountain or out of the canyon and take a calf when they can't catch anything closer to home. When it gets bad, a bunch of us goes hunting. A friend of mine on Buffalo Creek's got a pack of hounds." Graves was quiet for a while, then began to smile. "I won't have a problem at all when Henry gets his cows out here, 'cause he'll be between me and the canyon. The cats'll eat his calves before they get to mine."

Blue chuckled. "I believe you're right."

They kept a conversation going for most of the three-hour ride back to the ranch. Graves wanted to hear as much as Blue would tell about the fighting in Virginia, and seemed to find it odd that Litt did not know General Lee personally. It was the same with most of the men Blue talked with. Those who had not served on the battlefield simply did not understand the chain of command.

Graves spoke of the days when he had first come to the sparsely populated Uvalde County. He believed the county had even fewer residents now, for a few large ranchers, himself included, had bought out dozens of smaller ranchers who had found living in the San Antonio area more to their liking. The huge Graves Ranch itself was a conglomeration of seven smaller ranches, bought from men who had failed to make it for one reason or another.

Cattle rustling was not unknown to the area, for the Mexican border was only a two-day drive to the south. Such activity had slowed considerably in recent years, however, for those caught in the act, and a few who were merely suspected, had met swift punishment with a rope and a cypress limb. It was the unwritten law of the range, and such executions were rarely investigated.

When they returned to the ranch, Litt met Katie, the elder Graves's wife of thirty-five years. Blue had learned only a few minutes ago that the lady was an invalid. Rheumatism had rendered her lower limbs useless, and she had not taken a single step during the past year. Today, Rusty had brought her to the porch to get some fresh air, and to watch the sun sinking toward the western horizon.

"Pleased to meet you, Mister Blue," she said, when they were introduced. "Lord, if you ain't a good-looking young man I'll pay for lying."

"Thank you, ma'am. It's a pleasure to meet you." He took a seat on the porch swing.

Katie fanned her face a few times with the cardboard fan she held in her hand. "Rusty says Henry Miles is coming out here before the end of the year. I don't know the man myself, but John's been talking about him for years. I know that'll make him proud."

"Yes, ma'am. He's gonna stock some longhorns up north of here."

"Oh, I know the property," she said. "John showed

it all to me back when I could get around." Katie was a small woman, with a pretty face and fine features. She had light brown hair that was turning to gray, and large, blue eyes. Her complexion was very pale, and her hands tiny. Blue doubted that she had ever weighed more than a hundred pounds. She sat quietly for a few moments, then called Rusty to take her back inside the house.

John Graves was soon back on the porch, and handed Blue a glass of wine. "Made this myself last year, and it turned out pretty well. Had a bumper crop of pink plums, and I must have put up around forty gallons."

Blue tasted the wine, licking his lips a few times. "It tastes so good a fellow might be tempted to drink too much of it."

"Sometimes a fellow does," Graves said, pointing to himself.

They talked for close to two hours, with Graves refilling their glasses twice. It was close to sunset when the ranch hands began to arrive at the barn. As they cared for their horses then made their way to the bunkhouse, Blue counted seven men. Graves waved at the hands, then continued talking.

"We'll look at Henry's southern boundaries tomorrow," he said, "then you can prowl around till you decide where you want to put the buildings."

"I'll take my time, look it over good."

"I know you will," Graves said, taking Blue's empty glass. "We need to find out what kind of water we can get before you even drive a stake. Soon as you make your decision, I'll have the farmers dig a well."

"I'll help them dig," Litt said quickly. "And I'll pay their wages. Two Papas sent money; it's in the bank over in San Antonio."

Graves nodded. "Henry pays his way."

They ate an early supper, and went to bed shortly after dark. Blue slept in the same bed as last night, down the hall from Rusty.

In the morning, Blue accompanied John Graves to the cook house, where the cowboys and farmers were having breakfast. Putting his hand on Blue's shoulder, Graves said, "This gent's name is Litt Blue, men. He's gonna be our neighbor to the north. He represents a good friend of mine from east Texas, and he'll be scouting the area for a place to put the ranch buildings. Just didn't want any of you fellows to get anxious when you see him wandering around."

Nodding, the cowboys looked Litt over. Then Graves and Blue were out of the building quickly.

Two mornings later, Blue pitched his tent beside the Frio. Unburdening his pack animals, he placed the packs inside the tent, along with his bedroll. When he had picketed Ike and the yellow mule, he remounted Sox and headed north. Starting at the north boundary, he would crisscross the area until he made his decision. And he would be in no hurry.

The process of selecting a building site took three days. Shortly after noon on the third day he began to drive stakes in the ground, denoting the location of the ranch house, bunkhouse, barn, and corrals. The water well would be dug in the ranch-house yard, close to the porch.

Though Blue had given careful consideration to several locations, the site of his choice was a mile-wide plateau fifty feet above the surrounding terrain. Treeless, except for the two mountain cedars that would stand in the yard, the grassy plain gradually sloped toward the Frio, two hundred yards away. The river was only a few inches deep here, and could be forded easily. The view to the north, up the canyon and into the mountains, was nothing short of spectacular. To the south, the terrain was almost level, and nothing obstructed the view for several miles. Two Papas could watch most of his cattle while sitting on the porch, Blue was thinking. He drove the last stake in the ground, less than a mile from his tent.

"On that little plateau with the two cedars?" Graves asked, when told of Blue's selection. "I was hoping you'd find that place. It's the prettiest homesite in the county. Tomorrow we'll start digging for some good water. I've got a windlass in the barn."

Blue was more than willing to let John Graves take charge of the building process. Two Papas had said the man was a master, and Litt's own knowledge of construction was limited. Besides, Graves seemed eager to take on the job. He intended to see that his friend, Henry Miles, had a ranch of the highest quality, he said.

"You just tell me what to do, Mister Graves," Blue said. "I'm just another hired hand."

"All right, I'll do that. All the brick and most of the other materiels will have to be hauled in from San Antonio. That'll be your job. I'll give you two wagons and another driver. Two trips a week is all you can make, so you'd better get a head start on Rusty. He lays the brick pretty fast."

The following morning at seven, Blue and a forty-year-old man named Will Milo headed for San Antonio. Each man drove a stout, four-horse team, hitched to a sturdy wagon with a wide bed. They carried food, bedrolls, and grain for the horses, for they would spend two nights on the road: one coming, and one going.

Milo had been on the Graves spread for several years. Short in stature, with thick chest and broad shoulders, he had close-cropped brown hair and tobacco-stained teeth. He also had a sense of humor, and told Blue two "Yankee" jokes while they were hitching up the teams.

As they pulled onto the road, Milo took the lead. He not only knew the area well, he knew exactly where they were going, having been there before. Litt knew only that they were headed for a warehouse filled with kiln-dried brick, somewhere in the San Antonio area.

They made good time with the empty wagons, always moving at a fast walk, or, when on a downhill grade, at a trot. They traveled for two hours without seeing another human, then Blue brought his team to a halt. Milo had stopped up ahead to talk with the driver of another wagon, headed in the opposite direction.

They obviously knew each other well, for they talked for several minutes, laughing back and forth. Perhaps Milo was telling the driver the same jokes Litt had heard this morning. At last Milo moved on, and the driver nodded and waved his hand as he passed Blue's wagon.

They were more than halfway to San Antonio, and the sun was still an hour high, when they pulled off the road at a small spring to camp for the night. As each horse was unhitched it was allowed to drink from the spring's runoff, then fed a generous portion of grain. Afterward, the animals were picketed alongside the shallow ditch, where they could water themselves.

When he had tramped around and gathered an armload of dead wood, Blue kindled a fire beside his wagon. The men were soon eating cold food and drinking hot coffee. The beef and biscuits the cook had prepared were very good, and disappeared quickly.

Milo sat with his back against a wagon wheel, the firelight creating flitting shadows around his eyes. He blew into his cup, then took another sip of his coffee. "You pretty good with that Colt you're wearing?"

Blue did not answer right away. He took a sip of his own coffee, then thought for a moment. "Good enough," he said.

Milo, who wore no sidearm himself, asked no more questions. He dashed his coffee grounds over his shoulder and turned the cup upside down on a rock. Then, placing his bedroll under the lead wagon, he laid his rifle beside it and retired for the night. After extinguishing the campfire, Blue went to bed under his own wagon.

Just before noon the following day they reached their destination, on the western edge of San Antonio. It was not a warehouse at all, but merely a fifty-yard-long shed that contained mountainous stacks of red brick. A small building stood in front of the shed, and Milo stopped his team there. A sign proclaiming UP-TON & SONS, the owners of the business, appeared above the doorway.

"I'll have to make arrangements with Leroy," Milo said, after he had walked back to Blue's wagon. "Then we'll back the wagons under the shed. They'll load us up while we take care of the horses and feed ourselves."

"Be sure to tell them that Mister Graves only wants the wagons loaded five layers deep," Litt said.

"Five layers?" Milo asked, seeming surprised. He tapped his fingers against the side of the wagon. "Hell, we could have left these top sideboards at home, then. We'll do that next trip. No reason for the horses to pull 'em back and forth if we ain't using 'em."

Blue nodded in agreement. He stood beside the wagon while Milo talked with Upton.

Half an hour later the wagons were under the shed, being loaded by Mexican laborers. When the horses had been watered, Blue and Milo joined Upton in the office, where they were given hot coffee to wash down their biscuits and bacon.

"What's John building over there?" Upton asked. He was a big man, over six feet tall and probably weighed two hundred fifty pounds.

"He's building a ranch house for a man named Henry Miles," Milo said, nodding in Litt's direction. "This is Mister Blue, he works for Miles."

Upton refilled his cup from the coffeepot on the stove. "Name sure sounds familiar," he said. "I freighted with a fellow named Miles during the war."

"He was a freighter, all right," Blue said.

"Big fellow? Bigger'n me?"

"That's him."

Placing his empty cup on a nearby table, Upton handed Blue a sack of cookies. "Take these with you. They come in mighty handy when a man's wanting something to munch on."

Blue accepted the sack. "That's most of the time with me," he said.

As the men were leaving the office, Upton said, "I hope you'll tell Mister Miles that I'd like to see him again. Ask him to stop by, when he's in the area."

"I'll do that," Blue said. "Of course, he won't be out here till fall. He's still in northeast Texas."

Half an hour later they were headed west. The horses handled the heavy load very well, and took the relatively smooth road at a fast walk.

It was after sundown when they reached the spring, and a family in a covered wagon had already taken the choice camping site the two had used last night. They parked the wagons thirty yards west of the spring and began to set up their own camp hurriedly. When they had fed and watered the horses, and picketed them beside the ditch, darkness was upon them.

"We got more wood than we're gonna be needin'," the man camped beside them said. "You're more'n welcome to it."

"Sure beats hunting it in the dark," Milo said. He soon returned from the man's fire with an armload. Blue had already filled the coffeepot from the spring. He kindled a fire quickly, for the wood was very dry.

They ate the last of their beef and biscuits, then sat around the fire eating cookies and sipping coffee. They talked for half an hour about one thing or another. When it became clear that Blue did not relish talking about the war, Milo discarded his after-dinner chew of tobacco, washed out his mouth with water from the spring, and crawled under his wagon. A few minutes later, Blue also went to bed.

6

By the middle of May, the house and out-buildings were taking shape. The diggers had hit a good vein of water, and Rusty had built a brick curb around the well. The roof was already on the barn, and all of the workers slept there at night. The same two men who had dug the well now worked on the barn from sunup to sundown. Rusty wanted no help on the house, except one man to keep him supplied with brick and mortar.

Blue and a twenty-four-year-old redhead named Lon Bills had built the corral, using cedar posts and peeled poles. Today was Wednesday, and they had just hung the corral gate.

Bills, a Mississippian who had come to Texas with his parents at the age of ten, was a hard worker, and well-liked by all. He was also respected for his prowess with a six-gun. "Lon's the fastest draw I've ever seen," Rusty had said to Blue a few weeks ago. "Not only that, he's a marksman. He'll hit what he shoots at."

Working together twelve hours a day, Blue and Bills had become fast friends, sleeping side by side on their bedrolls. They ate their meals together, usually filling their plates and moving off away from the others. They were occasionally joined by Blackie Elam, a thirty-year-old who had grown up in Houston. Elam was a six-footer with coal-black hair, and weighed about two hundred pounds. He had originally come from Arkansas, and moved to Houston at the age of ten.

It was nearing sundown, and the three had just filled their plates and leaned back against the barn. "A few days ago, I celebrated my twenty-first birthday peeling corral poles," Blue said, sipping his strong coffee. "Tomorrow, I intend to go into San Antonio and do it right."

"Not without me," Bills said, pointing at Litt with his spoon. "I've been trying to think of something to celebrate for the past two weeks."

"I ain't had a beer in six months," Elam said. "I guess I could be talked into going to town myself."

"All right," Blue said, "you're both invited. I'll even buy you a drink."

Rusty had just cleaned his trowel, and was busy rearranging his scaffolding for tomorrow. When the men approached him with their suggestion, he thought for a moment, then began to smile. "If you'll put it off for one more day, I'll go in with you. I can finish up laying the brick on this west wall tomorrow. Friday morning we can load up in one of the spring wagons and all ride in together. That way, we won't have a whole bunch of horses to fool around with."

The festive mood of the hands was contagious. John Graves decided to go along with them. Rusty hitched the team to his father's buggy, then took his place in the driver's seat. At sunup, they took the road to San Antonio. Blue, Bills, and Elam followed the buggy in the spring wagon. Elam had been elected to drive.

John Graves had remained close to home for most of the past year, due to his wife's deteriorating condition. He had recently hired a full-time nurse for Katie, however, and now felt the urge to get out and about. A man could sit on the porch for only so long, then he must stretch his legs. And his eyes.

An hour before sunset, they camped for the night at the same spring Blue had used on his brick-hauling trips. While the horses were being fed and watered, and picketed along the ditch, Elam built a campfire. Scrounging around in the desert for fuel had been unnecessary, for Blackie had thrown several sticks of dry wood into the wagon before leaving home. The coffeepot was soon boiling, and when Elam had warmed up the food that had been prepared by the ranch cook, the men had a good supper.

They reached San Antonio the following morning at eleven. After stabling the horses, the next order of the day was food. There had been nothing to cook for breakfast this morning, and each man had settled for a cup of coffee.

"The food's about as good at Tom's Place as anywhere else," Graves said. "I've eaten there several times."

When they entered the saloon, Graves spoke with the bartender for a moment, then walked to Tom Hale's office. The saloon owner opened the door at

Graves's knock. Graves disappeared inside, then the door closed again.

"Hello, Pedro," Blue said to the bartender. "Got some hot food for four hungry men?"

Pedro nodded. "Yes, indeed. Take that big table back by the kitchen door. The waitress will be with you shortly."

The men moved to the table, and the bartender delivered a pitcher of beer. They drank to Blue's recent birthday, then each man ordered the "special" of the day: beef stew, highly seasoned with red pepper.

Today was Saturday, and more than a dozen drinkers were already in the saloon, all of them sitting on the same side of the bar. A situation that was no doubt appreciated by the bartender, for he could serve them all with a minimum of effort.

Several saloon girls had also begun their day. Though they mostly stood around making conversation among themselves, they moved about enough to make sure they were noticed by the drinkers. A middle-aged man walked across the dance floor and stepped onto the riser. Obviously the piano player, he tinkered with the instrument a while, then joined the drinkers at the bar.

Litt had not yet finished his stew, when he saw the bartender carry a bottle of whiskey to the office. When Pedro returned, he spoke for a moment with two of the girls, each of whom appeared to be about twenty years old. Then he returned to the bar. As inconspicuously as possible, the girls eased along the wall slowly, then entered the office quickly.

Though it was obvious that the girls had gone to visit the two men in the office, no one at the table mentioned it. Rusty turned his eyes elsewhere, and appeared not to notice. Littleton Blue could not have cared less what John Graves did. The man was not yet old, and his wife was an invalid. It was possible that Katie knew about these activities, and even approved. Since she herself could no longer take care of her man's needs, perhaps the two had an understanding. Blue discarded the matter from his thoughts, ordering another pitcher of beer.

Two Union soldiers stepped inside the saloon, walked around the bar looking the patrons over, then walked back outside.

Blue motioned toward the soldiers as they left the building. "I guess it's a little bit hard on them," he said, "knowing that some of us might be enjoying life these days."

"I don't know," Rusty said. "They're usually pretty good about leaving people alone, unless something gets out of hand. They've been ordered to occupy Texas, but they'd all rather be back home in New York or Pennsylvania. Most of the time they won't even interfere with a fight, as long as Texans are shooting each other."

Two hours later, John Graves was still in the office. So were the girls. Smiling at the thought, Blue pushed back his chair. "I'm gonna get a room at the hotel across the street, then hunt up a new pair of boots. Anybody coming?"

Nobody volunteerd.

He registered at the hotel, then began to walk the streets alone. A few minutes later, he entered a boot shop. Though the boot maker tried to sell him custom-made boots, Blue chose a pair right off the shelf, and the fit was perfect. He carried them under his arm as he walked back to the hotel.

He lay down on his bed to rest for a while. The beer he drank had made him drowsy, and he was soon asleep. When he awoke two hours later, he was in no hurry to get up. With his hands behind his head, and the pillow beneath his shoulders, he lay on the bed thinking for a long time. He believed the ranch buildings would all be completed by the end of June. So far, he had spent none of Two Papas's money. John Graves had taken charge of the operation from the start, saying Henry Miles would pay for the whole "shebang" in one lump sum. Litt supposed that the letter he delivered to Graves might have said something to that effect. Two Papas knew Graves was a builder, and might have asked him to take charge. At any rate, Graves had begun to speak with authority immediately after reading the letter. He had drawn up the house, laid it out, driven the stakes, and stretched the string in a single day, a feat which Blue suspected was no more than a grain of sand in his shovelful of building knowledge. Blue paid close attention, determined to learn as much as he could.

An hour after dark, Litt returned to Tom's Place. The crowd had tripled, and the merrymaking was in full swing. A majority of the men sat or stood with their backs to the bar, watching the activities on the dance floor. Several men were busy yelling and stomping the floor, jerking women around in what might loosely be called dancing.

Blue could see Lon Bills standing at the far end of the bar. His eyes were also on the dance floor. Litt made his way through the crowd and joined him. "I see you're still here," he said. "Where did everybody else go?"

"They started drifting out an hour or two ago. Some of them probably went to bed. Is that where you've been?"

"Yeah. I stretched out to rest, and dozed off." Blue

bought a shot of whiskey and drank it in one gulp. Then he leaned his back against the bar. "I'm hungry, Lon," he said. "I noticed that the restaurant across the street is still open. You want to join me for supper?"

"Yep," Bills said, turning to face the bar and inhaling the drink that had been sitting at his elbow. "Lead the way."

Bills had taken only one step toward the front door, when a bearded man stepped in front of him, blocking his way. The man was about Lon's own size, and appeared to be only a few years older. A .44 Colt rested in a holster that was tied to his right leg.

"Been watchin' you for a while, feller," the man said to Bills. "It's plain enough that you cain't take your eyes off that little redhead. You speak one word to her, and you've got me to fight."

Bills said nothing. He hit the man with a left-handed blow on the cheek that sent him sprawling. The beard went for his gun as he hit the floor, but checked his draw when he saw that he was looking into the barrel of Lon's Colt. After crawling a short distance, the man regained his feet and scampered from the building. Silently, Bills reholstered his gun.

Only a few men were close enough to actually see the altercation. Most of them stood with their mouths open, in awe of the fast draw they had witnessed. Littleton Blue was among them. All he had seen was a blur, then Bills suddenly had his gun in firing position, its barrel pointed at the space between the bearded man's eyes. The man on the floor had seen the same thing, and checking his draw had saved his life. Bills could hardly have missed at such a close range. Catching Blue's eye, Bills pointed to the front door, then led the way. As they left the building, they could hear a man with a loud voice in the background:

"Did y'all see that redhead empty that holster? Damned if I ever saw anythang like it. I tell you . . ."

They were soon seated at a table in the restaurant, where each man ordered beefsteak. The incident in the saloon was mentioned by neither man. Lon was as calm as Litt had ever seen him. Blue was impressed. He sat watching, as Bills carved his steak with the nerveless hands of a surgeon. Talk about self-assurance! Talk about sand.

They had paid for their meal and were about to leave, when Blue stopped just inside the front door. A placard on the wall had caught his eye: ONE HUNDRED DOLLARS! it proclaimed, then went on to say that a professional fighter would take on all comers tomorrow morning, with one hundred dollars going to any man who could last three rounds with the heavyweight billed as The Hammer. The place was a vacant warehouse on the west side of town, and admission was twenty-five cents.

When both men had read the poster, Blue said, "I sure could use that hundred, Lon. I think I'll take a shot at it."

"Really?"

"Really. I believe I can knock out any man I ever saw, if I get the right punch."

Bills smiled, looking at Blue out of the corner of his eye. "I believe you could, too," he said. "I would remind you, though, that prize-fighters are mighty good at keeping a man from getting that 'right' punch."

They walked to the hotel, where Bills rented a room of his own. Just before they said good night, Blue told Bills once again that he intended to take on the professional in the morning.

All five of the men met in the restaurant for breakfast.

The good times were over, and it was time to get back to work. When told that Blue intended to fight the professional, John Graves winked his eye. "Well, I guess it'll be worth a quarter to watch Litt knock that prizefighter around."

Two hours later, they were at the warehouse. They had parked their wagons and tied the horses a block away, for all the closer places had been taken. As they walked into the crowded building, the fight promoter was standing in the ring, making his spiel. The fighter was standing beside him with his hands taped, and wearing a robe. Men were standing on all sides of the ring, jostling for position.

John Graves pushed his way through. "We've got a challenger here!"

Blue made his way to ringside.

"Step right up, young man," the promoter said. "Tell me your name, weight, and where you come from."

Blue told him, then climbed into the ring and stripped to the waist. As the referee taped Litt's hands, the promoter was yelling again. "You all know my offer, but I'll repeat it. The rounds are three minutes long. If the challenger can stand on his feet for three rounds, he gets one hundred dollars."

"What does he get if he knocks your boy out?" Bills asked.

"An extra hundred," the promoter said.

Blue was standing in the ring with his hands taped, and much betting was going on at ringside. Graves noticed that, after taking a good look at the muscular youth, many of the men were betting on him.

The promoter came to Blue's corner and introduced him: "In this corner, weighing two hundred twenty pounds, from South Carolina, Littleton Blue!" A roar went up from the audience. Crossing the ring, the promoter continued. "And in this corner, from Dallas, Texas, weighing one hundred eighty-eight pounds, The Hammer!" A louder roar from the audience.

When the bell rang, they met in the center of the ring. It took the professional exactly two minutes to beat Blue to a pulp. He had broken three ribs, completely closed one eye, crushed his lips, and inflicted bruises too numerous to count. The last blow left Blue lying helplessly in the center of the ring. He was trying to struggle to his feet, when John Graves reached him.

"Get out of this ring, Litt," Graves said loudly. "That man will kill you!"

As they made their way through the crowd and out the door, the promoter was making his pitch again: "Normally, I don't fight my boy twice in one day. But due to the short nature of the preceeding fight . . ."

Never in Blue's life had he felt so humiliated. He had even heard some men booing him as he left the building.

When they reached the wagons, Graves said, "Let's find a doctor, and get you checked over."

"I'll be all right," Blue said.

"You should listen to Mister Graves, Litt," Lon Bills said. "You might have some broken ribs. They can puncture a lung and do a man in."

"All right, then. The doctor."

After taping up Blue's ribs, and administering to his many bruises, the doctor said, "The ribs are broken. I want you to keep this tape on for three weeks; give 'em a chance to mend before you do any work. Your face will heal in about a month. I don't believe you'll have any scars."

They camped by the spring on the way home, and

ate food they had bought in town. Blue, who had hardly spoken during the afternoon, sat staring into the campfire. "I know damn well I'm stronger than that fighter," he said, "and I know I can hit harder. But he made a complete ass out of me."

"Not exactly," Blackie Elam said. "The man is a trained fighter, and you weren't supposed to beat him. You would have stretched him out if you'd ever connected with one of them haymakers you were throwing, but I doubt very much that you could ever hit him with a good solid punch without some training."

"Blackie used to be a prize-fighter," Graves said. "Maybe he'll show you some things. Did you know The Hammer, Blackie?"

"Yeah, I know him. I fought him twice, and he beat me both times. He's the main reason I quit fighting. I got as far as I could go without beating him, so I gave up the game. The man's name is Bob Skinner. I tried to signal Litt when I saw who he was up against, but he never did look my way."

"I'm gonna do two things," Blue said, sipping the last of his coffee. "I'm gonna learn to fight, and I'm gonna get fast with a gun."

Graves took a sip from his small flask of whiskey. "Well, both things are good to know, but a man has to be careful not to let them get him in more trouble than he can get out of. Lon is the best among us with any type of weapon. Maybe him and Blackie will work with you."

Both men agreed to teach him.

The fire had burned low, and the men soon crawled into their bedrolls. Litt lay awake for a long time thinking of the beating he had taken. He had learned from it. The fighter had been a slick one, all right. Blue had thrown dozens of punches, but had been unable to lay a hand on the man. The Hammer had obviously put a lot of work into his craft: developing his skillful ring movements, learning exactly when and how to deliver his devastating blows. Blue believed that he himself could become that good. If Blackie would get him started in the right direction, Litt would do the rest himself with practice and determination. Just before he went to sleep, he promised himself that no man would ever put him down again.

Blue awoke at sunup, and walked to the fire, where Rusty was preparing breakfast. The others were sitting around sipping coffee. Litt filled his own cup.

"Did you sleep all right?" Graves asked.

"Woke up every time I turned over. These ribs hurt."

"They'll keep hurting for a week or two, then the pain will leave kind of suddenly." Graves refilled his cup, and seated himself beside Blue. "Don't know where the pain goes," he added, chuckling. "Guess it moves on to somebody else."

When they headed home, Lon Bills drove the wagon, with Blue sitting on the seat beside him. They were barely underway, when Litt mentioned the incident in the saloon. "I'm still trying to figure out how you got your gun into play so quick last night, Lon. Where'd you learn that?"

"It's not something that has to be learned," Bills said. "A man already knows how to do it. You make a fast draw the same way you make a slow draw. You just have to keep practicing till you get so it don't take you all day."

"I'm gonna get fast, Lon."

"I know. I've been paying attention to your movements ever since I met you. Some people are just naturally quick, and others are slow. You're one of the quick ones."

7

John Graves and his builders put the finishing touches on the ranch house and outbuildings the first week in June, and departed for their own homes. Using one of Graves's wagons, Blue had hauled several cots and a stove from San Antonio, and moved into the bunkhouse. He bought nothing for the big house, Two Papas would choose his own furnishings.

Litt believed that he had two months to kill, for there was simply nothing to do except keep an eye on the place. Two Papas had said the herd would arrive in late summer. Litt had no way of knowing how Rope Johnson and his men were doing with the gather, and doubted that Two Papas knew. Contacting him would change nothing.

Blue's ribs had healed nicely, and his face bore no scars from The Hammer's fists. He had not forgotten the beating he had taken, however. Blackie Elam had been true to his word. He had taught Litt as much as he could in such a short time, and had set up a heavy punching bag in the barn. Litt now spent a good part of every day pounding the bag.

And Lon Bills taught Blue the rudiments of the fast draw. He filed the front sight off Litt's Colt, then cut away part of the holster. "The rest is up to you," he said. "You've got to practice till your arm aches, then practice some more."

As the days turned into weeks, Blue, with nothing else to do, was constantly at work on the things the two men had taught him. As instructed by Bills, he had started out with his shells in his pocket, practicing with an empty gun. As his speed improved, he began to work with live ammunition. He had no problem hitting a target; he had been a good marksman for many years. He practiced the fast draw hundreds of times each day, and the blisters on his hand had long since turned to calluses. He was not yet as fast as Bills, he decided. But he would be.

Each night he spent at least two hours in the barn. He pounded the punching bag by lantern light, and practiced the fancy footwork Blackie had shown him. He retired to the bunkhouse after each workout in complete exhaustion, and usually slept fitfully. Once, he dreamed that he was back in the ring with The Hammer. Of course, in the dream, the fight turned out quite differently.

Today was Sunday, and Bills and Elam rode over to visit Blue. Both men had taken a strong liking to Litt, and decided to check on his well-being. Blue saw them coming half a mile away, and put on the coffeepot.

"We just got an urge to see your handsome face," Elam said, dismounting at the bunkhouse door. "Decided to ride over and check on you."

"Doing real well," Blue said, shaking hands with both men. "The worst thing about being alone is having to eat my own cooking. I guess the herd'll be here next month, then my vacation will be over."

"You can count on that," Bills said. He walked to the stove and filled a coffee cup. "When you drive a bunch of cows that far, they don't settle down too easy. Some of them are gonna be wanting to go on to California."

They finished their coffee, then walked around outside, for it was a beautiful day. When Blackie suggested that they go to the barn and work out on the punching bag, Blue was ready and willing. Bills declined the invitation, saying he would have another cup of coffee, then walk around for a while.

In the barn, the two men went to work. Blackie began by showing Litt some of the ways a man could use his feet to keep an opponent guessing. Then, after Blue had punched the bag for a while, they walked into corral and squatted on their haunches.

Elam began to draw diagrams in the sand with a twig. "In a brawl," Blackie began, "the idea is to get it over with as quickly as possible. In the ring, that's not necessarily the case. You take your time, and wait for the right opening. You should always avoid being pinned on the ropes or in a corner. Learn to slip off to the right or left, and never, never bounce directly off the ropes toward an opponent. It's a very dangerous maneuver.

"To slip out to the right, step to the right with the right foot, pivot, then follow with the left. To slip out to the left, reverse the process. There are times in a contest, when it's advisable to clinch. You should always clinch when you're off balance, or when you're tired or hurt.

"I didn't know how to beat Bob Skinner when I fought him, but I do now. I've had a long time to think about it. Anytime you square off against a man who stands flat-footed, remember this: You're facing a man who depends on his ability to hit hard with either hand. Bob Skinner is such a man. He always uses a flat-footed stance, and he can knock your socks off from either side. If you let him tag you many times, it's all over.

"A man can't hurt you when he's off balance, Litt, so that's exactly where you want him. Combine feints with actual leads. Feint at the head, hit at the body. Feint hooks, then score inside with straight punches. The second you know for sure that you've got him off balance, go in for the kill. You've got enough punching power to put any man in the world to sleep."

Blue nodded, and the men got to their feet.

Bills was standing in the doorway when they returned to the bunkhouse. "Let's walk down to the river, Litt," he said. "I want to discuss something with you."

Elam took the hint, and stayed behind. Bills sat down on the bank of the river, his feet almost dangling in the water. "This man you call Two Papas . . . the fellow who owns all of this. What's he like?"

Blue was silent for a moment, then smiled. "Well, he's as tall as me and a hell of a lot bigger."

"You know what I mean."

"Uh-huh." Litt sat down beside his friend. "Two Papas is a man first, and a businessman second. I don't know anybody who would speak ill of him."

They sat side by side, looking into the water for a

long time. Litt knew that Bills had more on his mind.
He waited patiently.

"I've been doing some thinking," Bills said finally.
"Do you think Two Papas is gonna be hiring any men
when he gets out here?"

"I don't know. It might depend on whether the men
bringing in the herd want to stay here or not. Or
maybe he'll send them back for another herd, and hire
a whole new crew for this place. Why? Do you know
somebody that's needing a job?"

"Yeah. Me."

Blue picked up a flat rock and skated it across the
water. "Hell, I thought you were happy working for
Mister Graves. He seems nice, and all of you get along
so well."

"He's a good man to work for, and I like everybody
over there. It's just that I feel like making a change.
I . . ." He got to his feet quickly. "Dammit, I just want
to be up here with you!"

Blue sat quietly for some time, deeply touched by
Lon's words. "I'll take it up with Two Papas as soon as
he gets here."

Shortly after his visitors departed, Blue headed for
the barn. He was soon working on the new things
Blackie had shown him today. As he moved about,
practicing the footwork, his mind returned to the
schoolboys he had fought during his growing years.
They had not known how to fight. Neither had Litt.
He had beaten them only because he was bigger and
stronger. The game men played was entirely different,
and Blue was determined to learn it. He pounded the
bag until dark, then walked to the bunkhouse and
went to bed.

He fed the horses at daybreak, then drew a bucket
of water from the well. He had coffee and oatmeal for

breakfast, then sat around for a while trying to think of something else that needed doing. A month ago he had considered building a chicken house and buying some chickens, but had second thoughts. Foxes and coyotes abounded in the area, and each animal would probably eat a chicken a day until there were none left.

An hour after sunrise, he saddled Sox and headed for Uvalde, a small settlement a few miles to the south. Once called Encina, the name had been changed only a few years ago. Though the town was little more than a wide place in the road, there was a blacksmith shop. Two general stores, dry-goods store, hardware, and a smattering of other merchants lined its single street.

Blue rode past the hardware, and tied the chestnut in front of a general store. A bell rang when he opened the door, and an elderly lady was at the counter quickly. "Good morning," she said. "Just look around. If I can help you, let me know."

The building was long and narrow, with an aisle down its middle. Blue moved down the aisle slowly, looking over the merchandise. Most of the things a man might need were there, even harness and horse collars. He returned to the counter. "I need some tinned soups and meats," he said to the lady. "Fish too, if you have it."

She nodded.

A basketful of eggs rested on the far end of the counter. "I'll buy some eggs," he said, "if you can pack them so they don't break on the ride home. And I was hoping to buy a smoked ham."

She nodded again. "I can wrap the eggs so they don't break, but I don't have the ham. Farther down the street, on the opposite side, is a small log building called The Smokehouse. They should have what you want."

After adding two pounds of cheese and three boxes of .44 shells to his order, Blue paid the lady, then headed for The Smokehouse.

The following morning, after a breakfast of ham and eggs, he saddled the chestnut and rode to the Graves Ranch. John Graves had insisted on lending Blue a team and wagon, along with a man to help him cut firewood. Litt had thought about building a shed for the wood, but remembered that the Box M had none. The fuel for the stoves and fireplaces was stacked right out in the weather. Blue would do the same here.

The man Graves volunteered for the wood cutting was a thirty-year-old named Trent Ives. Prematurely gray, Ives was of medium height, and very muscular. Obviously a man with little to say, he had merely grunted when introduced to Blue, then caught two large mules from the corral and hitched them to a heavy wagon. After loading two crosscut saws, two axes, a jug of coal oil, several wedges, and a sledge, he stood by the wagon for a few moments. Then, almost as an afterthought, he threw in two spare handles for the axes. He climbed to the wagon seat. "You got plenty to eat up there?"

Blue nodded. "Such as it is."

They headed north, with Blue taking the lead. When they reached the ranch, he loosed his chestnut into the corral, then heated ham and biscuits for their dinner. When they had eaten, he climbed to the wagon seat beside Ives, and pointed north. "Big stand of hardwoods on the hillside about three miles up."

Ives said nothing, and clucked to the mules.

When they had felled the first tree and chopped off the limbs, Blue moved on to the next.

"You ought not to take that tree," Ives said. "Nor

the one next to it. A man ought to take one tree and skip two. If you take 'em all, half the dirt on this hillside'll be down there in the river in a few years."

Blue thought for only a moment, then nodded curtly. Of course, the man was right. Litt skipped two trees, then began to notch the third with his ax.

They had twelve trees on the ground when they quit for the day. Tomorrow, they would saw the logs into blocks of different lengths: long for the fireplace, short for the cooking stoves. Then, as soon as the blocks were hauled to the house, Blue intended to dismiss his helper. He needed no help splitting the blocks and stacking the wood. Besides, he did not like the man. Earlier in the afternoon, in an effort to make conversation, Blue had asked Ives how long he had been working for John Graves. "About as long as I want to," Ives said. "The next time he sends me on a shit detail like this, I'll be long gone." Blue would make sure the detail did not last past tomorrow evening.

They sawed up the trees by noon the following day, and in midafternoon, delivered a wagonload of blocks to the ranch, dumping them in a pile behind the house.

Blue laid Graves's tools in the wagon bed. "I won't be needing you anymore, Mister Ives. Take the team and wagon back to Mister Graves, and tell him I appreciate the use of them."

"Why, there's at least eight more loads up there," Ives said. "You can't get that wood down here without this wagon."

"Sure, I can. I'll be heading for San Antonio tomorrow morning. When I get back, I'll have my own team and wagon. Axes and wedges, too."

Ives began to fidget. "Aw, there ain't no use in you doing that," he said, his voice sounding almost apologetic. "I'll just stay on till we've got that wood down here."

"You're not listening very well, Mister Ives," Blue said sternly. "I want you off these premises."

Ives never looked at Blue again. He climbed to the seat and whipped the mules south.

Litt stood in the yard till the man was out of sight. He wondered what kind of story Ives would offer if Graves began to ask questions.

Inside the bunkhouse, he kindled a fire in the stove. He dumped two handfuls of dried beans into a pot of water, then added a few small pieces of ham. Then he began to go over the things he had in the bunkhouse, making a list of the things he needed from San Antonio. He could think of nothing he needed in the way of food. He had plenty of beans, a big bucket of lard, a barrel of flour, cornmeal, oatmeal, eggs, jelly, and smoked ham and sausages. Plenty of wild game was also around for the taking. He had so far been reluctant to shoot a deer, for the weather was hot, and the meat would spoil quickly. He put no food on the list, but if he saw something he wanted, he would put it in the wagon.

Two days later, Blue was at the livery stable in San Antonio. "If ya gonna buy th' team an' th' harness," the liveryman was saying, "by jingo I'll jist about give ya th' wagon. She ain't exactly new, but she's solid. I greased th' wheels jist last week."

"How much?" Blue asked.

"Hunnert an' twenty. Hunnert an' ten fer th' team an' harness, an' ten dollars fer th' wagon."

Blue began to count out the money. "Write me a bill of sale, and I'll be on my way."

The liveryman stepped inside his office, and returned with a small tablet and a pencil. "I'd 'preciate it if ya'd jist write it yaself, an' let me sign it."

A few minutes later, Litt tied the team at the hardware store's hitching rail. He bought the tools he needed, along with a hundred feet of rope, a claw hammer, and a can of axle grease.

He bought coffee, rice, cookies, and sugar at the general store. Then, with the unsaddled chestnut tethered to the rear of the wagon, he took the road home at a trot. Remembering that campers had burned all the dead wood within walking distance of the spring, he continually cast his eyes about for anything that would burn. Each time he saw something, he would pull off the road and throw it in the wagon, atop the four sack of oats he had bought from the liveryman.

Blue had the campground all to himself when he pulled up at the spring, two hours before sunset. By the time he fed, watered, and picketed his animals, however, two more wagons arrived, headed in opposite directions. The drivers deliberately parked their vehicles a hundred feet apart. All types of people traveled the roads these days, and the man who trusted a stranger was rare. Most folks kept to themselves when traveling, and were almost always armed to the teeth. There was plenty of room at the ditch to water a dozen horses at a time. However, the second driver stood by his wagon holding his team till the first driver had watered his horses and returned to his own wagon. Only then did the second man lead his team to the ditch.

Blue sat by his fire waiting for his coffee to boil. A teenaged boy had to walk close to him to get a bucket of water, for Litt was camped near the spring. The youngster nodded, and Blue waved his hand. "Guess you folks could use a fire," he said. "I've got more wood than I need." The boy nodded again, and walked to his wagon.

After a short conversation with his family, he was back. "Pa says we could use a little o' that wood. That is if ya shore ya ain't gonna be needin' it yaself."

"I'm sure," Blue said. He piled the remainder of the wood on the boy's outstretched arms, then sat back watching as the family kindled a cooking fire. He ate a bag of cookies and drank most of his coffee, then extinguished his own fire. At dark, he spread his bedroll under the wagon and crawled in, his Colt close to hand.

He traveled from dawn to dusk the following day. It was already dark by the time he unhitched and unharnessed the team. He fed all of his animals by lantern light, and left their stalls open. The new team would quickly learn that they could walk down the chute that extended from the west side of the corral and water themselves from the shallow Frio.

At midmorning the following day, Blue had just thrown off a load of blocks and was about to head up the canyon for another, when he had company. Lon Bills rode around the corner of the house. "I see you're hard at it," he said.

Blue nodded. "Yep. Looks like you might be taking the day off."

Bills dismounted. "It's like I told you a few days ago. I'm in the mood for a change. I told Mister Graves I was coming up here; that if you didn't want me, I would head west."

Litt stepped from the wagon, and stood quietly for a moment. "The truth is, Two Papas told me to hire anybody I needed. I didn't mention it the other day because I didn't want Mister Graves feeling hard at me."

"Mister Graves don't give a shit," Bills said, loosening the cinch around his horse's belly. "He could hire a dozen men between now and sunup tomorrow. He even gave me a bonus when I left."

Smiling, Blue offered a handshake. "Put your horse in the corral, then climb in the wagon. We've got a lot of wood to split and stack."

8

lue was in the barn punching the bag, when Rope Johnson poked his head around the door. "Your friend at the bunkhouse said I'd find you down here," he said.

Blue stepped forward quickly, shaking Johnson's hand and hugging his shoulder. "Don't know when I've been so glad to see somebody, Rope. Did you bring the cows?"

"Bedded 'em down on the Sabinal yesterday evening. Spent most of today hunting you. Two Papas told me to follow the Frio north till I saw some new buildings, and here you are."

As they walked toward the bunkhouse, Johnson stopped for a moment, his eyes taking in the area.

"You chose this place well, Litt. Damn, this is nice. I sure didn't expect a brick house, though."

"Neither did I," Blue said. "It was John Graves's idea." He continued walking. "Come on, I'll warm up the stew and put on a pot of coffee."

A short while later, the three men were seated at the table, eating the highly seasoned food.

"Is this stew made from a rabbit?" Johnson asked.

"Nope," Blue said, smiling and shaking his head. "Two rabbits."

They sat at the table long after they finished eating, with Johnson telling the story of the longhorns. Recruiting the Mexicans to hogtie and drag the cattle out of the dense thickets, or ambush and capture them when they came out of the brush on moonlight nights to feed, had been the easy part, he said.

Though the Mexican vaqueros were excellent riders and ropers, most were totally averse to trail driving. The lure of the fiesta was simply too strong. Try as he might, Rope had managed to talk only three of them into making the drive. After much searching, Johnson had finally recruited fifteen riders, most of them teenaged boys, from the Beaumont area.

The drive itself had been much easier than Johnson expected. They had lost twenty head during a mild stampede, and lost half as many crossing the Colorado River. Otherwise, the longhorns had settled down after a few days on the trail, and, led by two old, well-domesticated oxen, moved steadily west, causing few problems.

"I consider myself lucky," Johnson said. "Easiest drive I ever made."

"When do you want to go after the cows?" Blue asked.

Johnson walked to the stove to refill his cup.

"Thought I'd sleep here tonight. It'll be dark in an hour, anyhow. I'd be leery about riding up on that herd at night. Every one of the riders is loaded for bear. Most of 'em are just kids, and they're jumpy as hell."

Blue nodded. "How many cows you got?"

"Thirty-five hundred head," Johnson answered, getting to his feet. "Give or take a few."

Johnson walked through the doorway, followed by Bills. Blue watched as the two headed for the barn, Johnson leading his horse. They were talking and laughing like old friends, and Litt was pleased. Earlier, when he had attempted to introduce them to each other, he found that Bills had already introduced himself, when Johnson first knocked at the bunkhouse door.

The three men reached the herd at ten o'clock the following morning. The cattle were up and grazing on the east bank of the Sabinal, a short distance north of its junction with the Frio. Several riders were posted on either side of the herd, which was strung out across the grassy plains and around a distant hillside. Johnson led the way across the shallow river, and two men from the herd rode out to meet them.

Rope introduced the riders as Getty and Turner. When the handshaking was over, Johnson spoke to Getty, who was the older of the two. "We'll take 'em across the river right here, then head 'em north. Ride down the line and spread the word. Get 'em moving as quick as you can, and push 'em hard. Keep 'em moving all day, and they'll be home by nightfall."

With little prodding, the old oxen led the herd into the water, the younger cattle willing and even eager to follow the older and supposedly wiser ones.

No swimming was required, for the water was only knee-deep.

Johnson himself rode point, and Blue and Bills tagged along, leading the herd due north toward Box M2 range, the brand that the cattle would soon wear on their hips. The cook, driving his grub-and-gear cart, rode well off to the side, avoiding as much dust as possible. The remuda of extra horses was the last to cross, two young riders yelling at their heels.

All day long they pushed north, and two hours before sunset, reached their destination. The cattle were watered from the Frio, then bunched on the wide, grassy plain below the ranch house, on the east side of the river. Tomorrow, the branding would start. They would be driven into the branding chute singly, touched on the hip with a hot Box M2 iron, then driven across the Frio, the river separating the branded from the unbranded. When the job was done, they would be allowed to scatter as their instincts dictated. Then the riders would be paid off in gold, and most would return to Beaumont.

Several days later, the riders followed Blue to San Antonio, where they were paid in full. Only two of the men chose to remain at the Box M2: Getty and Turner.

Joe Getty was a twenty-six-year-old Mississippian who had much in common with Littleton Blue. Getty had fought with Nathan Bedford Forrest, who had enlisted in the Confederate Army as a private, and risen to the rank of general. General Robert E. Lee himself had once called Forrest the most effective general on either side of the conflict. Getty had been with Forrest at Shiloh. He had also been there at the end, when in March 1865, Forrest was defeated by General James H. Wilson at Selma, Alabama. Forrest surrendered his army a few weeks later, in May.

Joe Getty returned to his home at McComb, Mississippi, but found no reason to stay. He had been hanging around Beaumont for half a year, when recruited by Rope Johnson. The fact that Getty had no experience with wild longhorns was not enough to deter Johnson, for he was hard up for men. Getty had learned on the job, as had the majority of the other riders recruited for the drive. He had grown up the hard way, working from dawn to dusk in the fields, and had been further seasoned by the long, drawn-out war. Dark-haired and brown-eyed, he stood five-foot-ten and weighed one hundred eighty pounds. He was broad-shouldered and very muscular, and, though he would never tell any of these men about it, the folks back home had nicknamed him "Scrappin' Joe."

Billy Turner was not yet fully grown. Pink-faced and showing no signs that he would ever be able to grow a beard, the youngster had turned seventeen only last month. He had light blue eyes, and blond hair that hung to his shoulders. Though this was the first job he had ever held, Johnson said the boy had more than carried his weight on the drive. When Turner asked for a steady job on the Box M2, Blue signed him on. He also noticed that the boy put his money in the bank, rather than going off carousing with the others.

Two Papas arrived ten days later. Blue was standing beside Rope Johnson at the bunkhouse door, when they spotted two covered wagons approaching from the south. As they closed the distance, Blue could see that Two Papas himself was driving the lead team, flanked by two riders. Any speculation Blue might have had as to who would ramrod Box M2 was quickly put to rest, for he recognized one of the riders as Cecil Hudson.

Kicking his big roan in the ribs, Hudson rode forward and dismounted, his right hand extended. "Good to see you, Litt." He pumped Blue's hand a few times. "Damn, what a layout," he added, his left arm waving around at the surrounding area. "Best ranching country I ever saw." Then he shook hands with Johnson, complimenting him for putting the herd together and getting it through.

Two Papas halted his team and stepped from the wagon like a much younger man, his face beaming. "You did a very good job, son," he said, addressing Litt, "and I'm plenty proud of you." He stood for a moment, looking down the slope toward the river. "You couldn't have chosen a better location."

"That's about all I did," Blue said. "Mister Graves took charge of the building."

"That's one of the things I asked him to do," Two Papas said. "John's a master builder." Handing the team's reins to Johnson, he walked to the main house and disappeared inside.

The second wagon was driven by a fifty-year-old man named Frank, who had signed on as the ranch cook. He brought the wagon to a halt and introduced himself. Blue pointed out to the man that there was no stove in the cook shack, that he would have to do his cooking in the bunkhouse till better arrangements could be made. The bald-headed, overweight man nodded and headed for the cook shack.

The second rider was a small, dark, bowlegged man from El Paso. Named Biff Collins, he was about thirty-five years old, and a seasoned ranch hand. When introduced, he stepped forward and shook hands, then returned to his horse, out of earshot of the conversation.

When Two Papas rejoined them he was still smiling. "Sally is gonna love this place," he said. "Especially the house. I tell you, John Graves thought of everything."

Blue nodded. "You'll have to settle with him on the cost, Two Papas. He footed the whole bill. I spent some of your money buying things for the ranch, then paid off the trail hands. The rest is in the bank in San Antonio."

"Good boy," Two Papas said, sqeezing Blue's shoulder. "How many men you got on the payroll?"

"Five, counting myself."

"Perfect. That gives us seven riders and a cook. The exact number I wanted. We'll unload these wagons tomorrow, then start hauling in the things we need from San Antonio."

Two days later, Blue signed the Box M2 account over to Henry Miles at the bank in San Antonio. When Two Papas paid him the five months' pay he had coming, Litt deposited it in his own account. Then they began to move about the town, with Two Papas selecting the things he wanted for the main house. He bought identical stoves with large, wide ovens for the main house and the cook shack. Litt helped load them on the wagons, knowing that the cook would be pleased.

They made three trips to San Antonio, using all three wagons, and Two Papas went every time. He completely furnished his own home and the cook shack, and bought tools and plows. The last trip Litt's wagon was loaded with grain for the working horses. The loafers got nothing but grass.

When they had unloaded the last wagon, Two Papas pointed to the large woodpiles beside the house and the cook shack. "Who's idea was it to cut all the wood?"

"I knew we'd be needing it," Blue said. "Decided to cut it early so it would be drying."

Two Papas took a step toward the house, then stopped, turned, and fished a gold eagle from his pocket. "Consider this a bonus for thinking about it," he said, as he laid the ten-dollar coin in Blue's hand.

Litt started to say something, then thought better of it. He stood watching as Two Papas disappeared inside the house. Shaking his head, he dropped the eagle into his pocket, making a mental note to share it with Lon Bills. Then he headed for the barn to punch the bag for a while.

Inside the barn, Litt made fifty fast draws with his Colt, then hung his gunbelt on a peg. Then he stripped to the waist and went to work on the bag, each punch an imaginary blow to The Hammer's midsection. It was easy to get caught up in the weaving, ducking, and fancy footwork Blackie had taught him, but Blue had no way of gauging what effect it might have on an opponent. The bag did not punch back.

Although Blue had never fought a full-grown man, and none of his combat during the war had been hand to hand, he had always been confident that because of his superior size and strength, he could handle himself against any adversary. The Hammer had quickly pointed out the errors in Blue's thinking. He had beaten Litt to a pulp, while dodging every defensive blow with ease. No, sir, Blue was thinking, as he hit the bag with another flurry of punches. Fighting was not just a matter of overpowering an opponent. Fighting was an art.

As Blue walked from the barn, Lon Bills led his horse through the corral gate and began to remove the saddle. He smiled, then motioned toward the punching bag. "About ready to take on The Hammer again?"

Litt shook his head. "Not yet," he said, then changed the subject. "I've been showing Two Papas the corner markers of his property. He wants every man on the ranch to know where they are, and I've been elected to do the showing. I'll start with you and Getty tomorrow morning."

Bills nodded, then led his horse to its feeding trough.

On Saturday morning, Litt remembered to tell Bills that Two Papas had given them a ten-dollar bonus for cutting the wood.

"Let's go down to Uvalde tonight and spend it," Bills said. "My mouth's been feeling dry for weeks."

"I'll talk to Cecil," Blue said. "I don't think he'll mind. Maybe Getty would like to ride down with us. He hasn't been anywhere since he signed on."

"I'll ask him," Bills said.

Getty agreed to join them, and the three men rode south in the afternoon. They reached Uvalde at sunset, and had supper in a small restaurant at the edge of town. An hour later, they tied their horses at the Buckhorn Saloon, a few doors down from The Smokehouse.

The building was almost square, with a low roof made of cypress shingles. Inside, a bar made of thick planks ran half the distance of the building, behind which stood a very busy bartender. Four-legged stools lined three sides of the bar, and all were taken, as was every table Blue could see. On the fourth side of the bar, nearest the front of the building, there were no stools, and several men stood there drinking.

Blue stepped forward and ordered drinks for himself and his companions. When he was served, he handed a drink to each man, then paid the bartender. Then the three stood leaning against the wall, sipping whiskey and listening to the tinkling of a piano at the rear of the room.

The room was crowded, and likely to become more so as the night wore on. As men kept coming, with nobody leaving, Blue noticed out of the corner of his eye that an additional bartender had moved behind the plank, and was busy tying an apron around his middle. Blue watched him closely for a long time, for the man looked very familiar. Finally, deciding that the bartender had probably lived here all his life, and merely resembled somebody Blue had known or seen, Litt pushed the matter from his mind.

"I'll get us another drink from the bar," Getty said, beginning to move in that direction.

Blue put his hand on Getty's shoulder. "Use this," he said, dropping money into his friend's hand. "The night's on Lon and me. Two Papas gave us a bonus for cutting a winter's supply of wood."

Getty accepted the money, and moved to the bar. He was about to order drinks, when a tall man shoved him aside. "Why don't you watch what you're doing?" the man said loudly. "That's the second time you've bumped into me tonight!" The man was obviously feeling his oats and trying to pick a fight. Getty had bumped him neither once nor twice. He had not even been near the bar.

Then the man backhanded Getty across the face. A mistake. The people back in Mississippi who called Getty 'Scrappin' Joe' had placed the nickname well. He was all over the tall man in an instant, attacking with a flurry of hard punches that were simply too fast for the eye to count. The last one was a devastating right hook that sent the man to the floor. He landed flat on his back and lay still.

Getty stood over the man for a moment, then backed away. The bartender, who had seen and heard everything that happened, stood looking at Getty for a moment. Then he smiled, and nodded curtly. "Very effective," he said, then moved down the bar to serve his customers.

Blue stepped forward and touched Getty's shoulder. "Let's get out of here, Joe," he said, and led the way. Back outside, they untied their horses and led them to the end of the street, turning the corner. Arriving at a saloon called The Barn, they retied the animals and walked inside. The building was aptly named, and indeed looked as if it had once been a holding place for livestock. Though the watering hole was larger than the Buckhorn, with a bar on each side, the crowd was meager, and the three had no problem getting a table. The bartender quickly served the beer and tequila that was ordered.

For the next hour, they sat drinking and talking of one thing or another. Getty's altercation had been mentioned only briefly, with both Blue and Bills complimenting Joe on bringing it to a hasty conclusion.

They had just ordered their third round, when the front door opened so noisily that it was heard by everyone in the building. The tall man was standing just inside the door, the welts and bruises from Getty's fists clearly visible on his face. He was accompanied by a dark-haired man who was several inches shorter, with a holstered Colt on his hip, the holster tied to his right leg with rawhide.

Looking neither left nor right, the two headed straight for Blue's table. "You the ones who ganged up on my buddy, here?" the shorter man asked.

Blue was on his feet quickly, as were Bills and Getty. "Nobody ganged up on anybody," Litt said, pointing to the tall man. "He picked a fight, and got his ass whipped. It's that simple."

The tall man began to shake his head. "No, no, Jess," he said to his companion. "That ain't the way it was. Somebody jumped me from behind. I didn't see much, but I know there was more'n one of 'em a-hittin' me."

The man named Jess began to sneer, looking Blue squarely in the eye. "I say you wuz the most mainest one," he said. "You're the only one big enough to knock 'im out like that."

Blue stood still, and said nothing.

"I'm callin' you, feller!" the man yelled. "Cain't you un'erstan' that?"

Blue understood. His mind raced to the warning Lon Bills had given him only a month ago. "When you know for sure that you're gonna have to fight a man," Bills had said, "make the first move yourself. It gives you an edge." Blue seized the edge. Making the fastest draw of his life, he shot the man in the mouth, sending him to the floor instantly. Then all was quiet. The man had cleared his holster, but had not lived to raise his shooting arm.

Still holding his gun in his hand, Litt spoke to the bartender: "You heard it all," he said. "You're a witness."

"Yep," the bartender said, "I'm a witness. Not that you're gonna need any. Ain't nobody gonna raise a stink about him. Somebody'd be more likely to bake you a damn cake." A hint of a smile appeared on his face. "His name was Jess Conners, and he's been pulling that kind of shit around here for a long time. Guess you put a stop to it once and for all."

They were about to leave the building, when Blue stopped suddenly. "Just a minute," he said to the others. He walked back to the body, where the man who had instigated it all stood looking down at his fallen companion. Swinging his right fist with all his strength, Blue knocked the tall man out again, then joined Bills and Getty at the door.

The men were soon headed north to the Box M2, riding three abreast. "That was mighty quick shooting back there, Litt," Bills said. "I intended to kill him if he got you, but I couldn't interfere. When a man gets called, he has to fight his own battles."

"I know," Blue said.

They rode in silence for a while, then Getty kneed his horse in closer to Blue. "I could have handled that job myself, Litt."

"I know that, Joe. But Conners singled me out."

They put their horses to a canter and continued north.

9

Two weeks later, Two Papas decided it was time for his wife to join him on the Box M2. He called Blue from the bunkhouse just before bedtime. "I want you to go back to the Box M and get Sally, Litt. Take one man with you, somebody who can handle trouble if it comes."

Blue nodded. "I'll take Lon Bills."

"I figured as much. You'll both be driving teams coming back. Fix the lead wagon up so Sally'll be comfortable, then she'll show you what to load on the second. She'll have at least a wagonload of stuff that you or I wouldn't give two cents for, but that's the way women are."

"We'll leave in the morning," Blue said, turning toward the bunkhouse.

"Here," Two Papas said. He laid four double eagles and two singles in Blue's hand, then disappeared into the house.

They saddled their horses at sunup. Bills was happy to be making the trip. As far as he was concerned, any deviation from routine ranch work was appreciated. The packsaddle the yellow mule had worn was readjusted to fit Ike, for Blue thought the mule's walking gait was too slow. Ike now carried food, bedrolls, cooking utensils, and a sack of grain. The cook had prepared enough food for the first two days.

A few hours later, they forded the Sabinal River and headed northeast. They would bypass both San Antonio and Austin, their route taking them several miles to the north of each town. Traveling almost on a straight line, the only towns they would encounter would be Waco and Corsicana. The ride to the Box M would take at least ten days, and returning with the wagons twice as long.

They traveled close to fifty miles the first day, and camped at Pipe Creek just before sunset. Each of the horses was fed a portion of grain before being picketed, for grass was sparse. Blue made coffee before dark, then kicked dirt over the fire. "Good idea," Bills said, speaking around a mouthful of beef and biscuit. "No reason to advertise our presence." They talked in low tones for a while, then retired to their bedrolls. They slept till dawn.

They continued to ride at a steady pace, making forty, and sometimes fifty miles a day, depending on the terrain. They reached Waco on the seventh day, arriving in late afternoon.

Litt led the way toward the livery stable. "We'll put

these horses up for the night and get them a good feed," he said. "Then we'll do the same for ourselves."

A few minutes later, they rented a room with two cots at the hotel, then went searching for a good meal. The Texas Saloon, a few doors down from the hotel, had a large sign outside boasting of excellent food. The men were soon seated at a table inside.

"Bring us two of your best beefsteaks," Blue said to the Mexican waiter, "and a pitcher of beer." He looked at Bills. "Is that all right with you, Lon?"

"It's very all right," Bills answered, chuckling.

They sipped the foamy brew for half an hour, then the waiter delivered large platters of steak, flanked by fried potatoes and red beans. "Can we eat all of that?" Bills asked, pointing to the platters and smiling.

"Uh-huh," Blue said, digging in.

After eating, they took stools at the bar, where they sat drinking for another hour. Neither man wanted to make a night of it, however. Both were weary from the long days in the saddle, and yearned for the softness of a real bed. They walked to the hotel and retired early. They would get an early start in the morning.

At Corsicana, they fed and watered their horses at the livery stable, then bought a sack of grain. Remounting, they continued their journey. It was only midday, and they could travel many miles before dark.

They made camp at Cedar Creek, knowing that tomorrow night they would sleep in the bunkhouse at the Box M. While Bills built a fire to heat supper and make coffee, Blue took charge of the horses. Though grass was plentiful in this area, he fed the remaining grain to the animals, mainly to relieve Ike of the burdensome bundle. Ike was a good horse. Though not particularly a good saddler, he was strong and tough and had no peculiar habits. And he had hauled Blue from South Carolina to Texas. Litt intended to hang on to the animal. When Ike's working days were over, he would be allowed to live out the remainder of his life in leisure.

"I'm ready," Blue said, as he neared the campfire. "You got something to eat?"

Bills pulled the skillet from the fire. "Bacon, potatoes, and crackers," he said. "Take it or leave it."

"I'll take it."

When they had eaten, Bills raked dirt over the gray coals, then began to break dead limbs over his knee for their breakfast fire. "Sometimes I wonder if I'm not a little older than I was taught to believe, Litt. By God, I'm tired. Tired all over."

"I feel the same way. I think it's mostly the heat. Fall is a little late in coming this year."

They spread their bedrolls and crawled in. Not another word was spoken.

They had more bacon and coffee at sunup, then stowed their gear in Ike's pack. Bills saddled both horses while Blue made adjustments to the pack-saddle and put out the fire. They would ride straight through today, for they were only a few hours southwest of the Box M. Blue mounted Sox, kicked the animal in the ribs, and set the pace.

Litt knocked at Sally Miles's door in the early afternoon. She opened the door quickly, and made a small sound akin to a gasp. Just as Blue remembered, she irradiated beauty that belied her years. No flab. No wrinkles. No crow's feet around her eyes. Standing straight and tall, her green eyes dancing, she pulled him inside the doorway. "Let me look at you," she said, hanging on to his arms with both her hands. "My, if you're not a handsome sight. Best-looking man I've ever seen." She moved closer. "Let me hug you." Wrapping her arms around his waist, she pressed her body against him. She kissed his cheek, then pressed her lips against his neck.

Deciding that the lady must be under some kind of spell, Blue took half a step backward. "Two Papas sent us to bring you to the Box M2," he said.

"Oh," she said faintly. "Oh, of course. I can't wait to see the new ranch."

Litt had by now backed out onto the porch. He motioned toward Bills, who was still sitting his saddle. "This is Lon Bills. He works at the Box M2."

"Nice to meet you, young man," Two Mamas said. "Get down and join us."

Bills touched the brim of his hat and nodded, then dismounted. He led both horses out of the yard and tied them to the hitching rail, then returned to the porch.

"You two must be half starved," Two Mamas said. "Stay close by while I fix you something to eat."

"We'll be at the barn looking the wagons over," Blue said.

As Two Papas had said, two of the wagons were already ribbed for canvas. They would grease the wheels tomorrow, then wait until the wagons were loaded to put on the covering. Blue found a grease bucket and placed it in one of the wagons, then walked around the corral, mentally selecting the horses that would make up the teams.

When Two Mamas called them to the house, they were inside quickly. Two large platters of food were waiting for them: thick slices of ham, gravy, hot biscuits, and stewed apples. A separate dish containing a thick slice of cake was beside each platter, along with a mug of steaming coffee.

"You men enjoy your dinner," Two Mamas said. "I'm going over to talk with Ellie."

Bills began to break his biscuits into small pieces, soaking them in the gravy. "Do they eat like this all the time around here?"

"Nope," Blue answered. "Usually better. She fixed this on short notice."

They ate their meal and walked into the yard just as Two Mamas returned. She was accompanied by Ellie Miles. "Oh, Litt," Ellie said, "it's so good to see you again. And you've gained back all the weight you lost during the war. You look good." She offered her tiny hand, adding, "Real good."

He took her hand. "Thank you, ma'am."

When she was introduced to Lon Bills, she nodded graciously. "You're traveling with good company, so you must be a nice man."

Bills nodded, smiled shyly, and said nothing.

"Mort's with the hands," Ellie said, speaking to Blue. "He should be in pretty soon, and I know he'll be anxious to see you. You men can sleep in the guest house. It's all made up with two good beds."

"Litt being so tall, he might rest better in Henry's bed," Two Mamas said. "It's a foot longer than the ordinary."

Ellie glanced at Two Mamas sideways. "Whatever he wants to do." She then excused herself, saying she had to start supper for her husband.

"I'll make out just fine in the guest house," Blue said quickly, making sure that Ellie heard.

He led Ike to the barn, where he removed the pack-saddle and turned the horse into the corral. Then the men rode to the creek, where they bathed, shaved, and changed into clean clothing. Afterward, they stabled and fed all three of the horses, then walked to the guest house, dragging up chairs and seating themselves on the porch.

"This is a nice place," Bills said, tilting his chair back against the wall, "but it sure ain't as pretty as the Box M2."

"Nope. Not many places are."

A few minutes later, five men rode in from the north, Mort Miles among them. He spotted the men on·the porch right away. He rode there and dismounted. "Seems like you've been gone for years, Litt," he said, holding out a callused hand. "We think of you often, and talk about you behind your back."

Blue laughed, and took the hand. He nodded toward Bills, who was on his feet now. "This is my friend, Lon Bills, Mort. He works at the Box M2."

The men shook hands. Then Mort addressed Blue again. "You two come after Mama?"

Blue nodded. "Two Papas says to deliver her to the Box M2."

"Well, I knew somebody'd be coming, just didn't know who. I sure can't think of anybody I'd feel better about her traveling with."

"Thank you, Mort. We'll see that she's as comfortable as possible."

When the ranch hands began to walk across the yard headed for the bunkhouse, Mort mentioned it. "Nobody in that bunch that you know, Litt. Whole new crew around here. Rope and Cecil are out there with you, and the others just drifted on."

"Don't really feel like talking to anybody anyway," Blue said. "Just gonna rest up. We'll load the wagons early in the morning, then leave whenever Two Mamas is ready."

"I'll say good-bye to her tonight, then. Don't guess I'll be around when she leaves tomorrow. You fellows take care of her and yourselves." Mort led his horse to the barn, then headed for the house.

The wagons pulled out of the yard at ten o'clock the following morning. Blue drove the lead wagon, which was loaded with a large trunk, sewing machine, folding table and chairs, and a thick stack of blankets, linens, and pillows, arranged in the form of a bed for Two Mamas. In the rear of the wagon was a stack of firewood for those times when none could be found. Directly behind Blue, and out of sight beneath the canvas, was a double-barreled, ten-gauge shotgun, along with the Henry repeating rifle. Two Mamas sat beside him on a blanket that she had folded to make the seat more comfortable. Ike and Sox were tethered on short reins at the rear.

The second wagon, driven by Bills, contained the men's bedrolls, saddles, and personal gear, along with several sacks of grain for the horses. The remaining space was filled with what the men, when talking among themselves, had quickly labeled "junk." Bills also had a rifle, and his horse was tied to the tailgate. Both wagons were covered with new canvas that was tied down past the lowest sideboards, and neither man thought they would leak, even if it rained long and hard.

Except on a downhill grade, when the team would sometimes trot voluntarily, Blue held them to a steady pace of perhaps three miles an hour. The trip would be a long one, and though he was confident that he had chosen the best horses in the corral, a man never knew for certain. At any rate, the last thing he needed was a winded, balky, or broken-down animal.

Riding horseback, they had traveled to the Box M almost as the crow flies. Returning, they would travel a much greater distance, for they would have to stick with the wagon road.

Blue spent much of the day answering questions. Two Mamas wanted to know all about his childhood and growing years. He did not mind, for talking about his earlier days gave him a good feeling. It brought back many memories, most of them pleasant. He talked about the parents he had scarcely known, and Uncle Charley and Aunt Effie, who had literally raised him and his sister. He did not mention the fact that Roberta had run off with the Yankees.

He was relieved that Two Mamas showed no interest in his war experiences. Most of the men he talked with wanted to hear every detail. Blue had no inclination to relive the war. He spoke only of the good times.

Then the lady launched the story of her own early life. Blue sat beside her nodding and grunting occasionally, as she told of a young girl named Sally Baker falling in love with a man named Henry Miles, who was the tallest, strongest, and most handsome young man in the county. Nodding again, Blue slapped at the horses with the reins. Smiling inwardly, he was thinking that the fact that Henry Miles was the only son of a wealthy couple had probably made him appear even more handsome.

Taking a deep breath, Two Mamas continued. She spent the next ten minutes talking about the young couple's journey to Texas, and how rough things had been. Blue listened patiently. He had heard the story from Two Papas more than a year ago, and the stories varied widely. Two Papas admitted that his money had paved the way, making the transition easy. Not that Blue thought Two Mamas was lying. Different people remembered things differently. She had probably told the story as she remembered it. Or imagined it.

They met several wagons and a few men on horseback during the day, and a fast-moving buggy passed them going in the same direction. The driver smiled and waved, seemingly unmindful of the cloud of dust left in his wake.

Blue selected a campsite an hour before sunset. Pulling off the road under the canopy of a large oak, he jumped to the ground and walked to a stand of small cottonwoods. "Good spring here," he said to Bills, who had stopped his own wagon. "We'd better make a night of it. No way in the world are we gonna make the Trinity before dark."

Bills nodded, and jumped to the ground.

Blue helped Two Mamas from the wagon, then placed one of the chairs under the oak. "Might as well make yourself comfortable while we get the chores done."

She stomped her foot in the sand. "Stop trying to make me feel so old."

The men unharnessed the horses and led them to water, then tied on the nosebags. When the animals had eaten, they would be picketed beside the runoff from the spring. Using kindling from the wagon, Bills soon had a fire going under the coffeepot.

"There's a box under the wagon seat, Mister Bills," Two Mamas said, rising from her chair. "If you'll get it, I'll heat up some supper. I made beef stew yesterday and sealed it in jars. The pot and eating utensils are right there in the box."

Bills placed the box near the fire, and got out of the lady's way.

She rearranged the fire for a moment, then poured two jars of stew in the iron pot and set it on the bright red coals. "I put up eight jars of this, so we'll probably get tired of it before we run out." From a cloth bag, she took biscuits she had made before daylight this morning, placing two on each of three tin plates. She gave the pot a final stir. "Guess this is warm enough to eat."

Blue was busy pouring coffee for Bills and himself. "You want a cup of coffee with your stew, Two Mamas?"

She shook her head. "Believe I'd rather have a cup of cool water from that spring."

Blue fetched the water.

Litt was soon enjoying the most scrumptious beef stew he had ever tasted. Both men complimented Two Mamas, and each cleaned his plate twice.

"Just made it the way I always have," she said. "To tell you the truth, that's Ellie's recipe."

Blue placed the plates, spoons, and cups in the empty pot, then headed for the spring to wash them. When he returned, Two Mamas stood beside her chair, stretching and yawning. "I think I'll turn in," she said. "It's been a long day."

Litt boosted her up into the wagon, then rejoined Bills at the fire. Keeping their voices down, they talked for almost an hour, then spread their bedrolls under the wagons. They were asleep quickly.

Sometime around midnight, Blue suddenly realized that he was not alone. He lay motionless as Two Mamas covered his mouth with her own. She began to lick his lips and massage his crotch gently with her hand, all the while making a soft sound not unlike the purring of a kitten. Litt knew that he must do something. And he must do it now, for his manhood was beginning to swell.

Rising to his elbow, he took her small face in his hand. "We can't, Two Mamas," he whispered softly.

"We just can't. Now, get back in the wagon. We'll forget this ever happened."

"Just let me—"

"Get back in the wagon."

She was gone quickly.

Blue remained on his elbow for some time, staring at the bundle under the second wagon that was Lon Bills. Sleeping soundly, Litt hoped. He lay on his bed thinking for what seemed like hours, waiting for the sleep that was slow to come. When he finally drifted off, he dreamed that he had not pushed Two Mamas away; that he had accepted her in his bed.

All three were up at daybreak. The men went about harnessing and hitching up the teams, while Two Mamas prepared breakfast. When they had eaten, Blue washed the utensils at the spring, then returned them to the box. "If you don't mind, Lon, I'd rather you drove the lead wagon. Seems like I should be bringing up the rear with the shotgun."

"Makes no difference to me. A wagon's a wagon."

Two Mamas dropped her head slightly and began to retie one of her shoelaces, as if she had not heard.

They traveled steadily throughout the morning, and reached the Trinity River two hours before noon. They allowed the horses to drink, forded in the knee-deep water, then pushed on till the sun was directly overhead. They made their noontime stop thirty feet off the road, beside a large hardwood tree. Bills kindled a small fire to heat the stew and make coffee, while Blue removed the bits from the horses' mouths and put on the nosebags.

They soon sat eating the stew, Two Mamas in her chair, and the men squatted on their haunches. Just as Blue cleaned his plate, he pointed down the road to the southwest. "See 'em?" he asked.

Bills nodded. Almost half a mile away, with two small hills in between, three riders were headed in their direction. They stopped for several minutes, appearing to be engaged in conversation, then rode on down the hill, disappearing from view. When they topped the nearest hill, there were only two riders.

"I don't like the looks of this, Lon," Blue said, keeping the tree between himself and the riders. "I don't believe they've had a chance to get an accurate count on us. Be on your toes and expect anything. I'll be in the second wagon. Maybe I can locate that third man from there."

With the tree and two of the horses hiding his retreat, Litt scampered to the wagon and climbed in, leaving the canvas flap up. He grabbed the shotgun and moved to the rear of the wagon. Doffing his hat, he took up a position behind a small desk, where he had a clear view of the area behind the camp.

A short while later, he heard voices at the tree, and knew that the riders had come in. Making small talk, Litt believed, trying to hold Lon's attention while the third man got the drop on him from behind. Then Blue saw the man. No more than forty yards away, he was bent at the waist, moving from tree to tree with a six-gun in his hand. Blue held his fire, as the man continued his stalk. Thirty yards . . . twenty. The shotgun bucked against Blue's shoulder, and the man went down instantly. As Litt jumped to the ground and whirled his weapon, he heard two quick shots at the tree. His eyes took in the scene quickly. Upon hearing the report from the shotgun, Lon Bills had made his lightning draw and shot both riders from the saddles. Blue had hit the ground in time to see the last man slide over the rump of his horse. Both men were dead.

Bills holstered his gun. "I was just waiting to hear

from you," he said. "One of 'em even had the gall to ask Two Mamas what was in the wagons."

Blue hurried to the man he had shotgunned. A small, bearded man with dark hair and complexion, he lay in a heap across a rotted log. He had taken a full load of buckshot, and now had the appearance of an oversized rag doll.

Litt could see the man's horse a hundred yards away, tied to a sapling. He covered the distance in long strides. He removed the saddle, then the bridle, and gave the horse a swipe across the rump. The animal reared, spun on its hind legs, and disappeared in the woods.

Then Blue walked to the tree and repeated the process with the other riders' horses. As they ran into the trees, he turned back to the business at hand. "Let's get these bodies and the saddles out of sight, Lon. I don't feel like answering any questions about 'em."

They dragged the bodies into a thick stand of bushes and piled the saddles on top of them, then returned to the wagons. Two Mamas stood there, clearly shaken. She threw her arms around Blue, and he hugged her to him. "It's all right, now," he said. "Everything's all right."

"I was just so . . . afraid." She took a step backward. "Are we going to bury them?"

"Do you think they intended to bury us?"

Color was returning to her face. "Oh. So you think they were going to kill us." It was more a statement than a question.

"I know damn well they were going to kill us. They intended to take everything we have and leave us exactly where we left them." Taking her elbow, he boosted her up to her wagon, and Bills followed. They took to the road at a trot, wanting to put as much territory behind them as possible before nightfall.

In late afternoon of the seventeenth day, they camped at the spring, between San Antonio and the Box M2. Having good horses and sound wagons, they had done much better than the twenty miles a day Blue had planned on. Tomorrow, their journey would be over. They built no fire tonight. The firewood they had brought from the Box M was long gone, and there was none to be had around the spring. Anyway, they had eaten dinner in a restaurant in San Antonio, then bought food that could be eaten without heating. They washed supper down with water from the spring, and, as darkness swept in from the east, the men spread their bedrolls under the wagons as usual.

Tired from the day's travel, Blue slept soundly. Several hours later, he was suddenly wide awake. He had heard something. He opened his eyes and lay still, then slowly closed his fingers around the butt of his Colt. He turned his eyes toward Two Mamas's wagon, for it seemed that the sound had come from there. Then the rear flap opened. Blue relaxed his grip on the Colt, for even in the darkness he could make out the form of Lon Bills stepping down from the wagon. Bills looked around in every direction, then crawled under the wagon and into his bedroll.

Two Mamas had finally gotten her itch scratched, Blue was thinking, glad that he himself was not involved. Though he knew this was probably not the only time Bills had visited the wagon, Litt would spend no time worrying about it. Nor would he condemn either party. Two Mamas had gotten what she wanted with no harm done, for she was well past the childbearing age. Two Papas had lost nothing; what he did not know would not hurt him. And Lon Bills was not the type to talk; the lady's reputation was safe. Blue smiled, and turned over in his bed. He wanted to grab another hour's sleep before daylight.

They were back on the road at sunup. They traveled all day, with their only stop being at the Sabinal River to water the horses. Two hours before sunset, the men delivered Two Mamas to her new home.

10

A week later, Blue rode in from a hard day's work just before sundown. After stabling and feeding his horse, he headed for the bunkhouse.

"Come over here a minute, Litt," Two Papas called from the porch of the main house.

Blue obliged, seating himself on the top step.

"Sally told me about the trouble you ran into on the trip," Two Papas said. "I appreciate the way you handled it."

"Just did what we had to do."

"I know, but I appreciate it just the same."

Blue nodded, and said nothing. He sat quietly for some time, thinking that Two Papas must surely have something else to say. He did.

"I'll be leaving for San Antonio in the morning," the big man said, "and I'd like for you and this Bills fellow to ride along. These are harsh times, Litt, and a man never knows what kind of riffraff he's gonna meet on the road."

"We'll be ready."

Two Papas continued. "Thought I'd go in and visit with Leroy Upton for a day or two. We freighted together during the war."

"He told me," Blue said.

"Well, anyway, I'm anxious to see him again. Besides, I still owe him for the bricks that went into this house. I already paid John Graves for everything else, but he charged the bricks to me."

Blue was getting to his feet. "Do you intend to ride a horse?"

"Lord, no. You and me will take the spring wagon. Bills can ride any of the saddlers he wants."

"About sunup?"

Two Papas nodded. "Sunup."

Blue walked to the cook shack, where he joined the other hands at the supper table. Fat Frank was a good cook, and the men ate well. Since the man's arrival, Blue had heard only one small complaint: One night as they sat eating supper, young Billy Turner said loudly, "I always thought cornbread was supposed to have a little sugar in it."

"Ain't gonna be no damn Yankee cornbread around here," Fat Frank said. "Not unless you cook it." There had been no more complaints.

After eating, Blue informed Bills of the upcoming trip to San Antonio. At the barn, they loaded nosebags and a sack of grain on the spring wagon, then Blue added two armloads of firewood for "The Spring," as the campground on the road to San Antonio was known.

They took to the road shortly after sunrise the following morning, and held a brisk pace all day. In the late afternoon, as they neared The Spring, Blue said, "Watch these horses, Two Papas. They know exactly where they are." Blue laid the reins aside. Sure enough, of their own accord, the horses pulled the wagon off the road at the campground, stopping under the tree. "They've done this so many times that they know the whole routine," Blue said. "They know their day's work is done."

They watered the horses and put on the nosebags, then Blue kindled a fire for coffee. Little food preparation was necessary, for Fat Frank had provided them with roast beef, beans, and boiled potatoes. Litt heated the food in a skillet, then the men enjoyed a very good supper.

At the brickyard the following day, Two Papas and Leroy Upton hugged each other like brothers, then disappeared into the office. Still sitting on the wagon seat, Blue chuckled. "Kind of funny watching them try to reach around each other. I guess between them, they must weigh about six hundred pounds."

"Pretty close," Bills agreed.

After half an hour, Two Papas returned to the wagon. "I'll be spending tonight and tomorrow night with Leroy," he said, handing Blue a double eagle. "You men enjoy yourselves, and meet me right here at sunup the day after tomorrow."

"We'll be here," Blue said, pocketing the coin.

Bills followed Blue to the livery stable, where they left the wagon and all three of the horses. Then they went in search of a good meal. Bills, who knew the area much better than did Blue, suggested a combination restaurant and saloon called Amigos, only a short distance from the livery stable.

Amigos was the largest saloon Litt had ever seen. There was no partition separating the saloon from the dining room, though an area close to the kitchen had been sectioned off with ropes tied to posts. There was a bar that reached half the length of one wall, and a shorter one in the middle of the room, with two bartenders behind each.

At the rear of the huge room were several rows of seats, all lined up in theater fashion with aisles in between. They faced a stage that was perhaps five feet high. Bills said that the saloon ran a show of some kind every hour on the hour. In fact, there was a comedy act on stage right now. All the seats were taken, but Blue could see the action very well. Two men were running around on stage wearing exaggerated versions of the Mexican sombrero, pointing and yelling at each other. Though they looked more Irish than Mexican, they must have been funny, judging from the reaction of their audience. Blue could not understand what they were saying, but he did get a chuckle out of reading their stage names: Hose-A and Hose-B.

Blue and Bills walked around the bar and stepped over the ropes, where they took a table close to the kitchen. A Mexican waiter soon took their order.

After eating, they took stools at the bar. While drinking tequila, they sat watching several women on stage dancing and kicking to the music of a pounding piano. "Shows every hour?" Blue asked. "I don't see how the house manages to pay so many people."

"They don't," Bills said. "The girls pay the house for the exposure, plus a percentage of the money they make from their sidelines."

"You think they're all whores?"

Bills took a sip from his glass, then nodded. "They're whores."

When the show ended a few minutes later, the men left the building. They rented a room with two beds on the first floor of the hotel, then began to walk the streets, stopping occasionally at a saloon for a drink. At Tom's Place, Blue said hello to the bartender, Pedro, and bought the man a drink.

They prowled around till almost dark, then settled on a small restaurant a few doors down from the hotel. As they ate their beef stew and sipped strong coffee, Blue seemed more thoughtful than usual. "You know, Lon," he said finally, "I've heard all of my life that a man never gets ahead as long as he's working for somebody else."

Bills was picking at his stew. He smiled now. "That's an established fact. What do you intend to do about it?"

Blue answered quickly. "I intend to run my own cattle in Frio Canyon."

"The hell you do. Didn't know you had that kind of money."

"I don't. But the way I've got it figured, I wouldn't need a fortune. I believe I can raise enough money to start slow, say a few hundred head. Maybe even a thousand."

"Did you get ambitious all of a sudden?" Bills asked, sipping the last of his coffee, "or has it been festering for a while?"

"I've always intended to eventually be my own boss."

"Well, a thousand head would sure give you a good start. If you take a herd in the canyon, you'll at least make the cats and the bears happy."

"I've thought of that. They will take some of the

calves and maybe a full-grown cow occasionally, but I still think a herd will do well in that canyon. A fellow could keep the predators awful nervous with a good pack of hounds. Might even chase some of them out of the area."

Bills pushed back his chair. "Sounds good," he said. "Hope you still know me when you get to be a big, fat rancher."

They left the restaurant and stood on the street talking for a while. Neither man had a desire to further explore the town. They walked to the hotel and went to bed.

Just before noon the following day, Blue left Bills at Amigos. Litt wanted to discuss his idea with his banker. The man listened to Blue's proposal attentively, then refused to lend him a single dollar. The banker had no interest in speculating in cattle. Now, if Blue owned some prime property as collateral . . .

Two weeks later, Blue brought up the subject to Two Papas, as they sat on the porch of the main house. "How much money would a man need if he decided to put a few hundred head of longhorns in Frio Canyon, Two Papas?"

The big man sat quietly for a moment, then chuckled. "I expected you to ask me that very question a long time ago, Litt. The truth is, I don't know. How much you got?"

"Seven hundred dollars."

"Well, that's seven hundred more than a lot of ranchers had when they started." Two Papas rose from his chair, walked the length of the porch, then took a seat beside Blue on the step. "Lots of room in that canyon, and the grass is good. I suppose you've given some thought to the predators."

"Yes, sir. But a man could take a pack of hounds and declare war on 'em if they get too bad."

Two Papas nodded. "I believe that'll be necessary. A man wouldn't have to buy but one section of land, though. There are miles and miles of free graze to the north, and ten times as much to the west."

"I intend to use some of it."

"John Graves owns some land up there," Two Papas said, getting to his feet. "I'll talk to him about it."

A week later, Blue bought six hundred forty acres of land at the mouth of Frio Canyon. It was the northernmost piece of property John Graves owned, and Two Papas agreed that the one-dollar-per-acre price was fair.

"Well, I've got me some land," Blue said, after the deal was done. "But it just about cleaned me out."

Two Papas laughed out loud. "Cleaned you out? You're twenty-one years old and talking about being broke? Hell, you've got another forty or fifty years to make some money. A man can either plant a tree when he's young or wander through life like some of these other fellows. First thing you know, you're fifty years old and own nothing but a saddle.

"You planted a tree this morning, Litt, and I'm proud of you. I feel . . . it's . . . almost like it was Ben." Two Papas turned his head and stared toward the canyon. "I won't offer you any advice I wouldn't have given to my own grandson." he added, sounding as if he might choke on his words. He stood quietly for a while, then regained his composure. "Guess you'd better start putting together a place to live up there. You gonna dig a well?"

"No. Not for a while, at least. Two clear-running springs right where I intend to build."

"Well, you go ahead and get the place ready. I'll be

making another raid on the Big Thicket in the spring, and we'll bring back an extra five hundred head for you. You can pay me for 'em when you sell 'em. I'll tell Cecil to start looking around for replacements for you and Bills. I know Lon will want to tag along with you."

"I haven't asked him."

"You won't have to," Two Papas said, heading for the house.

As Two Papas predicted, Bills did not have to be asked. "I think I'll be joining you up in the canyon," he said to Litt. "Unless you don't want me, that is."

"That's not the point," Blue said. The two were sipping coffee at the breakfast table, long after the others had eaten and departed. Litt refilled his cup, then reseated himself. "The point is, I don't believe I can pay you as much as you're making here." Blue sipped at the steaming liquid. "Would you work for twenty a month the first year?"

"Of course I would. You've got to have some help up there."

"Well, it could be that you won't lose anything in the long run. I'll try to pay you forty a month during the second year, so it'll average out to the same thirty you're getting now. Of course, that might be asking a lot of you, since you've never stayed that long in one place."

Bills drummed his fingers on the table, saying nothing.

"You see, Lon," Blue continued, "Two Papas made me a deal that would sound strange as hell to most people: He sold me a team and wagon on credit, and volunteered to lend me as much cash as I need to put my ranch in shape. Next summer he'll have five hundred head of longhorns delivered to me in Frio

Canyon. He has no way in the world of knowing for sure that he'll ever get his money back. The only damn collateral he has is my word."

"Your word is the only damn collateral he wants. The man trusts you. You fought with his grandson in Virginia, and the boy didn't make it back. Hell, you're the grandson now, Litt."

Blue sat for some time as if in deep thought. "Maybe so," he said, then headed for the door.

Later in the day, Litt laid out and staked the location of his cabin. Resting on a knoll five hundred yards from the canyon wall, the two-room dwelling would be built of cypress logs, and, for the present time at least, have an earthen floor. Blue would buy cypress shingles from John Graves for the roof.

The cabin would face the southwest. A grassy plain sloped ever downward to the Frio, a hundred yards away. Blue would build a shed and corral between the cabin and the river, with a chute made of poles leading down to the water. His animals could water themselves whenever they pleased.

He would build no fireplace or chimney. The same stove he used for cooking would heat the small building nicely, for he would chink the cracks between the logs with clay. The spring, twenty feet from the doorway, would be cleaned out and boxed with boards, and the brush and small saplings that surrounded it would be cleared away.

Litt would buy a good stove, table, and chairs. Everything else that went in the cabin, he would build.

Bills, who had helped Litt drive the stakes and stretch the string, now stood by enjoying the spectacular view. "This is the prettiest place I've ever seen," he said, casting his eyes toward the canyon and the green mountains beyond. Then he turned to face the river, waving his arm toward the wide valley on the other side. He kicked at a small stone, then chuckled. "After you get rich and build your mansion here, you're gonna have the showplace of the Southwest."

Blue chuckled along with Bills, but said nothing.

They loaded their tools on the wagon and headed for the Box M2. Tomorrow, they would move to the canyon for good. A cabin must be built, and there was no time to lose. Colder weather was already in the making.

11

Christmas had come and gone, and it was now the middle of January. The cabin was finished, and the roof had been tested with a week of rainy weather. Blue had quickly become dissatisfied with the earthen floor, and had bought seasoned lumber in San Antonio to remedy the situation. The shed, encircled by a pole corral, had been boarded up on three sides by rough planks, giving the horses refuge from the cold wind. A large, metal grain bin stood in one corner of the shed. The animals spent much of their time standing by and staring at it, for they knew what was inside.

Blue and Bills sat inside the cabin enjoying the warmth of the stove this morning, for the temperature outside was barely above freezing. Getting to his feet,

Bills walked outside for a while. When he returned, he pointed toward the corral. "The horses are sure enjoying this nippy air. Guess we ought to saddle up and work some of the vinegar out of 'em. You still want to see the saltpeter mine?"

"Now's as good a time as any," Blue said, reaching for his coat and hat.

The Confederate States of America Saltpeter Mine was actually a cave, located a few miles southwest of Litt's cabin, and was home to incalculable numbers of bats. The vast deposits of bat guano, which by natural decay became saltpeter, was the chief ingredient of gunpowder. Mixed with small amounts of charcoal and sulphur, the saltpeter powered both Confederate cannons and smaller arms.

The cave inhabited by the bats, the source of the guano, extended for twenty-three miles. One room in the great bat den was two hundred yards long and a hundred yards wide, with a forty-five-foot ceiling. A narrow-gauge railway with mule-drawn cars was used in the digging. There were also corrals for the mules, who never saw the light of day.

Blue stood in the huge den, holding a torch and looking toward the ceiling. "Do you mean that shit from these bats is what I was shooting at the Yankees?"

"Could be," Bills answered. "I know some of it was shipped east of the Mississippi."

"Humph," Blue grunted, pointing his torch toward the mouth of the cave. "Let's get out of here." Outside, he extinguished the flame and cast the torch aside. He stood for a moment rebuttoning his heavy coat, for it had been warm inside the cave. "Humph," he repeated, as he stepped into the saddle. "I remember a damn sergeant one time talking me into eating a handful of gunpowder. Claimed it would cure a cold. I guess what I was really eating was a handful of bat shit."

Bills began to laugh convulsively, slapping his leg and repeating himself. "Could be. I know some of it was shipped east of the Mississippi." He continued to chuckle occasionally for the next several minutes.

They had ridden about a mile, when Blue held up his hand and stopped at the top of a rise. He pointed to a meadow several hundred yards away. A single deer grazed there. Though the distance was too great to determine the sex of the animal, it appeared to be small, probably less than a year old.

"Think I should try to stalk it?" Bills asked.

Blue nodded. "If you get a decent long shot you'd better take it. No telling how many are down there that we don't see."

Bills unsheathed his rifle and kneed his horse around the side of the hill. Blue sat his saddle for the next half-hour, expecting to hear from Bills anytime. Several times, the deer raised its head suddenly and stared off into the woods for a while, then lowered its head and resumed its feeding. Blue knew that the animal had sensed Lon's presence, but had been unable to pinpoint his location. Then the deer jumped straight up, and began to run. A split second later, Litt heard the report of the rifle. When, after running no more than thirty yards, the animal caved in, Blue knew that Bills had once again lived up to his reputation as a marksman. Litt kicked his horse in the ribs and rode over the hill.

The deer, a young buck, was dressed out on the spot, and Bills placed the carcass behind his saddle. "As cold as the weather is, this venison will keep till we eat it up," he said.

At the cabin, Blue sliced a portion of the meat into small cubes and dumped it into a large iron pot. He added chili peppers, two cans of tomatoes, and several handfuls of red beans, then set the receptacle on the stove to boil. The concoction would feed the men for at least two days. He drove a nail into the highest log he could reach outside the cabin and hung the remainder of the deer there. As long as the weather hovered near freezing, the venison would keep almost indefinitely. He carried an armload of wood back inside the cabin and added a few sticks to the stove's firebox. After the mixture had boiled for a while, he chopped up several onions and dropped them into the pot. Then he seated himself in a chair, his long legs stretched out beside the stove. He would wait two hours before making his cornbread.

Bills returned from the shed, where he had been caring for the livestock. He stopped just inside the door, taking a deep breath. "Damn, that smells good. What is it?"

"Don't know," Blue answered, chuckling. "It just seemed like a good idea."

"It has to be. Anything that smells that good can't possibly taste bad." Bills walked to the stove, bent over the pot, and took another whiff.

The mixture turned out to be delicious, and fed the men for three days. Even as they emptied the pot, Bills was already thinking of another. "Guess you can do that again any time you want to, Litt. I can't think of anything a man needs to eat that wasn't in that pot."

A few days later, the men were in San Antonio. Blue had stopped by the bank to fatten up his account, for Two Papas had written him a check. Afterward, they rented the same hotel room they had used in the past. When Litt brought Bills up to date on his pay, Lon headed for the door, saying he was going to Amigos. Blue followed as far as the street, untied his horse, and stepped into the saddle. "I'm gonna ride around for a while, Lon. I've never really looked this town over."

He rode aimlessly for an hour. He soon left the seedy side of town, and guided his horse along the river for while. Most of the people he saw were afoot, some with fishing poles. Many of them smiled or spoke a friendly hello, and Blue answered their greetings with a wave of his hand. Evidence of the town's Mexican heritage could be seen at every turn. Most of the buildings in this area were adobe, and most of the people of Mexican descent.

He bought six tamales from a street vendor, then leaned against a building to eat them. Then he remounted and rode through a residential section that was obviously inhabited by the well-to-do. He sat his horse for a while staring at one German-built mansion in particular, wondering how it felt to live in such a place. He clucked to his horse and rode on down the street, deep in thought. Maybe someday . . .

At the Alamo, where one hundred eighty-nine Texas volunteers defied a Mexican army of thousands during a thirteen-day siege, Blue doffed his hat. The Alamo defenders had died to the last man, among them such storied names as William Travis, Davy Crockett, and Jim Bowie. The cost to the Mexican forces was dreadful. While Santa Anna dictated an announcement of glorious victory, his aide, Colonel Juan Almonte, privately noted: "One more such 'glorious victory,' and we are finished." The finish came April 21, 1836, when Sam Houston's Texans routed the Mexican army at the Battle of San Jacinto near Houston, and captured "the Napoleon of the West," as Santa Anna billed himself.

Blue continued to hold his hat in his hand for a while, trying to imagine the fierce battle. The defenders, facing an enemy that outnumbered them fifty to one, had been doomed from the start. Blue himself knew something of fighting against superior odds, but never had his back been pushed against the wall. The men at the Alamo had been unable to give up a single inch of ground. There had simply been nowhere to run, even if they had been of a mind to. He replaced his hat and rode down the street, knowing that he would never come here again.

He continued to prowl throughout the afternoon, even rode by the brickyard and said hello to Leroy Upton. At sunset, he left his horse at the livery stable and walked to the hotel. Lon Bills was there, sitting on his bed and sipping from a bottle of tequila.

"Looks like you've been having a good time," Blue said, hanging his hat on the bedpost and seating himself.

"Been over to Amigos getting my ashes hauled." Bills took another sip, and handed the bottle to Blue. "I tell you, Litt, that new girl over there knows how to clean a man's plow. I mean, you just gotta go over after a while and see her. This country hasn't ever seen anything like her. At least, not since I've been around here."

Blue was busy pulling off his boots. "Well," he said, chuckling, "if she's got you under all that big a spell, I guess it wouldn't hurt me to have a look."

"You'll probably do more than look, old buddy. She charges a dollar more than the others, but what the hell?" Bills fluffed up his pillow, and was soon snoring.

They ate supper at a small restaurant two hours later, then wandered into Amigos, arriving between shows. They ordered drinks, then stood with their backs to the bar. Bills motioned toward the stage. "You think we ought to get seats up front before the next show start?"

"I can see as much as I need to from right here," Blue said. "You go ahead."

Bills finished his drink and moved down the aisle, where the jostling for the best seats had already started.

Blue bought another drink and took a stool, his back to the bar. He could see the stage clearly, as most of the men, especially those in front, had removed their hats. Emptying his glass, and waving away the bartender's attempt to refill it, he leaned against the bar waiting for the show to begin.

At last there came the crashing sound of a cymbal, followed by several heavy chords from the piano. When the curtain opened, a man with a loud voice trotted on the stage and introduced the Christy Martin Dancers. A line of scantily clad girls danced onto the stage, keeping time with the music and kicking their heels higher than their heads. At center stage, they interlocked their arms and began to sing a well-known song, continuing to tease their all-male audience with bare flesh. The applause of the oglers was thunderous.

Blue himself was dumbfounded. There, dancing in the middle of the line, calling herself Christy Martin, and kicking the highest, was his sister, Roberta. Blue turned his back to the stage and sat staring at the bar for a long while. Then, sliding off the stool, he headed for the front door. He bought a bottle of whiskey at the hotel bar, then returned to his room.

Bills arrived half an hour later. "I looked all over that crowded saloon for you, Litt. Did you get a look at Christy Martin?"

Blue sat looking into his whiskey bottle with one eye closed, as if trying to read something at the bottom of the liquid. "Yep," he said finally.

"Well, what did you think? Ain't she got 'em all beat?"

Blue took a sip of whiskey, put the stopper in the bottle, and turned to look Bills straight in the eye. "Lon, I've got to tell you something, and this seems like the right time. There ain't gonna be any hard feelings between you and me, 'cause we've already been through hell and high water together. What you did earlier today was hump a whore. No more, no less. And you paid her for her services." Blue uncorked the whiskey, took a mouthful, and set the bottle on the table beside the bed. He swallowed the strong liquid, and exhaled loudly. "Christy Martin is my sister," he said, fastening his penetrating eyes to those of Bills. "She's a little over a year younger, and her real name is Roberta."

Lon's immediate reaction was to accept the statement in good humor, for the two pulled jokes on each other often. "Oh, yeah," he said. "Abraham Lincoln was my granddaddy, too." As he continued to look at Blue's chiseled expression, he decided the man was serious. "You wouldn't joke about something like that would you, Litt?"

"No joke, Lon. She's my sister."

Bills slammed his fist into the palm of his hand, and began to walk around the room. "I guess we might both be better off if I cleared out of the area, Litt."

"Nope. No reason for that."

Bills took a drink from Litt's bottle, then returned it to the table. He began to walk again. "Here I've been shooting my mouth off all day about doing this and that, when I should have been keeping things to myself."

"No harm done, dammit," Blue said. "The time she spent with you is just that much time somebody else wasn't plowing her garden. It's like I said before, you weren't humping my sister. You were humping a whore, and paying the asking price for the privilege."

"Well, I feel like hell about it just the same, and I'm sorry if I said anything to make it harder on you."

Blue lay awake long after Bills had gone to sleep. He remembered telling Aunt Effie that Roberta had made her bed when she rode off with the Yankees. Now, he supposed that she literally made the bed several times a day. Try as he might, he had no quarrel with that. His sister was a grown woman, and her body was her own. Likewise, she was free to choose her own occupation. He himself had slept with "women for hire," and each was likely somebody's sister.

What Litt found most difficult to pardon, was Roberta's changing sides during the war. Though he had heard only Aunt Effie's side of the story, he believed it, for although the lady cursed with every breath, she was known to speak the truth. And she had said that Roberta walked to the field and joined the Union soldiers of her own accord. When invited, she had climbed down into the ditch under her own power. Had her actions been the result of some strong female urge that she could not control? As the heifer seeks out the bull? Or was it because the Yankees had good food, and Roberta was tired of eating turnip greens and sweet potatoes? Whatever her reasons, she had ridden off and left the same two people who had raised her: one dead, the other frail and weak.

Before he finally went to sleep, Litt decided to seek answers to these and other questions tomorrow, for he had decided to confront his sister. Riding away and pretending he had not seen her was out of the question. And he must convince Lon Bills that the air was clear, that the actions of his friend were entirely excusable.

After a late breakfast the following morning, Litt bought a newspaper and returned to his room, for he had several hours to kill. Bills had made himself scarce when he learned that Blue intended to talk with his sister. Litt would wait till well past noon to visit the saloon, for Roberta had probably had a long night. He lay on his bed reading the paper till he became drowsy, then went to sleep again.

He entered Amigos at two o'clock. The saloon looked deserted, and Blue sought out the head bartender, whose name was Luke. Litt talked with the man for a while, then sat down on a barstool with a sigh.

He would not talk with Roberta today. Maybe never. She had skipped town in the middle of the night. "The other girls all said she left before midnight," Luke said. "Took everything she owned, and refused to tell them where she was going."

"Do you have any idea where she might go, Luke?"

"Not the slightest. She's got her own buggy and driver, a Mexican about fifty years old. She could be a long, long way from here by now. I know she's got a high-stepping roan, the kind that can trot all day and all night."

Blue headed for the livery stable. "Miss Martin's driver woke me up to get the horse and buggy," the hostler said, in answer to Blue's questions. "Little after ten o'clock last night."

"Did you see which way he went?"

"He went toward Amigos. To pick up his boss, I guess."

"I guess." Blue headed for his hotel room.

He first tried to finish reading his newspaper, but could not concentrate. He tossed it aside, and stretched his legs out on the bed, his back resting against the headboard. There could be but one reason for Miss Christy Martin leaving town in the middle of the night, he was thinking: at the same time Litt had seen her, she had seen him. And though it must have been difficult, she had gone on with the show, as attested to by Bills.

In one sense he felt relief that she was gone. In another, there was a deep ache in his heart. During their growing years the two had been practically inseparable, and had hugged and kissed each other often. At times, it seemed that Roberta was the only true friend Litt had. Always sympathetic to his problems, always seeming to understand. Would he have hugged and kissed her today? He did not know. He only knew that he still had a soft spot in his heart for his sister. In one fluid movement he was off the bed and out of the hotel, headed for the saloon in search of Lon Bills. And to get drunk.

Blue accomplished both, and it was close to midnight when the men went to bed. They awoke long after sunup, each of them with a big head. "Guess it's about time for us to be getting back to the ranch," Blue said, smiling at Bills, who was sitting on the side of his bed yawning. "Or did you want to make another day and night of it?"

"I don't think I could stand another day of it," Bills answered, shaking his head and easing himself into his pants. "It's like I told you once before: I believe I'm older than my folks led me to think."

Though they drank several cups of coffee at the restaurant, neither man felt like eating breakfast. Blue hired the cook to prepare some food for trail, and the men were on their way.

Though their horses were rested and frisky, and wanted to run, the men held the animals to a steady walk. There would be no jostling movement this morning. Nor was either man eager to talk. Occasionally taking a drink of water from a canteen, they rode quietly for most of the day.

The sun was about an hour high, and they were a mile from the campground, when Bills reached into his saddlebag. "Drink about half of this," he said, handing Blue a small bottle of tequila. "You'll be hungry by the time we get to The Spring."

"Damn, Lon," Blue said, accepting the bottle. "You're a lifesaver."

They camped at The Spring, and just as Bills had predicted, Blue was hungry.

12

Blue was sitting beside the stove mending a bridle, when he heard a knock at the cabin door. This was the last week in February, and the weather was cold. Litt was alone in the cabin, for Lon Bills had taken the shotgun and gone looking for small game for the pot. At the second knock, Blue opened the door, his hand close to his Colt.

The visitor was Two Papas, bundled up against the cold. "Come in and warm yourself up," Blue said, shaking the big man's hand. "I've wondered a few times if you'd ever come up here." He motioned toward the stove. "The coffee's bitter, but it's still warm."

Doffing his coat and hat, Two Papas took a chair beside the stove, accepting the cup of hot coffee he was offered. He sat quietly for a while, his eyes taking in his surroundings. "You boys have done a good job up here," he said finally. "It looks like you've got about everything you need."

"I expect to build a good barn sometime, and maybe a better house."

"That'll all come later. You've got all the time in the world."

Litt sat quietly waiting, for he knew the big man had something on his mind.

"Where's that Bills fellow?"

"Gone hunting. We're down to beans and onions."

Two Papas poured the last of the coffee into his cup. Blue washed out the pot, refilled it with water and a handful of coffee grounds, then placed it in the center of the stove. He added two sticks of wood to the firebox, then reseated himself.

"Rope Johnson will be leaving for the Big Thicket in two weeks," Two Papas said. "He's gonna take that Turner kid to drive the grub cart, and maybe do some cooking. I've hired two wranglers from Uvalde to handle the extra horses, and they'll be returning with the herd. The same two oxen that led the other herd out here will be used again.

"Once he gets to the Thicket, Rope will hire as many of the vaqueros as he can find, hoping to cut down on the time it takes to gather the herd. Counting your five hundred, I intend to bring out four thousand head this time.

"The rails are coming to Kansas, Litt, and I believe that Texans will have a ready market for longhorns there. It won't be much longer, either. Before this year is out, men will be driving whole herds north to the rails. I intend to be among them.

"I'll put Rope Johnson in charge of that operation.

He's a good man who knows what he's doing, and he'll be paid accordingly. I've known no man who understands cattle the way he does. He's wise to all their finicky ways, knows what they can stand and what they can't. Knows just exactly how much pressure you can put on a steer's neck before you break it. Watching that skinny bastard handle a rope is an education in itself."

Blue laughed. "That it is. I've watched him plenty of times. Guess that's how he got his nickname."

Two Papas nodded, and filled his cup with fresh coffee. "I've been thinking, Litt. With Rope and the Turner kid gone, I'm gonna be two men short for the spring roundup. Since you don't have anything more to do here, I thought maybe you and that Bills fellow might want to join us at the Box M2 till Rope gets back with you cattle.

"To tell you the truth, I sometimes get the feeling that the ranch is unprotected. I've got eight men on the payroll, and there ain't a fighting man in the bunch. Sally's beginning to act like a nervous wreck. She's suspicious of every stranger she sees. She never has got over that trouble the three of you ran into coming out here.

"I know she'd feel safer with the two of you down there, Litt. I know for a fact that you've got sand in your craw, and folks say that Bills fellow is mighty good."

Blue nodded. "I sure can't think of anything pressing around here, Two Papas. I'll talk to Lon about it, see what he thinks."

In the yard, Two Papas made three attempts to mount his horse before he managed to throw a leg over the saddle. Litt turned his head, trying to appear not to notice. The big man was aging fast, he decided.

"I'll be down there in about ten days," he said, as Two Papas reined his animal toward home. "You can count on me no matter what Lon decides." The big man waved good-bye, and kicked his horse to a canter.

Blue walked to the cabin shaking his head. Two Papas was even bigger than he had been a year ago, and looked ten years older. He moved about much slower, and his breathing could be heard from several yards away. Litt wondered if the big man was on his way out . . .

Blue and Bills returned to the Box M2 on the same day Katie Graves died. The beautiful lady had finally lost the long, hard battle with her crippling disease. Blackie Elam brought the word just before sundown, and stayed for supper. "I'm glad she passed on, Litt," Blackie said. "I mean, I knew her when she was the livliest thing on the place, running up and down the hillside like a little girl. Always had a big smile, and a good word for everybody. A man could tell by just watching her that all she wanted out of life was life itself. And she grew the prettiest flowers I ever saw.

"I also knew her when all she could do was sit on the porch for one hour a day, with tears in her eyes and the sad expression of a caged animal, barely able to lift her head. The biggest damn shame of it all was the fact that it took her so long to die." Elam stood at the hitching rail untying his horse. "The burial will take place on the hillside behind the ranch house tomorrow afternoon at two. Mister Graves says anybody who wants to come is welcome." He mounted, and rode off into the night.

Every person living at the Box M2 attended the funeral. Even Two Mamas, who had never met the lady, was present. Two Papas himself had only seen her once, on one of his visits to John Graves's ranch.

Blue stood on the hillside with at least fifty others, as the eulogy was spoken. Out of the corner of his eye, he spotted a small, yellow flower growing nearby that had somehow survived the cold winter. He walked to the flower and picked it, then dropped it into the open grave.

"Ashes to ashes, and dust to dust," the old preacher was saying, as Litt walked down the hill, still holding his hat in his hand. Lon Bills soon joined him. They stood by their horses watching, as John Graves led the crowd down the hillside.

"I appreciate you men coming," Graves said, "and I know Katie would."

Blue was turning his horse toward the Box M2. "It's the least we could do," he said, halfway saluting with his right hand. "We'll be looking forward to seeing you again under better circumstances." He kicked his horse in the ribs, and Bills was close behind.

Rope Johnson and his men left for the Big Thicket the following week. Billy Turner was the first to leave the yard, driving a two-wheeled cart containing food, pots and pans, clothing, bedrolls, and other assorted things. He stood in front of the seat, smiling and waving his hat to everyone.

When Johnson mounted to follow, Blue called to him: "Take good care of yourself, Rope, and look out for the cattle." A moment later, he added, "Especially my five hundred head."

Johnson smiled, then nodded. "How will I know which ones are yours?"

"They'll be fatter, and have the best dispositions."

"Oh." Johnson waved, and put his horse to a canter.

The grub cart and the horse wranglers were already disappearing in the east. Blue watched till the dust settled, then walked down to the Frio, where he seated himself on a large rock.

Sitting on the bank of the shallow, fast-moving stream, he began to think of his sister. Where would she have gone from San Antonio? Was she still practicing the same trade? Had she been driven by circumstances beyond her control? Or had she chosen that profession above all others, and of her own free will?

Accepting the notion that he might never know the answers to these questions was indeed difficult. He had merely assumed that since Roberta had ridden away with the Yankees, she had married one of them and was living somewhere in the North, having a baby a year. She herself had told him often that she would have a large family when she married.

Maybe she had married the man she rode north with, and the union had not worked out. Roberta was headstrong, bent on having her own way, and Litt knew that any man marrying her could scarcely look forward to a bed of roses. And he knew that she would surely attempt to dominate any man she lived with, as had beautiful women since the beginning of time. Maybe some hard-working Yankee had grown weary of fighting with her and left for parts unknown, leaving her to her own devices. The most lucrative profession for a woman as beautiful as Roberta was obvious, and would certainly not have escaped her hard-working imagination. The more Litt thought about it, the more he thought his sister had deliberately chosen her trade, even planned it.

"Everybody keeps talking about how beautiful I am," Litt could remember Roberta saying, when she was about fourteen, "especially the men. I'll tell you right now, if I've got the beauty when I get grown, I'll certainly use it to get the things I want. I just read a book that says there's no end to the things a girl can get if she's pretty enough, and knows how to spread herself around."

Spread herself around. Litt repeated the words in his mind. There was no doubt that Roberta was taking the phrase literally these days. He got to his feet, kicked a small stone halfway across the river, and headed for the bunkhouse. He lay on his bunk for a while reading an old copy of the San Antonio newspaper. In five minutes he was asleep, with the newspaper sliding from his fingers and onto the floor.

After supper, when most of the hands were playing cards in the bunkhouse, Blue was in the barn, practicing his fast draw by lantern light. He pulled the Colt more than a hundred times before hanging his gunbelt on a peg. Then he took off his shirt and began to pound the punching bag. Though the night was cool, he soon worked up a sweat as he danced around the bag, using all of the fancy footwork Blackie Elam had taught him. Blackie had shown him dozens of little tricks, all designed to confuse an opponent long enough for Litt to land one of his powerhouse punches.

Unknown to Blue, he had an audience. He had just knocked the bag off its hook and was busy rehanging it, when Lon Bills appeared at his side. "I've been watching for quite a while, Litt," he said, taking a seat on a nail keg. "If you attack a man the way you do that bag, he's gonna go down. I don't care who the son of a bitch is, he's going down."

"That's what Blackie says." Litt took off the light gloves he had been wearing to punch the bag, then took a seat on a tool box.

"I was watching you work with that, too," Bills said, pointing to Blue's gunbelt that was still hanging on the wall. "You're as fast as you need to be."

Blue stared at the toe of his boot for a moment, then looked the redhead straight in the eye. "Fast as you?"

"You're as fast as anybody," Bills said quickly. "It's like I told you a long time ago: You're just naturally quick. I do think you ought to learn to move as you draw, though, so you don't offer a man a still target. You see, you know which way you're gonna move, but he don't. It gives you a little advantage."

"Yes, sir," Blue said, smiling. "I'll work on it."

A few days later, Blue hitched his team to the wagon. He was headed north to check on his own place, and to cut and stack a year's supply of wood for the stove. Lon Bills, who would have normally made the trip, was off in San Antonio for reasons of his own. Sitting beside Litt on the wagon seat was the Box M2's newest hired hand, a twenty-five-year-old man named Alvin Werner.

Born in Zurich, Switzerland, Werner had been brought to America as an infant, and raised in Missouri's Ozark Mountains. He had been in Texas seven years, and like many Texans, his contribution to the Confederate war effort had been limited to driving supply wagons. Of medium height, and slightly on the heavy side, Werner had black hair and brown eyes. He was a likable man, with a ready smile for everybody. And though he called himself Al, no one else did. Among the hands, he was known simply as "Yodeler," which seemed to please him.

And the nickname was well placed. The man had a voice that was easy on the ears, and a falsetto of which he was in complete control. Though the syllables seemed meaningless, his melodies were beautiful, and he was often asked to perform in the bunkhouse at night. He had learned enough chords on the guitar to accompany himself nicely, and the instrument always hung on the wall behind his bunk.

By early afternoon they had felled two trees and sawed them into blocks. Shirtless, Blue was busy stacking the heavy blocks in the wagon. Yodeler stood by watching, a canteen in his hand. "Did you ever do any special exercises to build up all them muscles you got, Litt?"

Blue pushed the last block into place. "Nope. Just the same kind of work any other kid might do growing up on a farm." He placed the saw and the axes on top of the load. "I don't know how much all that has to do with muscles, anyway. Folks say my daddy was a very muscular man, and he never was known to lift a finger at anything."

Yodeler nodded, and climbed to the wagon seat. "Guess it just runs in your blood, then."

They stayed in the canyon for five days, till they had split a pile of wood half the size of the cabin. Then they stacked it in ten-foot ricks, only a few steps from the front door. They also built a corral for a garden behind the cabin.

Cecil Hudson had told Blue to take as much time as he needed with the wood, for there was little need for his services till spring roundup. In fact, the only work assignments Hudson had given Blue since his return to the Box M2 were small jobs in the immediate vicinity of the ranch house. Bills, too, had been given slack duty. Blue believed that Two Papas had instructed Hudson to keep the two young men close to home. Why? Was it because Two Mamas was less nervous, as Two Papas had said? Or was the big man himself expecting some kind of trouble? Litt supposed he would find out eventually.

When Blue and Yodeler returned to the Box M2, Lon Bills met them at the barn. He took charge of the team and wagon, for Two Papas had called to Litt from the porch, where he was sitting in a cane-bottom rocker. "How are things up at your place?" he asked, as Blue reached the top step.

"I don't think anybody's been fooling around up there," Litt answered, taking a chair himself. "I doubt that anybody knows where it is. We cut and stacked what I think is a year's supply of wood, and built a corral for a garden. I'll be planting my own vegetables there after the last frost."

"Good. What is it you decided to call the place? The Lazy Bee?"

"Yes, sir. Bee, for Blue."

Two Papas nodded. "Well, you'd better register the brand, and get some irons made up."

"I will. I'll do it before the month is out."

Two Papas called into the house for coffee, and his wife was quick to respond. Afterward, they sat quietly for a long time, sipping from expensive-looking cups. Even from where Blue sat he could hear the big man's heavy breathing, and, though Litt had never seen Two Papas using it, a walking stick rested against a nearby post.

"That Bills fellow's been staying around close ever since he got back from San Antonio," Two Papas said finally. "Makes Sally feel better. To hear her tell it, he's got sand."

"She's right, Two Papas."

"Well, I'd like for one or both of you to stay close to the house. We'll hire some extra men for the roundup, so you won't be needed there."

Blue nodded, and made no comment. He was now convinced that Two Papas was expecting trouble. He also believed that the big man knew where it would come from, that his anxiety had little or nothing to do with his wife's nerves.

"Are you expecting some kind of problem, Two Papas? Something I should know about?"

The big man averted Blue's steady gaze. "Well . . . it's just that these are harsh times. A man never knows what kind of riffraff's gonna come along."

Blue sat quietly for a moment. He had heard the same statement from Two Papas before, with no further explanation. And as before, Two Papas changed the subject completely, beginning to make small talk. Blue listened quietly for a while. Then, convinced that he would learn nothing more, he got to his feet. "At least one of us will be within shouting distance, Two Papas." He walked down the steps and headed for the bunkhouse.

"He wants one of us around all the time, huh?" Bills asked, when Blue had explained the situation. "Sounds like easy money. Guess we'll just have to flip a coin to see who goes to take a shit first every morning."

Blue walked to the cook shack to inform Fat Frank that he would have two extra mouths to feed at suppertime, then headed for the barn. And the punching bag.

Even as Litt pounded the bag, his mind was on Two Papas. The man was obviously uneasy about something, and was unwilling to discuss it. Had he done something in the past that was about to catch up with him? Doubtful, Blue decided. He was the kindest and most generous man Litt had ever known. Even in business transactions, Henry Miles was known to worry about whether the other fellow was getting a square deal. A man whose word was his bond, and Litt had met no one who disliked him. Even Two Mamas, who had known him longer than anyone, had been heard to say that he was too good for his own good. Would such a man have enemies? Blue supposed anything was possible. He took a final swing at the punching bag, then headed for the bunkhouse. He would keep a close eye on Two Papas, for he loved the man like a father.

13

A few days later, a man named Thurston Bull rode into the yard at the Box M2, accompanied by seven well-armed riders. Bull, a forty-five-year-old man who owned a horse ranch several miles south, in the Uvalde area, had been a freighter during the war and had crossed paths with Henry Miles on more than one occasion. He was now a successful horse breeder who was well known if not respected. A thick-chested man of medium height, with beady brown eyes and a complexion the color of old leather, he had been known to ride roughshod over many a man of lesser means. Those he could not buy out, he burnt out or simply chased out of the area.

Attracted by the sound of horses, Blue and Bills left

the bunkhouse in a hurry. They arrived in the yard in time to hear Bull yelling to Two Papas, who was standing on the porch: "I told you back in 'sixty-three to never set foot in this part of the country, Miles! I want you out of here, and I want you out quick!"

Blue climbed the steps to the porch, followed by Bills. "What's the problem, Two Papas?" Litt asked.

Thurston Bull answered the question. "The problem is him shystering me out of several freighting contracts during the war. Damn near sent me into bankruptcy."

Two Papas looked Bull straight in the eye. "The only thing I did was tell them I could do the job quicker for less money," he said. "I delivered."

Bull made no rebuttal to the statement made by Two Papas. Focusing his attention on Blue, he asked, "Are you his son? Or his grandson?"

"Something like that," Blue said, stepping between Two Papas and the riders. "He hasn't been feeling well lately. I'll be standing in for him today."

Bull sat his horse for a few moments, his beady eyes filled with hatred. Then he waved his arm toward his riders, who were all armed to the teeth. "I guess you can't count."

"I can count very well," Blue said, spreading his legs and bending his body slightly forward. "And I don't like the odds. But I'll promise you one thing, mister: If the shooting starts, you won't be around to see the outcome."

"Nor will you," Bills said quickly, speaking to the man on Bull's right. The redhead cast his eyes to the next man. "Nor you," he added.

A standoff. No man moved or spoke for a full minute. Blue finally broke the silence. "Get in the house, Two Papas," he said, never taking his eyes from those of Bull.

"There must be some way to talk this out," Two Papas said. "Maybe—"

"Get in the house, dammit," Blue interrupted. "These men are not talkers!" Two Papas obeyed, and Blue called after him. "Wrap your hands around that shotgun in the corner!" Whether there was a shotgun in the corner or not, Blue's words produced the desired effect. The riders began to fidget, and mumble among themselves.

Finally, one of the riders at the rear of the bunch spoke loudly. "I watched that redhead there operate one time, Mister Bull. Fastest gun I've ever seen." The man was quiet for a time, then added, "Ain't got no reason ta b'lieve th' one doin' th' talkin' is any slower. Figger 'em ta be birds uv a feather."

Bull sat his saddle for a while, then slowly began to turn his horse around. "It ain't over," he said. "You mark my words. It ain't over." He kicked his horse, and his riders followed him out of the yard.

Blue stood watching them out of sight. He knew very well that it was not over. He turned to Two Papas, who was standing in the doorway. "Did I hear one of the men call him Bull?"

"Thurston Bull," Two Papas said, stepping out onto the porch. "He was one of my competitors for freight contracts during the war. And I don't think he really believes I did anything underhanded. He just hates me because I wound up with some of the contracts he wanted."

"I believe you, Two Papas," Litt said. "And I'm sorry I snapped at you a while ago. It was a dangerous situation."

The big man nodded. "Think nothing of it. I just

appreciate you men being here when you were needed. Something like that can get out of hand mighty quick." He made three steps toward the doorway, then turned. "By the way, I don't have a shotgun in the house."

"I knew that," Blue said, stepping into the yard. "But they didn't."

The young men walked around for a while, ending up at the cook shack, where Fat Frank fed them plates of goulash.

"You think they'll be back?" Bills asked, sipping his third cup of coffee.

"Don't believe they'll ride right up to the front door again, but I certainly expect more trouble from them. Bull says it ain't over, and I think we'd better take him at his word."

"Me too. You got something in mind?"

Blue took another sip from his own cup. "I think we should start by taking stock of the way we do things around here. Most of the men ride about the ranch unarmed. Getty and Cecil Hudson are the only ones who even carry rifles on their saddles.

"All of them will have to be told about Bull's threat, and some of them might quit. Most of them are not fighting men. Even if they were, they might not feel obligated to stick with Two Papas in a quarrel that's several years old, and has nothing to do with the ranch." Blue got to his feet and headed for the door. "I don't believe Hudson or Getty will run, though."

Blue's thinking was correct: Hudson and Getty stayed. When told that trouble might be in the offing, the other five riders asked for their pay. The following morning, they rode off the premises.

The riders were scarcely out of sight, when Blue joined Two Papas at the house. "We've got to have some protection for the ranch, Two Papas. Men who are not afraid of their shadows."

The big man stood at the west wall, staring through the window at the river. "I don't know who to get," he said, without turning around. "Do you?"

"No. But you've got a man on the payroll who does. Lon Bills knows every fighting man in San Antonio, and we don't have any time to lose. Word'll get around quick that we lost most of our crew."

When the big man turned, his eyes still held a vacant stare. Finally, he nodded. "Guess so. Tell him to get eight men. We want men who'll stand their ground. Tell him not to hire anybody he doesn't know personally. Tell him to offer 'em sixty a month till this thing gets settled. One way or another, I intend to settle it. Once and for all."

Blue was out of the house quickly. He headed for the bunkhouse, where the three remaining men stood around outside talking. Hudson and Getty had not ridden out to work this morning, for Two Papas had told them not to. Litt spoke to Bills, motioned toward the barn, and began to walk in that direction. Bills followed.

They talked for ten minutes, then Blue stood by while Bills roped his horse. "Make sure everybody's got a rifle, Lon, and knows how to use it."

"I know what kind of men you want, Litt."

Blue nodded. Enough had been said.

Bills stopped by the bunkhouse for his bedroll, then walked to the cook shack. When he returned, he stuffed a two-day supply of food in his saddlebag, then headed for San Antonio.

Cecil Hudson watched Bills disappear from sight, then turned to Litt. "Is he gone after some help?"

"Uh-huh."

Hudson exhaled loudly. "Well, I know Two Papas don't want us out working, but we can't just stand here looking at each other. I'm gonna saddle up and stir around a little, maybe do some scouting." As he started for the corral, he spoke to Getty over his shoulder. "You coming, Joe?"

"Yep."

Both Hudson and Getty wore sidearms today. Blue watched as they saddled their horses, shoved rifles into scabbards, and rode south along the river.

A few minutes later, Blue walked to the big house. In his right hand he held a double-barreled, ten-gauge shotgun. In his left, he carried a full box of shells. When Two Papas opened the door, Litt walked to the nearest corner and leaned the weapon against the wall. "You've got a shotgun in the corner now, and it's loaded with buckshot." He handed over the extra shells. "At close range, it's the most devastating weapon known to man, and it takes no prisoners. The next time some son of a bitch rides into this yard bent on doing you harm, I expect you to use it. It's ready to go. Just pull back the hammers and you're in business." Blue closed the door before Two Papas could speak.

Litt got his Henry from the bunkhouse and checked its load. Then, with the rifle resting in the crook of his arm, he walked down to the river, taking his usual seat on the large rock. He had a wide view of the area. From his seat he could see at least a mile to the south, and half that far to the north. To the west, across the river, his view was unobstructed for several miles except for a few cedars here and there. His shortest vision was to the east, for the elevation rose steadily in that direction, then leveled off abruptly. A distance of about five hundred yards.

Casting his eyes in every direction, the only movement he could see was an occasional longhorn. Some were close, others farther away, and some were only specks in the distance. Sitting with his rifle across his lap, he was trying to figure out what Thurston Bull might do next, and wishing he knew more about the man. Was he all bluff and bluster? Or a vengeful man with no conscience, who would stop at nothing in order to gain revenge against a man who had bested him in a business deal?

Blue decided he was not bluffing. Though Litt was a young man, he had been around the mountain a time or two, and had long ago learned to take a man at his word until he knew otherwise. Recalling the hatred in Thurston Bull's eyes, Litt believed he might well be the type to shoot a man in his sleep, or burn him alive.

Blue did not believe that Bull would openly attack the ranch, for he would surely realize that it would cost him dearly. Besides, his quarrel was with Two Papas alone, not with the men who worked at the Box M2.

After thinking for a while longer, Blue began to face the fact that he had not the slightest idea what Thurston Bull might do. He had seen idiots leading fighting men before, sometimes needlessly to their deaths. Was Bull the type to regard the lives of his own men so lightly that he would order an attack? Blue had also seen that happen before. He uncrossed his legs, and got to his feet. Walking up the hill toward the bunkhouse, he began to lay his plans. He would make the cost of attacking the Box M2 so high that even a crazy man would be unwilling to pay it.

"Bull's losing the freighting contracts was a mess of his own making," Two Papas said, when Blue began to question him a few minutes later. "Some folks said he stole about as much as he delivered. I was not one of his accusers, however, even though he probably thinks so.

"He threatened to shoot me dead if I ever put cattle on this place, but I chalked that up to the heat of the moment. I learned from Leroy Upton that I was mistaken. Leroy says Bull's already made plans to put me out of business. Says he'll storm the ranch if necessary."

Blue shook his head emphatically. "That's not gonna happen, Two Papas. The storm will be waiting for him when he gets here."

The two men talked for an hour. When Blue heard the sound of approaching horses, he walked to the barn, where Hudson and Getty were unsaddling their mounts. He called Getty aside. "Two Papas wants you to make a quick trip to San Antonio, Joe. Hitch that blaze-faced bay to the buggy. He can trot the whole distance." He laid a stack of double eagles in Getty's hand. "Buy six double-barreled, ten-gauge shotguns and a dozen boxes of double-aught buck. Get 'em in as many different places as you can, so nobody begins to wonder about it."

Getty nodded, and dropped the money into his coat pocket. "I'll get Fat Frank to fix me enough food for a round trip, then pick up my bedroll. I don't believe I can travel there and back without some sleep."

"No. Just make it as quick as you can." Blue walked to the bunkhouse. Half an hour later, he heard the buggy leave the premises.

Blue and Hudson stayed close to the house for the next three days, during which time neither man saddled a horse. Then on the third morning, right after breakfast, the buggy rolled into the yard. Blue stepped from the cook shack and caught the bay's bridle.

Getty, looking red-eyed and haggard, jumped to the ground. "Been traveling all night."

"I know, Joe," Litt said, beginning to stroke the tired animal. "Let Fat Frank feed you, then get some sleep. I'll take care of the horse."

The shotguns and ammunition were in the buggy, wrapped in Getty's bedroll. Blue and Hudson carried the bundle inside the bunkhouse and laid it across Blue's cot. Litt picked up one of the shiny weapons, broke it open, and placed a shell in each chamber. "We won't saw the barrels off," he said, snapping the breech closed. "Cuts down on their range too much." He passed the weapon to Hudson, then loaded another for himself.

Bills arrived the following day at noon. Seven men rode into the yard behind him, bedrolls behind their saddles. A motley crew indeed. Each man wore a beard of a different color, a different type of clothing, and the horses they rode varied widely in color. What they did have in common was that a full cartridge belt circled each man's waist, a holstered Colt hung on his right leg, and his saddle scabbard contained a Henry rifle. Their ages appeared to range from twenty to forty.

Blue stood on the porch looking the men over. Bills was soon at his side. "Couldn't find but seven men, Litt. Not on such short notice."

"You did fine, Lon. We all appreciate it."

"Five of them I know personally, and they'll stick through hell and high water. The other two came highly recommended."

A few moments later Bills introduced the riders, who still sat their saddles, to Two Papas and Litt Blue. Then he introduced the riders themselves, pointing to each man as he spoke his name: "Will Christmas,

Razzy Hazelwood, Bob Jones, Rambo Stewart, Bill Jennings, Sam Lincoln." Bills paused for a moment, then pointed to the last man, who rode a horse as white as snow. "And this is Smitty. He's young, but he'll fight, and he's not smart enough to run." The remark brought a hint of a smile to Smitty's bearded lips.

Two Papas began to address the men: "I'm sure you've all been told why you're here. The truth is, we don't have any way of knowing what we might be facing in the very near future." He paused, and pointed to Blue. "Litt Blue, here, will be in charge. Completely in charge. He was an officer during the war, and he knows something about strategy. Any time he gives a man an order, I expect that man to hop to it." Then Two Papas was gone into the house.

Blue stood thinking for a while. He had not been an officer during the war, and Two Papas well knew it. However, the big man must have had a good reason for saying so. Blue quickly decided to let the statement stand. He eyed Smitty's horse for a moment, then spoke to the young man. "You can turn your horse into the corral, Smitty. Rope yourself one of a darker color."

"Naw, I'll just stick with Ol' Whitey," Smitty said, shaking his head. "He's a good horse."

"That might well be true," Blue said firmly. "But he can be seen for several miles. Even at night. No white horses!"

Smitty twisted in his saddle to face Blue, as his mouth broke into an unmistakable smile. He shrugged his shoulders. "No white horses," he said, turning his animal toward the corral.

Blue spoke to the remaining riders, none of whom had dismounted: "You fellows can put your horses in

the barn. You'll find grain and hay easy enough."
Some of the men nodded, while others mumbled behind their beards. All pointed their horses toward the
barn. Blue called after them: "Stake out cots for yourselves in the bunkhouse. The cook'll ring the bell
when dinner's ready."

Joe Getty rested most of the day, and went to bed
again right after dark. He was summoned by Blue
early next morning, and the two men walked down to
the Frio, seating themselves on the rock. "How good
an actor are you, Joe?" Litt asked.

"Never tried my hand at it," Getty answered. "Except maybe when I was a kid, trying to get my way
about something. Why do you ask?"

"Well, as you know, I've asked all the men to stay
near the bunkhouse. I don't want anybody to know
that they're here. But they're not the type to stay
cooped up for long. We've got a cow hunt coming up,
and calves to brand. We can't just sit here forever
wondering what Thurston Bull's gonna do. I think I've
figured out a way to make him show his hand, but I'll
need your help."

"You've got it."

Joe Getty rode into Uvalde at sundown. Tomorrow
would be his twenty-seventh birthday, so tonight he
would treat himself to some of the best liquor in town.
As he rode down the street he could see that most of
the stores were still open, with wagon teams from out-
lying ranches tied to the hitching rails. Nobody worried about being caught on the road at night, their
horses always knew the way home.

Getty was on his way to the Buckhorn Saloon, when
something else caught his eye. Three horses were tied
at the hitching rail of a small, run-down watering hole.
Each animal's hip had been burned with a Rocking

TB iron—Thurston Bull's brand. Getty tied his own horse, and stepped inside.

The building was about forty feet long, with a sawdust floor. Eight stools lined the crude bar, and two tables, with four chairs at each, sat off to the side. All three of the riders sat at the bar. Getty took the first stool inside the door. The bartender, a skinny man with a long blond mustache, was there quickly. Getty laid an eagle on the bar. "Give me a bottle of good whiskey."

The man reached beneath the counter for the bottle. One glance at the label told Getty that it was indeed good liquor. The bartender poured Getty's glass half full, then set the bottle on the counter. "Have a drink yourself," Getty said. Then motioning to Bull's riders, he added, "Give those fine gentlemen a drink out of my bottle, too. Tomorrow's my birthday, and I think everybody ought to have a drink."

The bartender complied, then lifted his glass. "Much obliged." Each of the riders lifted his glass into the air also, saluting Getty's generosity.

Getty nodded, and said nothing to the men. He spun himself of his stool and sat facing the counter, staring into his whiskey glass.

Getty was on his third drink, when one of the men spoke to him. Sitting three stools away, the bearded man wore a brown felt hat that had seen better days and ranchhand's clothing that he had no doubt worked in all week. "Ain't seen you around before. You just passing through?"

"Gonna be passing through," Getty answered loud enough that all could hear. "No, sir, I ain't fighting no man's personal battles. Gonna be getting myself to hell out of this part of the country." He poured himself another drink, then continued to stare into the glass.

"Battles, you say?" The man moved two stools closer. "What battles?"

"Old Henry Miles, up on the Box M2. Him and some fellow named Bull has had some kind of squabble going for several years. Bull ordered Miles out of the area, and I understand he ain't somebody to mess around with. I told the old man he'd be better off to round up his cows and move out, but he won't budge. Stubborn old cuss."

"You've been working up there, huh?"

"Yeah, but no more. Hell, I'm a ranch hand, not a fighter. The rest of the men weren't fighters, either. That's why they all quit, just like I did."

The man took a drag from his cigarette, then blew smoke toward the ceiling. "Whole crew quit, huh?"

"All but two, and they ain't worth a shit. Both of them are afraid of their own shadow." He took a sip from his glass, then began to drum his fingers on the bar. "Old Miles sent for some fighting men, but it'll probably be close to a week before they get in. I tell you, he's a sitting duck up there."

The riders were already getting to their feet. As they passed Getty's stool, the talkative one stopped for a moment. "Thank you for telling us all this, stranger. Now we won't go wandering around up north and get shot by mistake. You say Miles sent for more men this morning?"

"No, no. Sent for 'em two days ago."

The men walked through the front door. Moments later, Getty heard running horses. He waited ten minutes, then cut cross-country to the Box M2, convinced that Bull's riders had bought his story.

14

The attack came two nights later, just before midnight. The same moonlight Thurston Bull thought would give him an advantage worked against him. There were only two places south of the Box M2 where the Frio could be forded easily, and Blue had a man posted within seeing distance of each: Will Christmas at the north crossing, Joe Getty a mile farther south.

At ten o'clock, Bull and ten riders forded the river at the south crossing. Half a mile away, at the top of a hill, Joe Getty sat his saddle, concealed by a clump of cedars. He watched as the horses took to the knee-deep water, then scrambled out on the other side. Then, obviously wanting to save their horses, the riders pointed them north at a walking gait.

Will Christmas was already climbing into his saddle when Getty arrived at the north crossing a few minutes later. "They just forded the river, Will. Ten or twelve of 'em." Both men kicked their horses, and headed for the ranch at a gallop.

After hearing the news, Blue was busy passing out shotguns and ammunition. "We've been over it all a dozen times, men. I expect every man to stick to his station. Nobody fires till I do; we want 'em close." As the men headed for the bunkhouse door, he called after them: "Keep your wits about you, and don't jump the gun. If you lose your head you'll probably lose your ass." Then he blew out the lamp and began to fumble his way out of the dark building.

Three-foot-deep trenches had been dug around the main house, and on two sides of the bunkhouse. And though the excess dirt would have made good protection, Blue had ordered it hauled away to the river, for it would have given away the presence of the trenches. The area had been raked clean, and the ditches could not be detected at a distance of more than a few yards. The full moon was also in Blue's favor, for it hung at an angle behind the buildings, casting a dark shadow on the trenches. Blue did not believe they could be seen by the riders, even at a distance of twenty yards.

Thurston Bull halted his men two hundred yards away. They sat talking for several minutes, then advanced another fifty yards, stopping again. They sat their horses quietly for a long time. So long that Blue began to wonder if something or someone had tipped his hand. All nine of the Box M2 men were armed with Henry rifles and six-shooters. Seven of them held ten-gauge shotguns in their hands, the hammers cocked and ready. Fat Frank was in the main house with Two Papas, and both were armed with rifles. Two Mamas was tucked inside the rock fireplace, behind heavy oak furniture.

Blue had placed five men in the trench at the main house, and four at the bunkhouse. He himself had taken up a station at the corner of the bunkhouse, where he would have a clear view of the action, and could fire in either direction. The Box M2 men waited, the tension mounting. The only sound was the occasional stamping of a horse's foot at the corral.

At last the riders began to move forward. Fifty yards . . . forty yards. At thirty yards, they halted again. Then, using hand signals to direct his men, Thurston Bull unsheathed his rifle. His men followed suit, and all began to move forward slowly. At a distance of fifteen yards, Blue's shotgun bucked against his shoulder—twice. Two men fell from their saddles. Every man in the trench was firing now, and, even as he was busy reloading, Blue saw two more riders topple to the ground.

Totally confused, and firing their rifles wildly, the remaining riders spurred their horses past the bunkhouse, only to run into a curtain of fire from the trench surrounding the main house. When two riders galloped back past the bunkhouse and headed for the top of the hill, a barrage of fire from the Henry rifles emptied the saddles.

The sound of gunfire mixed with the squealing of horses ended as abruptly as it had begun. The battle, which had lasted less than two minutes, was over. Not a single Rocking TB rider had escaped.

Still in the trench, Blue got to his feet and began to call out the names of his men, waiting for each man's answer before calling another. The last name he called did not answer. Blue was out of the trench and to the south corner of the bunkhouse quickly. There, still holding his shotgun, with his hatless head resting against his knees, was Lon Bills. As Blue knelt and lifted his friend's head, Two Papas arrived with a lantern. The light showed that Bills had been hit squarely between the eyes, and was beyond help. Only one barrel of his shotgun had been fired, indicating that he died the moment the shooting started.

As Two Papas continued to hold the lantern, Blue allowed Lon's head to fall back to his chest, then sat staring at the body. How many times had this same thing happened during the war? How many times had he turned over a lifeless body only to recognize the face of one of his dearest friends? How many indefensible battlefields? How many unnamed creeks and swamps?

"The sons of bitches!" he shouted, getting to his feet. "All for nothing!" Then, taking Two Papas by the arm, he pointed to one of the bodies. "That'll be Thurston Bull," he said, almost at a whisper. "I made sure he wouldn't be around to reorganize."

Two Papas shone the light on the man's face. "It's Bull, all right."

Several lighted lanterns were bobbing about the hillside—Box M2 men looking over the carnage.

Three horses were also down. A big roan was struggling to get to its feet, but could not. Blue put a bullet in the animal's head to relieve its suffering. Then he shouted to the men, who were now clustered near the bunkhouse. "Leave everything just as it is! Don't touch anything."

Then he sought out Joe Getty. "You feel like taking another ride, Joe?"

"Guess so."

Litt pointed toward the corral. "Take that big buck-skin. He's the fastest horse we have. Ride to Uvalde and look up Sheriff Holloway. Tell him what happened, and tell him to bring the undertaker. He'll need two wagons."

Getty headed south ten minutes later.

With the help of Sam Lincoln, Blue carried Lon's body to the bunkhouse. Placing it on the redhead's own cot, he put a feather pillow beneath the head and covered him with a blanket.

He walked back into the yard just in time to over-hear a muted conversation between Razzy Hazelwood and Rambo Stewart. "Ain't no tellin' how much money them jaybirds got on 'em." Hazelwood said, waving his arm toward the scattered bodies. " 'Specially Thurston Bull.".

Stewart nodded. " 'At's right. And they damn shore ain't gon' be needin' it, neither."

Blue walked to the men quickly, standing close enough that he could have touched them. With azure eyes that seemed to suddenly turn to ice, he stared both men down. "Don't even think about it!" he said, loud enough for the others to hear.

Both men began to fidget. Then, dropping their heads, they turned their backs and walked to the bunkhouse.

The moon dropped behind the mountain, leaving the area in total darkness. Some of the men stretched out on their cots, but nobody slept. As the excitement of the battle wore off, and talk of the fight ceased, Fat Frank rang the bell. He had flapjacks, bacon, and hot coffee for all.

Two Papas took a seat at the head of the table. Refusing breakfast, he began to sip from a steaming tin cup. "I thank you all," he said, his eyes moving down the line, looking each man directly in the eye. "That sight out there is sickening, but it could just as easily have been us." His eyes rested on Blue's face for a long time. "You handled it perfectly, Litt, and it won't be forgotten. I'm sorry about that Bills fellow. He was a good man." Two Papas finished his coffee, then got to his feet. With the doorknob in his hand, he turned to face the men again. "No telling what Thurston Bull told his men in order to get them to fight like that. You can bet your boots that he didn't level with them." Then he was gone to the main house.

Joe Getty was back in the saddle before daybreak, headed for the Graves spread to invite Lon's friends to his funeral. Blue had chosen late afternoon for the burial because he believed that by four o'clock the bodies of Bull and his riders would be off the premises. The interment of Lon Bills would take place a mile north of the ranch house.

Sheriff Holloway arrived at noon, accompanied by a deputy and the undertaker. They had brought two wagons. A tall man, with green eyes and brown hair that was sprinkled with gray, Royce Holloway was about forty years old. He had originally come from Ohio, and though he had been in Texas for ten years, he had never picked up the Texas drawl.

The lawman sat his horse for a long time, staring at the bodies scattered about. "What the hell is this I'm seeing?" he asked of no one in particular. "I thought the war was over."

"It had nothing to do with the war, Sheriff," Blue said, stepping forward. "You can read the signs from where you're sitting. They attacked about midnight, and they're lying right where they fell."

The sheriff kneed his horse forward, looking down into the trenches. "Well, it's obvious that you were expecting them. How did that come about?"

"Bull rode up here with the whole crew a few days ago and threatened us. We kept an eye on his activities after that."

"Humph." Holloway turned his horse and rode down the hill for two hundred yards. Then, with his nose to the ground studying the tracks, he came back up the hill very slowly. Then he rode around looking at each of the bodies, and each of the dead horses.

He rode back to the corner of the bunkhouse and spoke to Two Papas, who was now standing beside Blue. "You'd be Miles, I suppose."

Two Papas nodded.

"Well, it doesn't take a genius to figure out what happened," the sheriff said, waving his arm around. "The signs are all there." He was busy rolling a cigarette. He licked the paper and gave it a final twist. "Would you mind telling me what brought it on?"

Two Papas talked for several minutes, with Holloway grunting or nodding occasionally.

"Well, I'll be damned," the lawman said, after listening to the story. "Let me get this straight. Thurston Bull first rode up here and threatened you, then turned right around and rode into your trap. Is that right?"

"That's right."

"Humph." The sheriff threw his cigarette butt into the trench. "Looks like self-defense to me, and that's what I'll report to the prosecutor. I don't expect him to push it. Will you have some of your men help us load the bodies?"

Two Papas nodded, and several men stepped forward.

The deputy and the undertaker, neither of whom had ever spoken, drove the wagons as the bodies were loaded. Then the saddles were taken from the dead horses and piled on top.

"Guess you'll drag those dead animals off somewhere," the sheriff said.

Blue nodded.

All hands stood in the yard watching as the wagons rolled down the hill toward Uvalde with their grisly cargo, Sheriff Holloway leading the way.

Blue ordered three men to hitch up teams and drag the dead horses toward Frio Canyon. "No use to bury them," he said. "The wild animals'll pick their bones clean."

Lon Bills was laid to rest two hours before sunset, a mile north of the ranch house. Twenty-three men stood on the grassy knoll as one of John Graves's riders, a devoutly religious man who always carried a Bible in his saddlebag, spoke a few words of praise and asked the Lord to be kind to the dearly departed soul at the Resurrection. Then the grave was filled in and covered with heavy rocks. That done, the men rode off the hill in small bunches.

John Graves and all of his riders had attended the funeral. Graves himself joined Two Papas in the main house, while the others congregated around the cook shack. Fat Frank had food for all.

Blackie Elam was taking the redhead's demise particularly hard. Sitting on the bench beside Blue, Blackie was sipping the last of his coffee. "I never met a man who had more sand than Lon Bills, Litt. Damn shame he had to go that way. You can bet your ass that there wasn't a son of a bitch in that bunch who could have matched his draw. Not even on Lon's laziest day."

"Somebody just made a lucky shot. Fired at Lon's muzzle flash, I suppose. I'm gonna miss him terribly, Blackie."

"Of course you will. We all will." Blackie drummed his fingers on the table for a moment. "I guess when your cows get here you'll be needing another man. How about me?"

"I already promised the job to Joe Getty. I expect to need more than one man eventually, though. If you're still available then, I'd like to have you."

Blackie chuckled. "Guess I will be. I sure don't have anywhere else to go."

Blue stepped to the stove and got the coffeepot. "I'll tell you what, Blackie," he said, refilling their cups. "If you really want to make a change, there might be an opening here at the Box M2 pretty soon. I'll be having a long talk with Two Papas in the morning."

Elam nodded, then raised his cup as if drinking a toast. "Go ahead and put my name in the drawing, Litt. I like it up here."

John Graves and Two Papas had decided against a community roundup, believing that it would be easier for each man to round up and brand his own calves. In country such as this, where cattle had everything they needed right under their feet, they had less inclination to wander, and most stayed on or near their home range. For the few head that did mix with the wrong herd, however, Graves and Two Papas each had several of the other's branding irons. Wherever it was found, a calf would be touched with whatever brand its mother wore.

Blue had coffee with Two Papas late next morning. He told the big man of the conversation he had heard between Stewart and Hazelwood. "They were talking about picking the pockets of Bull and his riders." Two Papas made no comment, and Blue continued, "I believe anybody that would rob a dead man would steal from a live one. I think you might be better off if they were somewhere else."

"I don't intend to keep any of them," Two Papas said. "They're not ranch hands, they're fighting men. The fight's over."

True to his word, Two Papas paid each of the men a bonus and sent them packing before the day was over. When told that Blackie Elam wanted to work at the Box M2, the big man nodded. "Hire him. Maybe he knows where we can get some men to help with the cow hunt."

"I would think so." Blue headed for the corral to get his horse. A few minutes later, he pointed the animal toward the Graves ranch.

Bringing two horses of his own that he would add to the ranch's string, Elam moved into the bunkhouse at noon the next day, saying that he indeed knew where to find hands for the roundup. "The men I'm talking about are not fighters, now, Litt," Blackie said. "They're ranch hands."

"Just the kind of men we need," Blue said. "It's like Two Papas said: The fight's over."

"It certainly is. Word gets around mighty quick, Litt. There ain't enough money around to hire a bunch of men to ride against this ranch now."

"That's just the way we want to keep it." Litt headed for the bunkhouse door, then stopped. Turning, he said, "Two Papas says to get at least six men. Eight if you can."

"Eight it is. I'll leave for San Antonio in the morning."

Next day at sunset, Blue, Getty, and Cecil Hudson were at the Buckhorn Saloon in Uvalde. The trip had been suggested by Hudson, who had been off the Box M2 for several months. A night on the town would do them all good, he said, and he also wanted to test the air, to find out in which direction public sentiment lay in regards to the shootout.

They did not have to wait long to hear conflicting opinions. Seated at a table in the middle of the room, they had no problem overhearing the conversation of a few drinkers sitting at the bar, twenty feet away. "I say Bull was a damn fool to go riding up there like he did," a bearded man was saying. "Especially with the moon as bright as day."

"Bull weren't no fool," another man said from the opposite side of the bar. "We prob'ly won't never know th' straight uv it, but I'd betcha he got suckered into it."

"Maybe so," a third man said. "Whatever the case, they were damn sure expecting Bull. Had trenches dug all over the place. The sheriff said it looked like Shiloh all over again."

A fourth man got to his feet, stood for a moment, and downed a shot of whiskey. "The damn truth of the matter is, Thurston Bull finally found somebody he couldn't bully. And that's what he rode up there for, just as sure as you're born. A man don't make a social call at midnight, and he don't take ten gunmen with him on a friendly visit."

"Ain't nothing but a bunch of war veterans running that place up there, and I hear tell that they've got a young ex-Confederate general leading them."

"I heard the same thing," the first man said. "I guess

every single one of the Box M2 men fought dozens of battles worse than that during the war. Probably seemed like old hat to them." He got to his feet and pushed back his stool. "I'll betcha one thing. I'll betcha nobody else don't go up there messing with them."

One of the drinkers suggested that they visit another saloon, and all agreed. They upended their glasses, then walked through the front door.

Blue, Hudson, and Getty sat at the table for more than three hours, during which time many men came and went. Most took stools on the opposite side of the bar, and sat staring. Blue had no doubt that the three had been recognized as Box M2 men, for their horses stood just outside the front door, wearing the brand. However, no one spoke directly to any of them. The men finally called it a night and bought a bottle for the road.

On the way home, Blue thought long and hard about the shoot-out. He supposed that by now it was the main topic of conversation throughout much of Texas. One of the San Antonio newspapers had called it the "Box M2 Massacre", and several other papers had picked up the term. Though Two Papas had chased two newsmen off the premises and the Box M2 riders had refused to talk to them, several men who had been involved in the fight and later discharged, talked to reporters freely. Litt had read two separate accounts and was surprised that both were for the most part, accurate. All except the part about "General" Blue.

Litt did not believe that any of the men who had fought the fight had called him a general. In fact, he doubted that any of them even liked him, and most had resented taking his orders. Nope, the newspapers had added the word "General" of their own accord, to give the story emphasis.

Nor did Blue believe that the story would die. Not in his lifetime, at least. It would be passed from the old to the young for many years to come, growing more bizarre with each telling. "General Blue!" Litt said disgustedly, to no one in particular. Then he reached for the bottle Cecil Hudson was offering.

15

B lackie Elam returned from San Antonio with eight riders, half of them teenaged boys. Speaking to Blue, Hudson motioned toward the youngsters. "Don't go judging them by that peach fuzz on their faces, Litt. They'll probably turn out to be the best hands on the ranch."

All of the riders had signed on knowing full well that their jobs would be terminated when the roundup and branding were done. Within the first hour, Blue made up his mind to keep an eye on a young man named Pete Nedd. Small, with blond hair and blue eyes, the seventeen-year-old was exceedingly handsome, with a perpetual smile that revealed rows of perfectly matched teeth. He sat his saddle as if he had been born in it.

"You pretty good with that, Pete?" Blue asked, pointing to the youngster's forty-foot lariat.

Fingering the rope for a moment, the boy nodded. "Uh-huh. I reckon the rope's the only reason I'm here." He sat his saddle for a while, gazing at the river and the longhorns grazing on the other side. "I know this job won't last long, but maybe I can earn a little money to help my folks out. My pa's on awful hard times, right now." Then he looked Blue squarely in the eye, offering the biggest smile yet. "Anyway, it's the first chance I've ever had to earn a dollar and a quarter a day."

At that moment, Cecil Hudson called the riders to the corral. Blue stood watching as Pete Nedd rode away. Litt had liked him immediately, and had a feeling that the young man would be on the Box M2 long after the roundup was over.

Two Papas called Blue to the main house shortly after supper. "We've got all the men we need for the actual roundup and branding, Litt," the big man said. "Your help won't be needed. What I want you to do is stick close to Cecil. Watch what he does, and listen to what he says. I'm not necessarily telling you to be like him, but you damn sure couldn't find a better man to learn from.

"Cecil knows it all; he knows when a cow's sick even before she knows it. I don't care if you don't lift a finger, just stay with Hudson all the way through. You'll learn a whole bunch of things you haven't been exposed to yet. Pay close attention to the way he handles men, 'cause there's nobody better at it.

"I suppose he'll have a big surprise for you right off, but don't come running to me. I don't want to discuss it. Now, get out of here and go learn something from the master."

"Yes, sir." Blue headed for the bunkhouse. Round-up would begin tomorrow at sunrise.

Blue's big surprise that Two Papas had mentioned came quickly next morning. Litt was standing beside one of the wagons, when he noticed the branding irons lying in the box. He picked up one and turned to the foreman. "These are my irons, Cecil. We won't be needing them till my cows get here."

"We'll be needing them today," Hudson said, continuing to hitch up the team.

Blue stood thinking for a moment, then laid the iron back in the wagon box. "You mean you're gonna put my brand on some of the calves?"

Hudson hooked the last chain to a singletree. "Two Papas says to put the Lazy Bee on all of them."

All of them! Litt stood frozen for a moment, then leaned against the wagon. "Hell, Cecil," he said softly, "we're talking about more than a thousand head of calves."

"Yep," Hudson said, then ordered some men to load dry wood in the wagon for branding fires.

Blue walked to the shed and took a seat on a nail keg, where he sat staring at the ground between his legs. What the hell was the big man doing? What did he have in mind? There was one quick way to find out, Litt decided. He was halfway to the main house, when he stopped in his tracks. "Don't come running to me," Two Papas had said. "I don't want to discuss it." After a moment, Blue slowly began to retrace his footsteps, knowing that the big man would eventually explain the situation without being asked. At the corral, Litt roped the chestnut and cinched down his saddle. As he mounted, something Lon Bills had said several months ago came to his mind: "You're the grandson now, Litt," Lon had said.

As he had been ordered, Blue stayed with Hudson all day, watching silently as his own brand was burned into the hides of the bawling calves. Just before noon, as Blue sat on his haunches stoking the fire, Hudson laid on several more sticks of wood. Litt rearranged them, and sat staring into the fire. "I still don't understand why Two Papas is putting my brand on the calves."

"Seems obvious to me," Hudson said, remounting. He turned his horse and added over his shoulder, "Use your noggin. You should be able to figure it out."

Blue paid close attention to Pete Nedd. The kid was an excellent roper. Maybe not as good as Rope Johnson yet, but it was obvious that in time, he would be. His long loop seldom missed, and then only because a calf made a sudden move just as the loop was released. Then, building another in what might have been record time, the youngster would bring the calf to a halt quickly, and drag it toward the branding fire.

Occasionally, a bawling longhorn cow, her head and horns dropped down in a position to do business, would charge both men and horses in answer to her calf's bellowing. All hands would scamper to safety till the cow was roped and dragged away. Then the calf would be branded and allowed to return to its mother. Irate longhorn cows were fully capable of killing either man or horse, and it was a possibility that ranch hands were constantly on guard against. Even so, more than one man had been sent to an early grave by a mother cow trying to protect her offspring from the branding iron. These days, there was always somebody present who had a firearm. If a cow could not be bluffed into halting her charge, she would be shot.

Blue also spent some time watching Blackie Elam and Joe Getty. Either man could pick up a two-hundred-pound calf and take it to the ground in one fluid motion. And they could do it all day long. Even when the day was done, neither man seemed tired. After Fat Frank served beef and beans for supper, the men sat around the campfire. "Guess you're about white-eyed, Blackie," Blue said. "You've put in a hell of a day."

"Not especially," Elam said, then pointed to Getty. "I guess Joe might be. He did most of the work."

Getty shook his head, and dashed his coffee grounds into the limbs of a small cedar. Then he picked up his bedroll and walked away in the darkness.

Blue lay awake in his own bedroll long after the fire died, thinking of the workers he had watched in action today. It had been teamwork at its best, and every man knew his business. Elam, Getty, and even young Pete, were a pleasure to watch. Just before going to sleep, Blue made himself a promise: If he ever became a successful rancher, men such as those would be paid well. Two Papas himself paid wages well above the average, but Blue would pay more.

And Litt wanted to keep Pete Nedd on the payroll no matter what Two Papas was up to. The only complaint the young man had made was that the cowboys talked too "nasty" around the campfire. "All they want to do is see who can cuss the most," Pete had said, "and talk about all the different things a man can do with a woman. I've had a few women myself, Litt, but I sure didn't go off talking about it."

Blue chuckled. He liked Pete Nedd, and hoped to meet his folks someday.

* * *

When the roundup was over, twelve hundred twenty-six head of calves scattered to the four winds, all wearing the Lazy Bee brand. Two Papas paid the riders off on the porch of the main house. Each man said that he was well satisfied, and offered his thanks for the opportunity to earn some cash money. Then, with the exception of Pete Nedd, all headed for San Antonio. Following Blue's recommendation, Two Papas had given the youngster a year-round job. With a smile even wider than usual, Pete expressed his gratitude, saying that he would ride to San Antonio to give his earnings to his folks, then return to his duties as a regular ranch hand.

"If you'll wait till tomorrow we'll ride together," Blue said to Pete. "We all need a break from the steady grind."

Shortly after sunrise next morning, Blue, Elam, Getty, and young Pete headed for San Antonio. Saying he had lost nothing in the "big town," Cecil Hudson declined the invitation to join them.

At The Spring, the men only stopped to water themselves and their horses. Then they continued on to San Antonio, arriving long after dark. Pete Nedd headed straight for his father's shanty, while the others stabled their horses, then rented a hotel room with three beds.

They had supper at Tom's Place, then sat at the table, drinking one pitcher of beer after another for the next three hours. Business was slow, with only a few drinkers coming and going. Several times during the night the Box M2 men were the bartender's only customers.

By the time they called it a night and returned to the hotel, the beer had loosened their tongues. They sat on their beds talking for a while, with Elam tugging at his boots. He finally got one of them off, then decided to rest. "Did you see the placard on the door down at Tom's, Litt?" he asked.

"Uh-huh." It was the same placard Blue had seen a year ago, but the wording had changed. Bob Skinner was up to his old tricks, only this time the challenger would have to put up some money. And this time it would be a fight to the finish, with the promoter betting two-to-one odds that no man could beat the professional. The time would be ten o'clock tomorrow morning, at the same vacant warehouse on the outskirts of town. The admission price for spectators was thirty cents.

Blue took off his boots and dropped them to the floor, then fluffed up his pillow. "I think I'll take him on again, Blackie."

Finally free of his other boot, Elam began to pace the floor in his stocking feet. "Well," he said, stopping at the foot of Litt's bed, "I have no doubt that you can whip his ass if you remember everything I showed you. If you forget any of it, he'll hurt you again." Beginning to pace the floor again, he continued. "You and him both are a year older, now. In your case, that's good. In his case, it's bad. I know for a fact that he's at least thirty-two years old."

"You think he's slowed down some?"

"Of course he has. Time takes care of that. He'll still be quicker than most men though, and he'll still have punching power. If you make a mistake, he'll knock fire from your ass.

"He's tough and he's smart, Litt, but you can beat him. I've already shown you enough to get the job done if you can remember it." Elam stopped his pacing, took off his clothes, and sat down on his bed. "I don't intend to talk all night and overload your mind, but let me just get a couple more points across. Don't trade punches with him, Litt; he's a damned expert. And if you get in a situation where there's nothing to do but stand toe to toe with him, take the same flat-footed stance he always uses. It gives you a whole lot more punching power."

Joe Getty, who was an excellent scrapper himself, had sat on his bed nodding as Elam spoke. Apparently he agreed with everything Blackie had said.

Long after the others were asleep, Blue lay on his bed thinking, trying to remember everything Blackie had taught him in the barn. Litt had fought Bob Skinner before, and knew that the man would not go down unless literally beaten to the floor. Skinner was several inches shorter than Blue, and Blackie had said to make a shorter man bring the fight to you, that you could hurt him more when he was coming in. He said Skinner could knock a man out with a twelve-inch punch and advised Blue to use his longer reach to keep a constant jab in the man's face. And never, never let him get inside.

Next morning, it was decided that Joe Getty should be the one to set up the fight, for there were hard feelings between Elam and Skinner's promoter. Getty left the hotel shortly after sunrise.

Then Blackie had more words of advice for Blue: "Skinner's not only a hard puncher, Litt, he's a good actor. He'll act like he's hurt a lot worse than he is, then nail you when you come after him. I made that mistake with him myself. Twice.

"Watch his eyes, Litt. When a man is hurt bad, his eyes take on a look that's impossible to fake. They might roll up in his head, and he'll start looking around trying to figure out exactly where you are. He's clearly out of focus, and that's when you go in for the kill. You've got to move instantly, or the moment will pass. Then he'll be brand-new again."

At the restaurant, Elam bought a large breakfast, while Blue had only pie and coffee. Blackie sopped at his egg yolk with a biscuit. "When his eyes turn glassy, get after his assy," he said, chuckling at his silly rhyme. Then he turned serious. "I'll be at ringside, Litt. I don't know that you can hear me above all the noise, but I'll be telling you when to take him."

Blue nodded, and said nothing.

Getty returned an hour later. The fight was set for ten o'clock this morning. Joe had found the promoter, a man named Haygood, at a hotel farther down the street, where both he and his fighter were staying. Haygood would indeed bet six hundred dollars to Getty's three hundred, and the money must be deposited with the referee before the fight began.

"I'll put up the three hundred myself," Blue said. "I don't want you fellows taking chances with your hard-earned money."

"The hell you will!' Getty said loudly. "I intend to bet fifty dollars on you."

"Me too," Elam said, then began to count his money. The three hundred quickly materialized on the bed, and Getty shoved it into his pocket. "Guess we should walk to the warehouse," he said, looking at Blue. "It'll give you a chance to stretch your muscles a little."

The warehouse was crowded, and Elam, who would act as Blue's second, shouldered his way through. Skinner and the promoter were already in the ring. The fighter stood in his own corner talking with his second. His hands were taped, and he wore a bright red robe.

Getty deposited his money with the referee, who assured him that Haygood had done the same. The winner-take-all pot would be held by a deputy marshal.

Blackie Elam climbed into the ring first, then parted the ropes for Blue to enter. Then Elam began to tape Litt's hands. Skinner recognized both men. He nodded, then sat on his stool, eyeing them.

"This event will be a fight to the finish!" the promoter shouted from the center of the ring. "Unlike London prize-ring rules, which say that a knockdown must occur before a round ends, these rounds will be three minutes long. A timekeeper will be positioned at ringside."

Then he walked to Blue's corner and lifted Litt's hand above his head. "In this corner, weighing two hundred twenty-five pounds, from South Carolina, Littleton Blue!" A small amount of applause followed.

Haygood crossed the ring to the opposite corner. The applause began before he even lifted Skinner's hand. "In this . . ." the applause was deafening. "In this . . ." He led Skinner to the center of the ring, motioning to the crowd for silence, which was soon restored. "In this corner, weighing two hundred ten pounds, from the great state of Texas, Bob Skinner!" Men were immediately shouting and whistling again.

Then the referee took over, and the promoter, along with the seconds for both fighters, jumped out of the ring. The referee, who had not been introduced by name, called both fighters to the center of the ring, where he talked to them for a moment, then sent each man to his corner.

When the bell rang to signal the beginning of the fight, they met in the center of the ring and began to circle each other. Blue remembered that the first time he fought Skinner, the man charged him immediately. It did not happen this time. Bob Skinner was no fool.

He respected Blackie Elam as an excellent fighter, and knew that any man Elam was seconding had had some training, and might well be a problem. Though confident of his own ability, Skinner could see with one eye that the muscular young man circling him now was a powerful machine, and clearly dangerous. He took a left-handed poke at Blue's jaw, and missed.

Neither man scored a telling blow during the first two rounds. So far, the fight had been little more than two cautious men feeling each other out.

During the next five rounds, both men gave and received several hard punches, and it was beginning to show. Several times Skinner had hurt Blue, but each time Litt had managed to get away. Blue's mouth was bleeding and his right eye was cut, but Skinner looked no better. Just as the seventh round ended, Blue scored well with a fast flurry of punches, and saw Skinner's legs buckle and his eyes roll. "Not yet!" Blue heard from just outside the ring, recognizing the voice of Blackie Elam.

When the bell rang for the eighth round, Blue stabbed Skinner's face three times with left jabs, then feinted him into an opening and crashed a short right to the jaw that sent him toppling to the floor. He was up quickly.

Blue's viperish jabs were beginning to take their toll on the professional. Raw, red gashes gaped above both his eyes, his lips were bleeding freely, and his mouth was puffed completely out of shape. Even to the most inexperienced onlooker, it was obvious that Skinner was a beaten man. The crowd had grown silent as Blue took charge of the fight.

Even now Skinner kept coming doggedly, but the force had gone out of his blows. He was floundering and groggy. Blue, ever cautious but confident, now took a hand at forcing the issue. He staggered Skinner with right-hand smashes over the heart and jabbed him incessantly, making the man's head bob back and forth as if it were on springs.

Worried and desperate, Skinner resorted to rough-house tactics. Blue continued to circle the weary fighter, and dance away from the harmless blows. He scored with a right hand to the mouth and followed with a vicious blow to the right side that sent Skinner panting into the ropes. The man pushed himself off the ropes and began to look around for his opponent. "Now!" Blue heard from ringside. He waded in, scoring with a left then a right to the head that sent Skinner to the floor. Though the game fighter was still trying to get to his feet, his second—realizing Skinner's helpless condition—threw in the towel. The fight was over.

Getty and Elam were in the ring immediately. Then a few quiet cheers turned into a thunderous ovation for the winner.

Elam was busy wiping the sweat from Blue's face with a towel. "I knew you could take him, Litt. He's gained a lot of weight, and that slowed him down."

Two saloon girls appeared in the ring with a pan of water and a dry towel, mopping, wiping and commenting about Litt's perfectly proportioned body. "Not an ounce of fat on him," one of them said, feeling the muscle of his arm.

Skinner was on his feet now. As he left the ring, he stopped and stared at Blue for a long time. Then his battered face broke into a smile. He nodded, gave Litt an understanding wink, and stepped through the ropes.

A young newspaper reporter stepped into the ring with pad and pencil in his hand. "You sure taught him a lesson, Mister Blue. Would you say a few words for the paper?"

"I guess I will," Blue said, reseating himself on the stool. "First of all, I didn't teach him a damn thing. He already knows everything I know, and then some. I don't know a single trick that he hasn't been using for years.

"He's reached what is considered an old age for a fighter, but he still hits hard and he's quick. He jarred me from my head to my toes several times with each hand. If he could call back ten years, I wouldn't stand a chance with him.

"Bob Skinner is one salty son of a bitch, and I don't want any more of him." Blue was on his feet now, buttoning his shirt. "The better fighter lost the fight, my friend." He stepped through the ropes and jumped to the floor.

An old man wearing overalls, slouch hat, and faded flannel shirt, tapped Litt on the shoulder. "That wuz some awful good scrappin', son," he drawled. "An' I heerd all them good thangs ya said about Skinner. That wuz white uv ya. Mighty white."

Blue stared at the old-timer for a moment, then nodded and left the building.

16

A week later, Two Papas sent the cook to the bunkhouse for Blue. The big man answered Litt's knock on the door, and pointed to a chair. Then he limped across the floor with his cane and dropped his bulk onto his own cushioned seat, wheezing loudly. After a few moments, he began to breathe quietly. "I want you to take Sally back to the Box M, Litt. Her nerves are getting worse by the day, and she'll never be able to adjust to this place."

When the big man paused, and raised his eyebrows, Blue nodded. "Yes, sir," he said.

"There are a lot of things we need to talk about, Litt, and I guess this is as good a time as any. I know you've been wondering why I had them put the Lazy Bee brand on all of the calves."

"Yes, sir."

"Well, the answer is not all that complicated. The shoot-out put a stigma on the Box M2 that'll last a hundred years. I'm sure you've already read about the so-called Box M2 Massacre."

"Yes, sir."

"I can't do anything about the stigma, but I can get rid of the Box M2. The railroad is laying track west every day. When they get to Kansas, there's gonna be a real strong market for Texas longhorns. When that happens, I'll send the cows we've got now north to the rails. The calves wearing your brand will be weaned by then.

"When Johnson gets here with the herd he's gathering, we'll put your brand on them. I intend to sell you this ranch at a price you can afford, then the Box M2 will no longer exist. Added to that section you've got already, you're gonna have a fine spread.

"Pay me half your profits each year. Not half the money you take in, now, half the profits. I won't write a mortgage, because I trust you fully. We'll change the name to the Lazy Bee and put it in your name right away. If I should die before you pay it off, it'll be yours free and clear."

Blue sat frozen, stunned at the things he was hearing. "Free and clear?" he managed to ask. "What about Mort?"

"Mort's financial future is secure, Litt. My own father saw to that."

Blue sat speechless for some time, then said the only thing he could think of. "When does Two Mamas want to leave?"

"Any day, now. Guess you should take another man with you."

"I'll take Pete Nedd; let him drive her wagon."

Two Papas heaved himself to his feet and followed Blue to the door. "By the way, Litt," he said. "I heard about you whipping that professional fighter's ass."

Blue ignored the remark, and stood on the porch just outside the doorway. "Why do you treat me so good, Two Papas? I mean, why are you making it so easy for me to buy the ranch?"

The big man leaned against the doorjamb. "Well, the truth is, I never intended to build a ranch house here. I bought this property for Ben. Weren't you and Ben big buddies? Didn't you fight a war together?"

"Yes, sir."

"Well, all right, then." Two Papas closed the door.

Blue headed for the bunkhouse with Lon Bills's words ringing in his ears once again: "You're the grandson now, Litt."

The trip to the Box M began two days later. Pete Nedd, who had never been farther than fifty miles from home, was willing and eager. The covered wagon was loaded much lighter than before, containing only a large trunk, dry wood, grain for the horses, a bed for Two Mamas, and the bedrolls of the men. Pete Nedd's saddle and enough food for several days lay under the seat.

Just after sunrise, Pete clucked to the team and the wagon began to roll east. All residents of the Box M2 stood in the yard waving as it disappeared over the rise, a saddle horse and a pack horse tethered to its tailgate. Two Papas watched the longest, then returned to his house without speaking.

Only Fat Frank went near the main house for the next several days, then only to carry food. Everybody sensed that Two Papas should be left alone with his feelings. For almost a month, the only times the big man was seen by the hands was when he walked to the cook shack for coffee.

Then Blue and Pete Nedd returned from the Box M, and, Two Papas, all smiles, was in the yard to greet them. "Did the trip go all right?" he asked.

"No problems at all," Blue answered. "Didn't even rain on us but once." He patted the neck of the big chestnut. "I guess we made close to fifty miles a day coming back." Blue followed Two Papas to the house, and remained there all day—and all night.

During the first week of July, Rope Johnson and young Billy Turner rode into the yard. Johnson announced that he had twenty-three men camped on the east bank of the Sabinal, guarding four thousand head of longhorns. "Not as easy as it was last time, Two Papas," he said. "The Big Thicket's full of cowboys, and the cattle are all spooked and going deeper. We got most of our herd out of the brakes along the Neches River."

Two Papas nodded. "That's to be expected. You did very good, Rope, and you'll be rewarded. Let's build a chute on the east side of the Sabinal and brand them before they cross the river. Put the Lazy Bee on all of them."

Johnson looked at the big man questioningly. "All of them?"

"All of them," Two Papas repeated. He shrugged his shoulders, then added, "We're changing the brand."

Cecil Hudson took charge of the branding operation. Next morning, Blue took Two Papas for a long buggy ride. The big man wanted to go first to Uvalde, then on to San Antonio. When they left Uvalde in the early afternoon, Littleton Blue was the sole owner of the former Box M2, now the Lazy Bee, and such had been entered into the county records.

An hour before sunset, Blue pulled off the San Antonio road into a cluster of cedars that hid the horse and buggy well. He watered the animal from a small spring, then fed it from a nosebag. There would be no grazing tonight. He built a small fire for coffee. Cooking was unnecessary, for Fat Frank had filled a large bag with palatable food, including dried apple pies.

Two Papas ate a large meal, then sat beside the gray coals drinking coffee. "You told me once that Ben was a good soldier," he said, after sitting quietly for a long time. "Did he take foolish chances?"

"No," Blue lied. "He stood his ground, though." Then Litt was on his feet. He took the bedrolls from the buggy and spread them side by side on the level ground. Both men called it a night without another word.

"I've got several things to do in San Antonio," Two Papas said, as soon as they were on the road next morning. "I want to find out how far west the rails are, and there's a small association of cattlemen that I want to meet with. I believe the time to start moving cattle north is right on us, Litt. Might already be some herds on the trail, for all I know.

"And then I want to go to the bank. I'd like to pay Johnson's riders off in cash. Nothing makes a cowboy feel as good as having gold coin in his pocket."

Blue tapped the horse's rump with the whip. "Then there's the matter of the doctor. I'm taking you to a doctor."

Two Papas sat quietly for a while, then chuckled. "Do you think it'll do any good?"

"Hell, yes, I think it'll do some good. Something's bothering you, Two Papas. I think we can at least find out what it is."

"Maybe so."

In San Antonio, Blue rented a room in a good hotel at the center of town, insisting on the ground floor of the three-story building. Walking tired Two Papas quickly these days, and climbing stairs was out of the question. With the big man ensconced comfortably in the hotel room, Blue went looking for information on a new group of men calling themselves the South Texas Cattle Marketing Association.

His search was a short one. At the Texas Bank, he learned that the banker himself was a member, and had provided the group with a meeting room in his own building. A few of the members would be meeting tonight, and Henry Miles and Littleton Blue were welcome to attend if they wished. Blue returned to the hotel to pass the information to Two Papas.

Only three members attended the meeting: Thomas Eden, the vice president; Haskin Rogers, the secretary; and Seth Calloway, who owned a small spread east of San Antonio. As Henry Miles introduced himself and Littleton Blue, it became obvious that the members had heard the names before. Each man had no doubt read or heard about the "Massacre." However, it was mentioned by no one.

"The Box M2 no longer exists," Two Papas informed the men. "I sold it to Mister Blue, here. His brand is the Lazy Bee." The members nodded.

The secretary took the floor. "The rails are moving west at a fast clip," he began, "and they'll reach Abilene, Kansas, before any of us can get a herd up there." Then he produced a printed circular and passed it around. "This was handed to me two days ago by a man named Whitley, who represents a cattle buyer in Abilene. As you can see, the poster says that a man named Joseph McCoy will buy every cow he can get, and pay top dollar."

Seth Calloway spoke. "I ain't got enough cows, Haskin. What do you think about a few of us pooling our cattle to make one big herd?"

"I'm sure some of that'll be done," Rogers said. Then, turning to face Two Papas, he said, "What do you think of that idea, Mister Miles?"

"It's an excellent idea, and it's bound to happen. It won't work in my case, though. I already have as many cows as my riders can handle."

When the meeting adjourned, Blue and Two Papas returned to the hotel. Litt had joined the association, coughing up twenty dollars for the initiation fee. As he handed Blue a receipt for the money, the secretary smiled. "I was in the warehouse the day you whipped Bob Skinner, Mister Blue. You did a masterful job." Litt said nothing, and pocketed the receipt.

Two Papas sat on his bed studying a map he had bought from the secretary for five dollars. "No way of knowing how accurate this thing is, but Whitley was down here from Abilene, so he's obviously traveled the trail himself. According to this, Abilene's almost on a straight line north from San Antonio, maybe just a little bit east. Even the rivers are named and clearly marked." He handed the map to Blue.

Litt counted the rivers between San Antonio and Abilene, then read them aloud. "The Colorado, Brazos, Trinity, Red, Washita, Canadian, North Canadian, Cimarron, Salt Fork, Arkansas, and the Little Arkansas. Eleven rivers, Two Papas, not counting the Sabinal."

"I know," the big man said, reaching for the map.

"But if it can be done, our men will do it." He thumped the map with a forefinger. "Just as soon as we can round them up, I intend to bet thirty-five hundred head of longhorns on Rope Johnson."

Blue nodded. "It sounds like the right time to me. If your drive goes well, I'll probably send the Lazy Bee cows up the same trail next year, after they wean their calves."

"I'll probably have to leave some of mine here because their calves are too young to make it on their own," Two Papas said, folding the map. "But every cow with a calf that can look after itself is on her way to Kansas."

After poking and thumping around on Two Papas next morning, the doctor decided that the big man was wheezing when he breathed. "Just a little weakening of the lungs," he said. "Goes along with getting older." Reaching into a cabinet, he produced a bottle of brown liquid. "Take a little sip of this every once in a while, it'll make you feel better."

Back in the buggy, Two Papas opened the bottle. "Smells like alcohol," he said. He took a small sip. "Tastes like it, too. Hell, I didn't need a doctor to tell me I could feel better by getting drunk." He pointed up the street. "Stop up there at Tom's Place and get me a case of whiskey."

At the bank, Two Papas withdrew enough money to pay off Johnson's riders, then fattened up Blue's Lazy Bee account. "Should be enough there to last till the ranch starts paying its own way, Litt. You can make withdrawals or write checks anytime you need money."

Shortly thereafter, they headed home. The buggy had traveled less than a mile, when Two Papas put the doctor's medicine under the seat and uncorked a bottle of whiskey. By the time they reached The Spring, both men were feeling better.

When the branding was done, and the cattle pushed onto Lazy Bee range, Two Papas paid off the riders, giving each man a bonus. Then he passed several bottle of whiskey among them. "Drink up and enjoy yourselves, men!" he shouted. "And there's plenty of food in the cook shack. Tomorrow, I'll have a brand-new proposition for you."

Rope Johnson, who was standing near the big man's elbow, spoke softly, "I've already talked to them about the drive north, Two Papas. They've all agreed to go."

"Oh. Well, all right, then. Do they know it's gonna be eight hundred miles?"

"They know."

The big man nodded, then disappeared inside the house.

The drive, consisting of three thousand, two hundred head, began during the first week of August. The remaining Box M2 cows were left to a life of luxury on Lazy Bee grass, because their calves were too young to fend for themselves. Prompted by shouting cowboys, the herd crossed the shallow Sabinal easily, then headed north. Their dust cloud could be seen for the next two days.

Johnson had decided that he needed only twenty-one men for the drive, and Blue hired the remaining two as regular ranch hands: thirty-five-year-old Grady Henry, and his sixteen-year-old son, Lanny. A man of medium height and weight, Henry had twice gone broke with outfits of his own, possibly one of the reasons for his prematurely gray hair. His first venture had been a small spread only a few miles north of the border, where Mexican cattle thieves quickly rustled him into bankruptcy. Then he tried a horse ranch in eastern Texas, only to learn that he could scarcely give the animals away. Broke and disgusted, both he and his teenaged son had eagerly signed on with Rope Johnson. Henry was a widower who had lost his wife to pneumonia more than ten years ago. And though he had had some formal schooling, young Lanny was less than literate. Seldom living in proximity to a schoolhouse, he had received a different type of education while sitting in the saddle, and, though only a boy, was an excellent cowhand.

"We appreciate the job, Mister Blue," the blond-haired youth had said this morning. "It's good to have someplace to be." Fidgeting, he stared toward the river for a moment, then added, "We're good at what we do, me and Pa both."

"I know, Lanny. And we're glad to have you at the Lazy Bee. But I won't be the man you have to answer to. Cecil Hudson's your foreman; he'll decide what needs doing. And by the way, I don't like that Mister Blue stuff. Just call me Litt."

"Thank you, sir." The youngster headed for the bunkhouse.

The Lazy Bee herd now numbered well over five thousand head, and would need additional grass. Several hundred head would be driven into Frio Canyon, while the others would be allowed to drift farther west. All of which dictated that Blue hire more riders. He was in no hurry to hire, however, for men would soon be riding about the area seeking work. Litt wanted to eventually have ten men on the payroll, for overgrazing must be prevented at all costs. He remembered a discussion he once had with an old man at a saloon in San Antonio.

"A damn cow ain't gonna overgraze nothin' if she's got some room ta move," the old-timer had said. "Room," he added emphatically, "that's the answer." He took a sip of his rotgut, then a suck on his cigarette. "Take yaself, for instance. If ya wuz eatin' a big bowl of soup that ya liked, would ya ruther eat it with a thimble, or a big spoon?" He took another drink, then answered his own question. "Ya'd take the spoon, 'cause ya'd want bigger bites. Well, it's the same thang with a cow. She ain't gonna stand in the same old place feelin' around for a few little sprigs of grass. Not when she knows she can walk a hundred yards and git a whole damn mouthful with one swipe. Give 'em room ta move; they won't overgraze. Overstockin' is what causes overgrazin'."

Though Litt had gotten a chuckle out of the simple comparison, he knew that the old-timer's words contained a lot of common sense. Tomorrow, they would begin to drive some of the older cows into Frio Canyon. Blue expected the bears to take a few head. But the cats, who loved to prey on calves, would quickly learn that their mamas and papas were not such easy pickings. Indeed, any cat that managed to bring down an angry, full-grown longhorn would definitely earn his meal. Litt would put his two teenaged cowboys in the cabin for a while, to keep an eye on things in the canyon.

After much prodding from Two Papas, Blue moved his things into the main house, taking a room across the hall from the big man's sleeping quarters. "A ranch owner does not sleep in the bunkhouse with the cowboys," Two Papas had said. "And the hands don't expect it. Truth is, they don't want the boss anywhere around after they get their day's work done.

"They feel comfortable enough sleeping next to

their foreman, because he's one of them. And they know he's not gonna come running to you if one of them calls you a no-good son of a bitch."

With no further argument, Blue built a rack on the wall for his guns, then settled into his new home. He would continue to eat his meals in the cook shack. There was no reason to cook in the main house these days; Fat Frank brought all of the big man's meals to him, along with a pot of hot coffee. "The hands all know that you and me eat the same food they do, Litt," Two Papas had said. "That don't hurt matters none."

An hour after dark, the big man broke out a jug of white wine and poured two glasses full. Sitting at the table sipping, Blue could see through the window that the lamp was still burning in the bunkhouse. He did not have to wonder what he was missing. Night after night the topic of conversation was the same: women. One man would talk about the dozens of beautiful women who had chased him all over Texas begging him to marry them. Another might boast of the time when a young woman in a whorehouse had been so pleased with his performance that she almost gave him his money back—almost.

He lay awake for a long time that first night. His bed was the best he had ever slept on: several inches longer than his tall frame, and the mattress was firm. Lying in the darkness, he began to think of the old farm back in South Carolina, and Uncle Charley. What a man. Even with his physical handicap he had managed to scratch a living for four people out of the infertile clay. And Aunt Effie. A woman who cursed with every breath, she was nevertheless a good-hearted soul and had even tried to give Litt the farm after the war.

And Uncle Caleb. Though of no blood relation, he

had always treated Litt like a son. The land he owned was superior to that owned by Uncle Charley both in quality and quantity, and Caleb had prospered over the years. And he had long been known to share with others. The man's generosity had been directly responsible for Litt's being in the right place at the right time. Tomorrow, he would post a letter to Uncle Caleb and Aunt Effie, telling them of his good fortune in acquiring a ranch of his own. When times were better, and he could see farther ahead, he would send money.

And Roberta. Litt wondered if he would ever see her again. When he saw her at the saloon in San Antonio, she was as beautiful as ever. She was also showing more of her body than he had seen since they were young children at the old swimming hole. That she was using the name Christy Martin in the saloons had come as no surprise to Litt, for she had had a fixation for the name since childhood. One of the two dolls that leaned against the pillows of her bed all day was named Christy Martin. Christy Martin and Julie Brown. In his mind Litt could still see the dolls with the big eyes and yellow hair, their name-tags hanging from their necks.

He closed his eyes and went to sleep.

17

The cattle had been in Frio Canyon for a month, when Blue decided to ride up and look them over for himself. He stopped at the cabin, had coffee with Pete Nedd and Lanny Henry, then continued to ride north. Even after three hours of looking, he had seen few cattle. Unlike the Lazy Bee range to the south, which was relatively flat and to a large degree, treeless, vegetation in the canyon was dense. The thick stands of cypress, cedar, bushes, and brush provided a thousand places for the animals to hide.

Shortly before noon, he dismounted and dropped the reins to the ground. He walked a few steps, then stood looking at the beautiful scenery the canyon offered. From this location, near the top of the mountain, the view was almost breathtaking, and he could see several bunches of cattle grazing below.

He was standing thinking about what a difficult job lay ahead at roundup time, when he heard something behind him. He whirled. Too late he saw the huge, brown-and-white-spotted bull come from behind a cedar, charging like a mad rhinoceros. Just before the point of contact Blue drew his Colt and put a bullet between the animal's eyes, but the charge continued. Litt's body was tossed about like a rag doll, finally coming to rest against a cypress log. Then the wild-eyed beast died in its tracks, no more than ten feet away.

Just before sunset, Pete Nedd and Lanny Henry were about to unsaddle their horses for the day, when Blue's chestnut walked into the yard, holding its head sideways to keep from stepping on the trailing reins.

"Hey!" Pete shouted, trotting to the animal and grabbing its bridle. "This is Litt's horse." Both men walked around the animal, looking for any sign of a struggle. "The reins ain't broke," Pete said, "so I guess he wasn't tied. Something's wrong, Lanny; maybe something bad. This horse is trained to stand when the reins are dropped to the ground."

They unsaddled the chestnut and turned it into the corral, then mounted and began to backtrack the animal, which was both difficult and time consuming. The horse had wandered about crazily as it meandered through the canyon, always seeking a bite of the best grass. The young men had made little headway when darkness closed in.

"Ride to the Lazy Bee and tell the men," Pete said to Lanny. "I'll get the lantern from the cabin and keep trying to track the horse."

The men in the bunkhouse had just blown out the

lamp and called it a night, when Lanny arrived. "All hands in the saddle!" Cecil Hudson ordered, when the youngster had told the story. "Take lanterns and move as quietly as you can. No use to wake Two Papas unless it becomes necessary."

The men saddled their horses and left the yard at a walk. As soon as they were out of earshot of the main house, they put the animals to a canter. At the cabin, they stopped for only a moment. "Pete said he was gonna keep looking," Lanny said. "The lantern's gone, so I guess we should just ride into the canyon and look for his light."

The riders headed north even as the youngster spoke. As the unruffled plain gradually gave way to dense vegetation and uneven terrain, they had to slow their horses to a walk. Sometime around midnight, Hudson spotted a flickering light to the northeast, near the top of the mountain. "Up on the mountain, there!" he shouted to his men. As they guided their horses in its direction, the light stopped its flickering and became a steady beacon.

"Hello the light!" Hudson shouted, as they came near enough to be heard. There was no response to his call. They sat their saddles quietly for a few moments, then each man drew his gun. In a loose formation, they eased their mounts forward. There, sitting on a rock and sobbing like a child, was young Pete Nedd. "Li . . . Litt's dead," he stammered. "Damn bull killed him."

Following the boy's point, the men walked into the darkness. Holding their lanterns high above their heads to light up a larger area, they came on the scene quickly: With the dead bull and Blue's Colt lying on the ground nearby, and Litt's face buried in the leaves beside the cypress log, the story could be read easily.

One of Blue's legs was draped across the log lifelessly, and his back was covered with dried blood.

"Looks like Litt got lead into the bull," Blackie Elam said, "but he was too late. Dammit all to hell."

The men stood around staring in disbelief for some time. They had all loved Blue like a brother, and nobody seemed eager to touch the body. "We can put the body on my horse," Joe Getty said. "I'll lead it as far as the cabin. We can pick up Litt's chestnut there."

Grady Henry was the first to walk forward. He moved Blue's leg off the log, then touched one of his arms. "Hey!" he shouted. "A dead man's supposed to be cold and stiff after a few hours. This man ain't stiff. He ain't even cold." He raised his eyes to meet those of Hudson, who had by now begun to walk forward. "This man ain't dead!"

"The hell you say!" someone shouted. All of the men had gathered around. Hudson turned Blue's body over and began to feel for a pulse, while Getty checked for signs of breathing. "I can't tell for sure, Cecil," Getty said, "but I believe I can feel air coming out of his nose. Feels mighty weak, but I believe it's there."

"Of course, it's there," Grady Henry said. "A man quits breathing, he dies. When he dies, he turns cold and white. This man ain't done none of that. This man's alive."

Blue was indeed alive—barely. The thousand-pound bull had hit him full force, and the fact that the animal was charging downhill added to its momentum. The shot between the eyes had probably disoriented the bull, and the tips of its horns passed on either side of Blue as first contact was made. Tossing Litt into the air, the animal had made a second attempt to gore him, but succeeded only in penetrating the flesh about an inch or so, just below the left shoulder blade. The wound that had done the bleeding was not the problem: Littleton Blue had a concussion.

Hudson ran his hand along Litt's cheek, and could feel the warmth of life. "We'll have to carry him off the mountain," he said. "We can't lay him across the back of a horse; no telling how bad he's hurt." Then he began to bark orders: "Pete, go back to your cabin and hitch up the wagon. Bring it as far up the canyon as you can." Then he turned to Getty. "Ride to Uvalde and get a doctor, Joe. Tell him to meet us at the Lazy Bee."

Litt was lying on his own bed before noon. His clothing was cut from his body with a scissors, and his pants taken outside for burning. When hit by the bull, Litt had defecated in them.

Pete Nedd washed Blue's body from head to toe, then sat beside the bed with his head in his hands, his eyes swollen from crying and lack of sleep. "Litt's gonna make it," he said, staring at the floor. "He's got to make it." Since being found on the mountainside, Blue had never fluttered an eyelid.

When Doctor Lipscomb arrived, his first act was to pick the small bits of cloth out of Litt's wound, then pour in some kind of healing powder. That done, he bandaged the wound, then ordered everybody else out of the room. After spending an hour alone with the patient, the doctor walked in the den, closing the bedroom door softly. "He's not going to make it," he announced, shaking his head. "I believe it's just a matter of time, now. Probably won't be long."

"Are you sure, Doctor?" Two Papas asked anxiously. "Are you sure there's nothing we can do?"

"His brain is already dead," the doctor answered. "The body usually follows soon after." Accepting his ten-dollar fee, the doctor bade them all farewell and walked through the door. In the yard, he untied his horse, climbed into his buggy, and headed for Uvalde.

For the next two days someone sat beside Litt's bed around the clock. Pete Nedd drew the watch most of the time, for there were enough normal ranch activities to keep the other men occupied. Midway through the second day, Pete burst into the den. "Litt's brain ain't dead, Two Papas!" he said loudly. "His brain ain't dead. He just peed all over the bed. Wet the whole thing."

The big man did not get out of his chair. "It's a natural bodily function, son. Don't reckon a man needs a brain to do it."

"Maybe not. But it looked to me like he was straining a little bit. That takes a brain, don't it?"

Two Papas raised his eyebrows. He heaved himself to his feet and followed Pete to the bedroom. He put his hand on Litt's face and began to call his name, first softly, then louder. He got no reaction. "We've got to get some water down him," the big man said. "A man can't last long without water."

Without a word, Pete walked to the kitchen and filled a tin cup with water. He soaked a clean cloth in the cup, then squeezed a few drops onto Litt's lips. The reaction was immediate. Without moving another muscle, Blue licked the water off his lips. Pete's face broke into a big smile. As he raised his eyes to meet those of Two Papas, a tear fell on the youngster's cheek. "He's gonna make it," he said.

"Part his lips and squeeze some on his tongue," the big man said. "See if he can swallow."

The boy complied, and Blue swallowed.

"Keep it up," Two Papas said. "Give him as much

as he'll take." The big man was out of the house quickly, headed for the cook shack. "Make some beef broth, Frank," he said to the cook. "Make it as strong as you can. Litt's started swallowing water, and he needs some nourishment."

Fat Frank nodded, and reached for a pot.

For the next week, Blue was given a cup of broth every two hours, day and night. Of late he had begun to swallow the broth easily, then seek out another spoonful with his tongue. But he had not moved his body, spoken, or opened his eyes. Indeed, all concerned had reconciled themselves to the idea that Blue might well be in a vegetative state for the remainder of his life. All except young Pete Nedd, who watched over him like a mother hen. He bathed Litt daily, and usually kept a damp cloth on his forehead. At first he heated the strained soup every two hours, but ceased after he discovered that the patient seemed to like the broth better at room temperature. And Pete shoveled it in, sometimes giving Litt two cupfuls at each feeding.

Unlike most people who recover from a concussion, Blue's brain did not begin to function gradually. It began all at once. Pete Nedd had gone to the cook shack for more broth. When the boy returned, pot in hand, Blue was sitting on the side of his bed, looking around for his clothing. Pete set the pot on the table, and screamed like a woman. He rushed to the bedside and threw his arms around Litt, sobbing like a child.

Blue finally pushed the youngster away. "Dreamed I was fighting a damn bull," he said, his deep voice as strong as ever.

Alerted by the kid's scream, Two Papas now stood in the doorway, beaming from ear to ear. "Did you hear that, Two Papas?" Pete asked loudly. "Litt said he dreamed he was fighting a bull." Laughing and crying at the same time, the kid ran from the building to spread the good news.

Two Papas continued to stand in the doorway smiling, trying to figure out how many of Blue's faculties had returned. "You gonna be all right?" he asked, stepping into the room.

Blue got to his feet unsteadily, then sat down again. "I'm looking for my clothes," he said.

"Get some out of your drawer, there," Two Papas said, pointing. "You ruined your clothing when the bull hit you."

Litt gave him a blank stare. "Bull hit me? I thought I dreamed that."

"He got to you, all right; got you up in Frio Canyon. Gored you right under your left shoulder blade. You've been unconscious since then."

Blue ran a hand along his shoulder, wincing as he touched the wound. "Unconscious?" he asked, reaching into the drawer for clothing. "How long?"

"Today is the fifteenth day. You shot the bull and killed him, but he got to you before he died."

"Fifteen days?" Blue sat on his bed, holding his pants across his lap. He began to shake his head. "And I didn't even get a chance to eat the son of a bitch that gored me," he said with a sigh.

Two Papas smiled, then laughed aloud. Littleton Blue had returned. He was going to be all right. The big man wiped Litt's hair out of his eyes, then hugged him as a father hugs a son. "We all thought we were gonna lose you, Litt. The bull hit you mighty hard. Guess you can thank Pete Nedd for nursing you back to health. He's been right by your bed for two weeks, shoveling beef broth down your throat."

Blue pulled on his jeans and got to his feet weakly, then nodded. "I'll do that," he said. He struggled into his boots, then walked outside without a shirt. He moved back and forth across the yard for a while, lifting his legs as high as he could and stomping his feet against the ground. Then he leaned against the hitching rail. "My legs don't seem to want to work," he said to Two Papas, who had followed him into the yard. "They're as heavy as lead."

"They'll feel that way for a while. You need to do a lot of walking; get 'em used to carrying your weight around again."

Blue walked in circles for a while, then opened the door at the cook shack. "You got anything for a hungry man, Frank?"

Fat Frank stood at the stove stirring the contents of an iron pot. The cook had long had a standing rule: No man who was not wearing a shirt could enter the cook shack. This time he made an exception. "Have a seat," he said, beaming broadly. "I don't know that I've ever been quite as happy to feed a man." He reached for a large bowl, adding, "This stuff is already done, guess I was just stirring it out of force of habit." He placed the food and a hot cup of coffee on the table, then pointed to the bowl. "I don't rightly know what to call it. I just put some of everything we've got into the pot and added salt and water."

"Smells good, Frank. Thank you."

Two Papas took a seat and accepted the cup of coffee he was offered. He sat watching, almost counting the bites, as Blue devoured the food. The big man felt good. It was almost like he was watching his own grandson come back to life.

Blue handed his bowl to the cook for a refill. "Whatever that is, don't forget how to make it, Frank."

When Blue finished his meal, he walked down to the Frio. Still shirtless and hatless, he walked north along the river's east bank slowly, forcing one foot in front of the other. His legs were nervous and shaky, but he continued to push on. An hour later, he took a seat on a fallen cypress. He had never felt so weak and helpless in his life, but he knew that Two Papas was right: He must force his body to move until it regained its strength.

He sat on the log thinking for a long time. Two weeks! He had been lying on that damn bed for two weeks, growing weaker by the day. The upper portion of his body felt strong enough, but his legs simply did not want to carry him. Even now he could feel them tightening up and getting sore. He knew there was but one remedy: He must walk until the legs gave out, then walk some more. He figured that by the time he got back home this afternoon he would have covered at least four miles. Tomorrow he would walk twice as far.

He sat on the log trying to recall events leading up to his blackout. He could remember the bull. In his mind he could plainly see the red-eyed critter darting from behind the cedar, both nostrils flared for war. And Blue remembered drawing his Colt and firing the shot that Two Papas had called a literal "bull's-eye." He did not remember the bull hitting him.

Nor did Litt blame the bull. The animal had done no worse than its natural instincts dictated. The poor bastard had been hog-tied and dragged out of his home in the Big Thicket and left without grass or water for several days to weaken his resistance. He had been whipped and herded across four hundred miles of strange country, chased into rivers where he had to swim for his very life, then had his hide cooked with a hot branding iron. Small wonder that the big beast had regarded all humans as enemies. Sitting on the thick log, Blue thought about the incident for so long that he began to feel sorry for the bull.

Knowing how close he had come to death, Litt resolved to be more careful in the future. Never again would he dismount in cattle country unless he could see for a considerable distance in every direction. He would stay in the saddle in brushy terrain, for although an old, angry bull might sometimes charge a rider's mount, a well-trained cutting horse was much quicker, and could easily outdistance any longhorn.

Blue stood beside the log, moving his legs up and down as fast as he could for several minutes. There was no pain, just a weak, nervous feeling. Nor did his shoulder hurt. The only time he noticed the wound was when he touched it with his hand.

He walked much faster going home, and it seemed that his strength was returning with each step, though the nervous feeling was still with him. Two Papas was sitting in the back yard with his chair facing north. He had been concerned, and was awaiting Blue's return anxiously.

"Feeling better?" the big man asked, as Blue walked up the hill at a fast clip.

"I think so. Seems like the faster I walk, the better I feel."

"You're gonna be all right," Two Papas said, getting to his feet. "The Almighty smiled on all of us today. The Lord didn't want to take you, He just wanted to teach you a lesson that might very well save your life one of these days." The two walked to the porch, where they parted.

"I'm gonna raid Fat Frank's pot again." Blue said. "Whatever that damn stuff is, it's good."

"Eat all you can as often as you can," Two Papas said. "Your body needs the nourishment."

18

In late August, Blue, Joe Getty, and Pete Nedd were in Uvalde. They sat at a table in a new saloon called the County Seat, where a guitar player named Dean Dykes entertained the drinkers nightly. Dykes, a sandy-haired native Texan with a constant smile, played his instrument expertly, and could sing most any song a man could name. On slow nights Dykes sat on a stool in the center of the room to entertain. When the saloon was crowded, and his voice could not be heard above the din, he strolled from one table to another singing whatever song was requested. Tonight, he stood at Blue's table, yodeling.

"I like that, Dean," Litt said when the song was over. "And you're very good at it." He dropped a coin into the singer's vest pocket. "Can you sit down and have a drink?"

Dykes handed his guitar to the bartender, then returned. "I have been known to take a sip now and then," he said, toeing a chair around to face the table. "Don't know that it's all that good for my health, but these nights can get to be mighty long, sometimes."

Litt stepped to the bar for another glass, then poured it full. "Do you travel around much, Dean?"

"I used to," the singer said, taking a sip of whiskey. "I've been in Uvalde ever since this place opened. Traveling around gets to be expensive. When I stay in one place for a while I seem to get ahead a little."

Blue poured another round of drinks, then spoke what was on his mind: "Dean, do you happen to know a woman named Christy Martin?"

Dykes nodded. "Beautiful lady and a good singer. Good dancer, too."

"Do you know where she is nowadays?"

"Not at the moment. I played guitar for her last spring at a place called Smokey's, in Fort Worth."

Smokey's. Blue repeated the name to himself. Roberta had gone to Fort Worth after leaving San Antonio.

"It's like I said," Dykes continued, "Christy is a good singer. The only hard part of the job was that she'd rehearse you to death. Every little thing had to be just right."

"That's her, all right," Blue said.

Dykes took another drink, then began to shake his head. "I don't think it's her so much as it is that fellow that controls her. I mean, he watches every move she makes, and orders her around like a slave. She might be a slave for all I know. She told me herself that he beats the hell out of her, and takes every dollar she makes."

Blue sat in his chair seething. That Roberta had become a whore of her own free will was one thing. The thought that some son of a bitch might have forced her into it was quite another.

"What's the man's name?"

"I don't know. Nobody knows. If anybody asked, he'd tell them it was none of their business. He always hung around backstage, and very few of the customers ever saw him. He ordered the musicians around just like he did her, and we all stayed away from him as much as possible."

"What does this fellow look like?" Blue lifted the bottle to pour the singer another drink.

Dykes placed his hand over the top of his glass to signal that he wanted no more. "About like any other bully, except that he's good-looking. Big, black-haired fellow with blue eyes. Guess he's about the same size as you. Talks with a Yankee accent." He pushed his chair away from the table. "Got to get back to work now. Thank you for the drinks." Pretty soon, he could be heard singing at another table.

Pete Nedd was pouring himself another drink. "That man's a good singer," he said, slurring his words. He upended his glass. "This Christy Martin, Litt. Is she one of your old girlfriends?"

"Nah," Blue said. "Just somebody I once knew."

They stayed in the saloon for two more hours. Litt wanted to talk with Dykes again, but there had been no chance. The singer was a busy man. When Dykes finally put his guitar away again, Litt approached him at the bar. "I've got a special reason for wanting to find Christy Martin, Dean. Do you know where I might start looking?"

The singer took a sip of beer, then wiped the foam from his lips. "She might be back at Smokey's by now.

She's not always Christy Martin. Sometimes she works under the name of Julie Brown."

Blue nodded. He had expected as much. "Does she have any particular place that she calls home?"

"I don't know, but I do know that she travels around a lot. She's got her own buggy and a Mexican driver, but that big fellow is always mighty close by. I believe he follows her on horseback."

Blue motioned for the bartender to refill Dykes's mug. "Is there anybody around Smokey's who might know more?"

"You can check with a man named Dixie Hall. He books all of the entertainment. Makes sense that he'd know how to get in touch with her. Get in touch with the big fellow, I should have said, 'cause Christy don't make any of her own decisions. You won't get to talk to her, either. Not unless you go through him."

"Thank you, Dean," Blue said, dropping a second coin in the man's pocket. "The big fellow's the one I want to talk to, anyway."

The three had one more drink, then called it a night. As Pete Nedd got to his feet, he had to hang on to the table to keep from falling. "I'll be all right," he said sheepishly. "My foot just went to sleep." He took a few steps, then bounced off the bar and slid to the floor on his backside. Both Blue and Getty were there quickly. With each man taking an arm around his shoulder, they hauled Pete from the saloon. The outside air seemed to revive the youngster somewhat, and he needed only a little assistance getting into his saddle.

"That foot woke up yet?" Blue asked, laughing.

He received no answer.

They rode toward the Lazy Bee in silence. Litt's

mind was occupied with the things he had learned during his conversation with Dykes. Blue believed every word the singer had said, for the man would have no reason to lie. Litt would definitely go looking for his sister. When, he had not yet decided. Maybe after winter arrived, when there was little else to do.

"You feeling better, Pete?" he asked, after they had ridden a few miles.

"Some."

"Well, I've got a job for you and Lanny tomorrow. Hard work's the best thing I know to get a drunk feeling good again." Blue chuckled, and Pete said nothing.

The job consisted of hauling the dirt back up the hill from the river and filling in the trenches that surrounded the buildings. Each of the ditches now held standing water, and had become a hatchery for mosquitoes. Blue had left the trenches open these many months because he thought they might be needed again. But the fight was now history, and it was time to replace the dirt and pretty up the yard.

Sunrise found both of the teenagers down by the river loading a wagon. When they brought the first load up the hill, Litt doffed his shirt and began to help shovel the red earth into the ditch behind the bunkhouse. Blue was in excellent condition these days, both mentally and physically, and the incident with the bull had been all but forgotten. Pete Nedd stood by watching the muscles ripple across Litt's broad back, as Blue threw heavy loads of dirt into the trench with his oversized shovel. "Must be nice to have a body like yours," the youngster said, shaking his head.

Blue continued to shovel, and said nothing.

As the boys turned the team downhill for another load, Two Papas walked around the corner of the bunkhouse. "I've been wondering when you were gonna do this," he said.

"I don't suppose we'll need 'em again," Blue said, patting the dirt into a mound with the shovel. "They certainly served their purpose, though."

"Yes, they did," Two Papas agreed. "Don't guess anybody but a military man would have thought of it." The big man stood quietly for a while, leaning heavily on his cane. "I was thinking you might want to join me for some coffee," he said finally. "Or maybe you'd rather have a glass of wine."

Blue shook his head. "I'll drink the coffee while you have the wine, Two Papas. I had enough to drink in Uvalde last night to last me for a while."

Blue propped his shovel against the building and followed the big man to the house. A pot of hot coffee was already on the back of the stove, and Blue filled his cup. Two Papas poured himself a glass of wine, then both men sat down at the table.

Two Papas did not drink right away. He sat staring at the window for a long time, then wet his lips with the wine. "Lord, I miss Sally," he said, as if talking to the window.

When nothing else was said for a full minute, Blue said, "You want me to take you to see her?"

"No, no, not yet. Got to give her time to get her garden plowed." He tipped his glass and emptied it in large gulps, then continued. "You see, Litt, Sally takes other men when she can find one who's willing. I'm surprised that she didn't try you when you were bringing her from the Box M."

Not knowing whether Two Papas was fishing for

information or simply unburdening himself, Blue said nothing.

The big man refilled his glass, then continued. "I knew about her lovers before we married, and I've known about a lot of 'em since. Don't know whether she knows that or not.

"I'm not blaming her, Litt. It must be frustrating being married to somebody like me. You see, I never could please a woman; never could last long enough. I mean, when I satisfy myself, I'm done; don't even want to see a woman for a day or two.

"I could always tell when Sally'd found herself a willing ranch hand by the way she acted. Quick as I could figure who the hand was, I'd make it easier for 'em: I'd assign him some kind of duty around the house or the barn, then take myself to the back country. Then she'd be happy for a while. At least till the new wore off."

Two Papas was obviously on his way to getting drunk. He refilled his glass and took a large gulp. "Yep," he said, "I'm surprised that she didn't take after you. As many nights as you two had on the road together, I'd have thought she'd be trying to crawl into your bedroll. Told me herself that you were the best-looking man she'd ever seen."

Blue sat staring into his cup. He now believed that the big man knew. Maybe Two Mamas had even confessed her actions under the wagon. "Nothing happened between Two Mamas and me, sir. Nothing has ever happened."

Two Papas took another drink, then looked Blue straight in the eye. "She didn't try to crawl into your bedroll?"

Litt was trapped. He now knew that he was being

tested. "Yes, she did, Two Papas. But like I said, nothing happened."

The big man nodded. "I knew you would tell me the truth if I asked you straight out. It's just like Sally said: You're a man with principle." He tamped the cork back into the neck of his wine bottle, and, with the help of his cane, got to his feet. "Guess I'll take a little nap; didn't sleep very well last night." With slow, deliberate movements, he walked down the hall toward his bedroom.

Blue added two sticks of wood to the stove's firebox; the coffee would be hot when he came back to check on Two Papas after a while.

Litt sat on the porch for a while, watching the boys fill in the trenches. But his mind was on his recent conversation with Two Papas, and wishing it had never happened. He wondered if Two Mamas had confessed her actions hoping to make the big man try harder. Had she told him about Lon Bills? Did Two Papas know about the nights "that Bills fellow" had spent in her wagon? Maybe. And maybe Two Mamas was losing her mind. Maybe she did not fully realize how much hurt such knowledge could bring to her husband of more than forty years. Maybe the lady had been going downhill mentally for a long time. Hadn't Two Papas himself said that she was a nervous wreck? That she had not been herself during the past year?

Blue sat on the top step nodding at his thoughts. Two Papas had put him on the spot, all right. The big man had shrewdly maneuvered the conversation around, then asked a point-blank question that required a direct answer. Hoping that Two Papas already knew the answer, Litt had spoken truthfully.

His concentration was broken by the sound of a single gunshot across the river, maybe a mile away. A few minutes later, Joe Getty splashed across the Frio and began to unsaddle his mount at the corral. "Came in to get a team and wagon," Getty said, as Blue approached. "Had to shoot a young steer with a broke leg. He's prime beef for the cook shack." He threw an ax into the bed of the wagon. "I'll have to hurry, though; the coyotes and buzzards'll find the carcass mighty quick."

Blue helped Getty harness and hitch the team, then climbed into the wagon. "I'll give you a hand," he said.

They skinned and beheaded the animal on the spot, and Getty quartered the carcass with the ax. "Don't guess Fat Frank'll have much choice but to serve some good steaks for the next day or two," Getty said, as he threw the last hind quarter in the wagon. "I'm not complaining, but sometimes I think I've had enough beans to last me a lifetime."

A lifetime? Blue sat on the wagon seat thinking about Getty's words. It was very true that the man was not a complainer. "How often does Fat Frank serve beans, Joe?"

"Most of the time," Getty answered, whipping the team to a trot. "Sometimes the only things on the table at suppertime will be red beans and cornbread. Maybe an onion apiece."

Blue sat quietly for a while, thinking. He knew of no men who worked harder than the Lazy Bee crew, and none had to be reminded that an honest day's work was expected. To a man, the crew knew their jobs; even Cecil Hudson had said that they needed little supervision.

Blue had not eaten supper in cook shack for quite

some time. His food, along with that eaten by Two Papas, was brought to the main house on large trays. Never once had the cook brought a tray that contained only beans and cornbread. "I'll look into the food situation, Joe," Litt said.

They hung the butchered carcass in the smokehouse. Then, taking a pail and a broom, Getty drove the team back down to the river to wash out the wagon. Blue headed for the cook shack. He helped himself to a cup of coffee, then got right to the point: "Do you feed the hands the same thing you feed Two Papas and me, Frank?"

The cook had been reading a magazine. He laid it aside. "Well, some of the time. I—"

"I want it to be all of the time, Frank," Blue interrupted. "Every breakfast and every supper. And I want them to leave here every morning with a decent lunch in their saddlebags."

The cook's round face took on the expression of a scolded child, but he looked Blue straight in the eye. "I don't always have enough of everything to go around, Litt. It's been that way every place I've ever worked."

Blue nodded. "Well, it's not gonna be that way from now on. Make a list of everything you need. I'll see that it's delivered. I want our crew to the be the best-fed bunch around." He dropped his empty cup in the dishpan, then headed for the door. "We just hung a beef in the smokehouse," he said over his shoulder. "When it's gone, we'll butcher another one."

Blue joined the hands in the cook shack for supper, and the food was excellent. The cook served hot biscuits, gravy, and mashed potatoes along with the tender beefsteak. When they had eaten, each man complimented Fat Frank before heading for the bunkhouse.

"Can you spare Grady Henry and his son for a few days, Cecil?" Blue asked, as Hudson rose from the table.

"Guess so," Hudson said. "Nothing pressing."

Blue followed Henry to the bunkhouse, where the man was already undressing for bed. "Do you know how to smoke meat, Grady?"

Henry sat down on his bunk, removed his socks, and nodded. "Guess you could say that I'm pretty good at it. Tried to turn it into a business once, but I never could sell enough to make a go of it."

Blue pulled up a chair. "I want to fill that smokehouse with meat, Grady. I'm turning that chore over to you and your son."

"You want beef, or pork?"

"Both. You can buy live hogs in Uvalde."

Henry fluffed up his pillow and slid under the covers. "I'll have to build a crate to haul the hogs in, then rig up a brine barrel. Lanny can haul in the wood while I'm doing that."

"What kind of wood do you need?"

"Green mesquite's the best. Makes more smoke, and adds a flavor all its own."

Blue got to his feet and returned the chair to the card table. "You can get started in the morning, Grady. Fat Frank's gonna have a list of the things he needs. If eggs, butter, and jelly are not on the list, get 'em anyway. You can come by the house for some money when you get ready to go to town."

Propped up on his elbows, Henry lay on his bunk, nodding. "I'll take care if it, Litt. Smoking meat is something I like to do, anyhow."

Blue joined Two Papas for his nightly glass of wine and some light conversation, then called it a night. He lay on his bed for a while thinking about the next few days' activities. He would not crowd Grady Henry, or give the impression that he was looking over the man's shoulder, but he would watch close enough to learn something about smoking meat.

19

I n the middle of October, Blue decided to take up the hunt for his sister. Since talking with Dykes, in Uvalde, Litt had thought on the matter daily, and now believed that Roberta was not in her line of work by choice; that she was the victim of an overbearing flesh-peddler of whom she was deathly afraid. That would account for her sudden departure from San Antonio in the middle of the night. Maybe she had seen Litt at the same time he saw her, and had been afraid for both herself and her brother. Hadn't Dykes said that the big man beat her up often and took every dollar she earned? He was obviously good at battering women. Litt intended to find out how the handler would stack up against a man.

He saddled the horse named Sox at sunrise, then

rode by the cook shack to pick up a four-day supply of food. He had fed his horse a double portion of oats at daybreak, for he would pass few livery stables on his northeastward journey. Most of the time the animal would have to make do with whatever graze was available.

He carried two blankets and a change of clothing wrapped in his slicker, and his trust Henry rifle rested in the saddle scabbard. An hour after saying good-bye to Fat Frank and Two Papas, he crossed the Sabinal. Skirting Frio Canyon, he pointed his animal north by northeast, knowing that he might not come in contact with another human for a hundred miles.

He camped on Pipe Creek the first night. He picketed the chestnut on good greass, then spread his blankets under the canopy of a cottonwood. He would build no fire tonight, for he had brought no coffeepot. A campfire attracted attention, and he wanted none. Just before sundown, he found a straight stick and laid it beside his saddle, pointing in his desired direction of travel. If it was cloudy tomorrow, and there was no sun by which to get his bearing, the stick would clearly point the way.

Late afternoon of the second day found him at the Pedernales River, which he forded easily. A family of campers had a fire going beside a covered wagon nearby, and Litt waved to them. His greeting was returned. Two white mules were hobbled north of the wagon, and Blue picketed the chestnut in the same area. The mules were in poor condition, suggesting that they had pulled the wagon a long way. The job would certainly not get any easier for them, for wagon travel in the Hill Country was difficult at best.

Blue had just made himself a bed of leaves and spread his blankets, when a youngster of about ten years approached. "Pa says ta tell ya that we got plenty o' stew 'n coffee, if ya want some."

Blue eyed the boy for a moment, then nodded. "Sounds good. I'll be over there shortly."

The youngster stood his ground. "Pa says ta come now."

Nodding again and chuckling to himself, Blue got to his feet. "Lead the way," he said.

The man introduced himself as Zack Perkins, and his wife as Belle. He did not introduce his two young sons. Blue was soon sitting beside the fire enjoying a large bowl of tasty stew, along with cold biscuits and hot coffee. "This is very good," he said, speaking to the lady. "First hot food I've had since breakfast yesterday morning."

The lady opened her mouth, but before she could speak, her husband was talking. "Belle can make sump'm good out'n a little o' nothin'," he said. "I shot th' rabbits this mornin', an' we had ta cook 'em right on th' spot. Meat won't keep ver' long atter th' sun comes out, ya know."

Blue nodded. "I know."

Perkins said that he and his family had come from the Arkansas Delta, and had been traveling for six weeks. They were headed to the town of Fredericksburg, where they had kin.

"Well, your journey's about over," Blue said. "A man on horseback could make Fredericksburg in less than a day, but it'll take you longer with the wagon."

"Shore, it will. But if'n th' mules hold out an' th' wagon don't break down, we'll be a-pullin' in there 'fore long."

"Yes, sir," Blue said, getting to his feet. "You're just about home. Thank you again for the food, and good night to you all." He walked back toward his bedroll.

"Good night yaself," Perkins called after him.

Litt lay on his bed thinking of the folks who had just shared their food with him. He had meant it when he told the people they were almost home, for they were they type who would stay. Perkins and his boys, with their worn-out overalls and brogans, and the wife, with her plain, cotton dress, probably owned little more than the clothing they wore. But they would make it. It was people like them, Southerners for the most part, who would populate this part of the country and make it great. Perkins appeared to be no older than thirty-five, and seemed to be in good health. He had many good years left, and when he found his place he would become a producer. His sons would soon grow into strong, young men with their own ambitions. Litt smiled at the thought. He promised himself that he would look the family up in a few years.

The ride to Fort Worth took seven days. He rode into town a little past noon, and headed straight for the livery stable. He unsaddled the chestnut, then handed the animal's reins to the hostler. "Treat him good, now," he said. "He's had a hard week."

The man nodded. "He'll be good as new when you want him."

With his change of clothing tucked under one arm, Blue unsheathed his rifle and laid it across his shoulder. It was unlikely that he would need the long gun here in town, but weapons left in livery stables sometimes had a way of sprouting wings. Especially a Henry in good condition.

Less than a block from the stable, he entered a barber shop, where he bought a haircut, shave, and a hot bath. When he left the establishment an hour later, he looked and felt like a new man. He had soaked the trail dust and tiredness from his body and donned clean jeans and his favorite blue shirt. The week-old, itchy stubble was missing from his face, and the barber had even volunteered to brush his hat.

He rented a hotel room across the street and left his belongings inside, then walked to the nearest restaurant. The noontime rush hour was over, but the waiter was still serving dinner. Blue ordered roast pork and sweet potatoes, and his meal was there quickly. The food was very good, and he ate leisurely.

Even after the waiter had taken his empty plate, Litt sat at the table for half an hour, drinking several cups of strong coffee. He was thinking about his conversation with the barber. The man had given him directions to Smokey's, only two blocks away, and said that the establishment did not open until four o'clock in the afternoon. The girls began doing their shows several hours later, he said.

When Blue left the restaurant, he headed straight for Smokey's. Walking back and forth in front of the huge, oblong building, he was more than a little impressed with its size. Standing on the corner, its depth reached halfway to the next street. Litt walked down the side of the saloon to have a look at its rear. Across the alley there were three small, neat cabins, behind which was a huge parking lot containing at least a dozen hitching rails. The saloon itself had two rear doors with well-worn paths leading to each of the cabins. Supposing that his sister's tiny feet had tread those paths many times, Blue kicked an empty can, then headed for his hotel room. Once there, he slept the afternoon away.

"Don't have no girls this week," the bartender said, when Blue visited Smokey's at sundown. "Julie Brown'll be startin' ag'in next Monday night."

Monday! Blue repeated to himself. Today was only Thursday. "Know where I can find Dixie Hall?" he asked.

"Shore do," the pudgy, gray-haired man said. "You're lookin' at 'im. Sump'm I c'n do fer ya?"

Litt had been expecting a man of a different type. He sipped at his beer slowly. "Well, I don't guess I had any special business with you," he said. "Mostly, I just wanted to talk with you about this Julie Brown. A guitar player named Dean Dykes told me to look you up; said you'd know when she was coming back to town. Dykes says she's the prettiest woman in Texas."

"I remember Dykes," Hall said, pouring himself a drink of whiskey. "He a fine musician, and there damn shore ain't nothin' wrong with his eyes. Julie Brown's got 'em all beat."

Blue laid money on the bar to pay for Hall's drink, then sighed. "Don't guess there's any chance of an ordinary fellow like me ever getting to know her," he said. "Spending a little time with her, I mean."

Hall rolled his eyes toward the ceiling. "Ya'd hafta take that up with Horse," he said, finishing off his drink.

"Horse?"

"Horse Hathaway. His name's Clyde, but ever'body calls 'im Horse. 'Count o' his size, I guess."

Blue pushed his mug forward for a refill. "What does this Hathaway do, Dixie? I mean, what kind of business is he in?"

Hall chuckled. "Why, he's in th' Julie Brown business," he said, placing the full mug in front of Litt and wiping at the bar. "Some folks say he wuz a Union officer durin' th' war, but I shore ain't never heerd nobody ask 'im about it." Hall chuckled again.

"Is Hathaway easy to talk to?" Blue asked.

"If ya got money in ya han' he is. If ya ain't, he ain't." Hall pointed to the far side of the bar. "Ever' time she goes on th' stage, he'll come an' set right by that post there. All ya gotta do is walk right up an' make a deal with 'im."

Blue finished his beer and got to his feet. "Maybe I'll try that sometime, Dixie. Nice meeting you, and I guess we'll see each other again."

"Good ta meet you too, big feller. Julie'll be startin' Monday night about ten."

Next morning, Blue took a room at a run-down boarding house on the edge of town, well off the beaten path. There he would remain until Monday night, taking no chances that he might be seen by his sister. Litt did not believe that Roberta's handler would know him from Adam. In fact, the success of Blue's plan depended entirely on his not being recognized by Horse Hathaway.

Litt left the boarding house at eight o'clock Monday night. He walked first to the livery stable, where he could see his chestnut standing idly in the corral. A big roan was also there, and a black buggy with red wheels was parked out front. Probably his sister's transportation, Blue thought.

Keeping to the shadows, he walked at a fast clip to the hotel, where he rented a first-floor room with two beds. A glance at his watch told him that the time was a few minutes past nine. He sat down on the bed to wait. He would not leave the room till after ten.

It was ten minutes past the hour, when he walked through the front door of the saloon, on the heels of a man almost as tall as himself. Stooped at the shoulders, with the brim of his hat pulled low, he made a quick left turn to the far side of the bar, where he could not be seen from the stage. Two bartenders were on duty, and neither of them was Dixie Hall. Blue leaned against the bar and ordered a beer, which was served immediately.

Litt could easily recognize his sister's voice above the pounding of the piano, as she belted out a song the two had sung together as kids. And there, down at the dark end of the bar, beside the post, sat a man who had to be Horse Hathaway. He was a big man, probably as tall as Blue himself, and twenty pounds heavier. With dark, curly hair that was neatly trimmed, he was good-looking and clean shaven, and the holstered Colt tied to his right leg was in plain view.

Leaving his beer on the bar untouched, Litt walked past several stools and took up a position on Hathaway's left, where the lighting was even dimmer. "I've been wanting to talk to Miss Brown," he said softly. "Been told that you're the man to see."

Hathaway turned his head to look at Blue, who was leaning over the next stool. After barely a glance, his eyes returned to his drink. "Costs money," he said.

"I'll pay."

"Twenty dollars," Hathaway said, finishing off his drink. "Twenty dollars for twenty minutes."

Blue thought on the proposition for only a moment. "I'm a slow talker," he said. "I believe I'd need more than twenty minutes."

"Fifty dollars for an hour," Hathaway said quickly.

"I believe an hour is just about how much time I'll be needing," Blue said. "Who do I pay?"

"You pay me," Hathaway said, holding out his hand. "In advance."

Blue fished two double eagles and a single from his pocket and handed over the money.

Hathaway dropped the coins into his vest pocket quickly. "Go out the front door and walk along the side of the saloon," he said softly, with no trace of a Northern accent. "Across the alley, you'll see three cabins. Go in the first one and wait. The lamp's already burning, and the door's unlocked. Miss Brown'll be with you as soon as she's finished here. Your time starts when she leaves the building."

Blue saw no one as he walked toward the alley. All of the men in the immediate vicinity were probably in the saloon watching the show. He stood for a moment watching the cabin, then after one last look around the surrounding area, crossed the alley. The tiny building had a flimsy curtain covering its only window, and a solid wooden door. After a twist of the knob and a gentle shove, Litt was inside.

The cabin contained only the bed, two small tables, and one chair. One table held the lamp, the other a pan of water, a sponge, and a towel. Blue dragged the chair to the window, where he sat peeking around the edge of the curtain. He could see both rear doors of the saloon plainly, for the light shining through the cracks outlined them perfectly.

He sat for what seemed like a long time, though a glance at his watch told him that only twenty minutes had passed. At last one of the doors opened partially, and Litt could see his sister slip through. She stopped in her tracks momentarily, as the door swung wider to reveal Hathaway standing in the doorway talking. Giving Julie Brown her instructions, Blue supposed.

When the door closed, she began to walk toward the cabin. Litt made his move. He stepped from the cabin quickly and closed the door, then met her halfway across the alley. At his approach, she made an attempt to reverse her direction, but he grabbed her hand firmly. "It's Litt, Roberta," he said softly. "Keep quiet and follow me."

He led off down the alley at a fast walk, his sister having to trot to keep up. More than once she made an effort to dig her heels in, but he yanked her on. "We can't do this, Litt," she said finally. "He'll kill you. He's done it before." He continued to drag her down the alley. "He . . . he'll beat me to death," she said. "He—"

Litt put his hand over her mouth, hugging her to him as he had in the old days. Holding her head against his chest, he kissed her forehead. "Hathaway's not gonna kill anybody, Roberta. He'll never lay a hand on you again. Now, come on, and be quiet." She began to trot by his side obediently, and did not make another sound.

The desk clerk was away from his post when they entered the hotel, for which Litt was thankful. He walked down the hall and unlocked his door, gently pushing his sister inside the room. He looked at his watch and saw that he had fifty minutes left. Plenty of time. He leaned against the door. "I want to hear one thing from you, little sister. I want you to tell me that this is the kind of life you want to lead."

She was crying now. She put her arms around his waist and hung on. "No, no, Litt. I wanted to be an actress, but never . . . this." She sobbed against his chest for a few moments, then continued. "You can't imagine how bad it's been, Litt. He's lied to me so much and beaten me so often that I don't even have a mind of my own anymore. Broke my arm once, and put me in the hospital another time. Said he was gonna make enough money off of me to retire in five years."

Litt held her tightly for a long time, all the while thinking of Horse Hathaway. The son of a bitch was going to retire all right, but in considerably less time than five years.

Litt looked at his watch again, then led Roberta to a chair, informing her that he wanted to hear the whole story. She stopped crying and wiped her eyes with the backs of her hands, then began to talk.

Her departure from the farm had not been anything like it appeared to Aunt Effie, she said. Lieutenant Hathaway had told her that the soldiers would burn the house down with Aunt Effie in it, if Roberta did not go with him. They had already killed Uncle Charley, so Roberta believed him. The war was practically over at that point, and she soon found herself in New Jersey with Hathaway.

He had then taken her west, claiming that he was going to help her bercome an actress. The type of acting he had in mind became clear very soon. They had not even passed all the way through Ohio, when he forced her to take on three men in succession, calling that her "initiation dance."

She was crying again. "It's been that way ever since, Litt. I quit trying to have a private thought a long time ago, 'cause all I ever get out of it is a beating. He's mean, Litt. He killed a man in Arkansas just for trying to talk to me."

Litt looked at his watch again. It was time. "Can I trust you to stay right here till I get back, Roberta?"

She raised her head and wiped away another tear. "Where are you going?"

"I've got to find Hathaway before he finds you. Will you stay in this room?"

She crossed the floor quickly and had her arms around him again. "He's good with that gun, Litt. I'm . . . so afraid."

He halfway carried her back to the chair. "I've got to

go now. Lock the door and don't open it for anybody but me. Will you do that?"

She dried her eyes, then nodded. "Yes," she said.

He was out of the hotel quickly, and walked the two blocks to Smokey's at a fast clip. Just outside the door, he moved his Colt up and down a few times in its holster to make sure it was riding easy. Then he was inside the door. The show was over now, and the room was relatively quiet. Blue stood in his tracks for a while, adjusting his eyes. After a few moments, he saw Hathaway at the back of the room.

The man had also seen Blue. Hathaway came lumbering between the tables, kicking a chair out of his way. He stopped thirty feet away, for he could plainly see that Blue had assumed the gunfighter's crouch.

"Where's Miss Brown?" Hathaway asked loudly. "What have you done with her?"

Blue stood with his legs apart and bent at the knees, every muscle ready to spring like a coiled snake. "Your game is over, fellow," he said.

Hathaway stood very still, as if he knew that any sudden movement might cost him his life. "What . . . who are you?" he asked.

Litt's sky-blue eyes had turned to ice. "I'm that tough son of a bitch that you think you are, Hathaway." When a few men laughed, Hathaway's sullen face began to look even more threatening, but he made no move.

Keeping his eyes locked on those of Hathaway, Blue began to speak to the men around him. "Let me tell you fellows a few things about this no-good bastard. He was a Union officer during the war. He kidnapped my sister in South Carolina and forced her to become a whore. He's been living high off of her body ever since." A loud murmur echoed throughout the room.

Hathaway's face changed colors again, but still he made no move. Then Litt began to wonder why even he himself was waiting around. "Always make the first move yourself, Litt," Lon Bills had told Blue on many occasions. "It gives you an edge." Who would know more about it than Lon Bills? Blue asked himself. Then he made his move. He whipped the Colt from his hip with lightning speed. He pumped two shots into Hathaway's chest, but not before the man got off a shot of his own. Litt had felt the wind from the slug as it passed his cheek and knew that Hathaway had come close to killing him. Blue also knew that he owed his life to the fact that he had taken the advice of his now-dead friend, Lon Bills, for Hathaway had been at least as fast as Litt.

Hathaway staggered at the first shot, and the second put him down quickly. He now lay with his head halfway under a table.

Blue sensed somebody standing to his left, and turned to see Dixie Hall. "I heerd some o' what ya said, big feller." Hall said. "If Hathaway done all that stuff ya said, then I'd say ya done whatcha had ta do. By the way, what's yore name?"

"Littleton Blue."

Hall was silent for a few moments. He dusted tobacco in a paper and began to fashion a cigarette. "I've heerd th' name plenty o' times," he said. "You th' Littleton Blue that ramrodded th' Box M2 Massacre?"

Though Blue did not like the term, he answered the man's question. "I was there," he said.

Hall began to chuckle, motioning toward Hathaway's body. "I'll bet ole Horse didn't have the slightest idear who he was up ag'inst."

At the moment, the town marshal walked through the door. He was a tall, skinny man named Ben

Rankin, and, like Dixie Hall, was a native of Florida. As the lawman drew nearer, Hall spoke to Blue. "Let me do th' talkin'," he said.

"What happened here?" the marshal asked, looking from one man to the other.

Dixie Hall spoke quickly. "Justifiable shootin', marshal. Pure an' simple." He motioned toward Blue. "This here's Littleton Blue." He lowered his voice, and added, "He's th' feller that masterminded th' Box M2 Massacre." Then, raising his voice to its normal volume, he continued. "Ya see, th' deceased wuz guilty o' kidnappin' Blue's sister an' turnin' 'er inta a whore. Then when Mister Blue come ta try ta take his sister home, th' deceased tried ta kill 'im. Now ain't that self-defense, Ben?"

"O' course it is," the marshal said, stepping forward and beginning to go through Hathaway's pockets. He immediately extracted a large roll of bills. "Powerful lot o' money here, Dixie," he said.

"Everything he has belongs to my sister," Blue said quickly. "The money should be given to her."

"Naw," the marshal said, shaking his head emphatically. "Cain't do that. Gotta be some studyin' done on it. Awful lot o' studyin'."

Dixie Hall stepped in front of Blue and spoke to him softly. "Don't push ya luck, big feller. Th' best thang ya c'n do is git ya sister an' git th' hell out o' this town."

Blue thought on the matter for a moment, then decided to take the man's advice. "Thank you, Mister Hall." He was out the front door quickly.

When told of Hathaway's demise, Roberta began to cry again.

"Hey," Litt said, handing her a towel. "Why the tears? I thought you hated the son of a bitch."

When she raised her head, she was laughing. "I did, Litt. Oh, you don't know how much. I guess I was crying because it's over." She got to her feet and hugged her brother tightly. "It's over," she repeated, whimpering softly.

They sat on the bed talking for an hour. Roberta was both surprised and happy to learn that Litt had his own ranch nowadays.

Roberta said that she had not seen Litt in San Antonio. Her sudden departure in the middle of the night had been because Hathaway had a falling out with some man over money, and believed that he would face overwhelming odds if it came to a showdown.

"Is that your buggy down at the livery?" he asked. "The one with the red wheels?"

"Yes. It's the only thing I've ever owned."

"At the first hint of daybreak, I want us to be in the buggy headed west."

"To your place?"

"To my place."

"I'd like that, Litt," she said, kissing him again. "I'd love it." She sat down on her own bed and leaned back on her elbows. "It's finally over," she said.

20

An hour before daybreak, Litt left the hotel, his saddlebags draped across his shoulder. His sister held tightly to one of his hands, the other was wrapped around the Henry. The liveryman complained loudly about being awakened at such an ungodly hour. "I don't know what th' world's comin' to," he said.

"I'd like my horse and buggy," Roberta said to the man. "The big roan."

"Well, now," the hostler said, scratching his head and shaking it at the same time. "I don't know so much about that. I was told not to—"

"You're getting told something else, now," Litt interrupted. "Hitch her roan to that buggy. Then you can trot my chestnut out here." Litt moved one step closer to the man.

"All right," the man said, reaching for a rope. "All right." He headed for the corral without a backward glance.

Litt dumped his saddle and his bedroll in the buggy, then stood by while the liveryman hitched up the roan. After dropping a sack of oats into the vehicle, Blue helped his sister aboard, then paid the liverman for the boarding of both animals. The hostler stared at the money in his hand for a moment, then realized that he had been given a little something extra. "All right," he repeated. "All right."

Blue climbed aboard and placed his coat over Roberta's shoulders, then clucked to the roan and headed south. "First chance we get, we'll buy some grub and something to cook it in. Then we'll get you a bedroll and something to wear. You especially need a warm coat." He knew that they would pass several places where food and utensils could be bought. As for the bedroll and clothing, it would have to wait. They would be in Hillsboro sometime tomorrow morning, and he would give his sister money there, trusting her instinct to buy things that were both pretty and practical. Roberta had nothing. She had been rescued from Horse Hathaway's clutches with no more than the clothes on her back, and flimsy they were.

They found a store just before noon that sold both food and cooking utensils, and bought the things they needed for the trip. Litt also placed a jug of water in the buggy. The store had no bedding or blankets.

They camped at a spring two hours before sunset. Litt gathered a large pile of dead wood, for he knew the night was going to be chilly. He kindled a fire, then watered the horses and put on their nosebags. All the while, Roberta was busy around the fire. A short time later, they sat with their backs against the buggy wheels, eating thick slices of smoked ham. They also had cheese and crackers, and a bag of cookies to go with their coffee.

A few minutes before sunset, Litt spread his tarp behind a cluster of small bushes, then added his blankets and saddlebag. "We're both gonna have to sleep under that tarp and share the blankets," he said, when he returned to the fire. "Otherwise, we'll freeze."

Roberta sat staring into the amber coals. "I can still remember when we slept together every night. Didn't have but one bed."

"Me too," Litt said, exhaling loudly. "Seems like it's been a hundred years, though. I think I was eight years old the year Uncle Charley built that addition out of slabs from the sawmill." He began to chuckle. "The first night you slept by yourself you whined for what seemed like hours. Wouldn't shut up till Aunt Effie agreed to leave the lamp burning in your room all night." He chuckled again.

Roberta failed to see the humor. "It was the first time I'd ever been by myself. I was afraid, Litt. Can't you understand that?"

"I can now," he said. "I couldn't then."

Litt kicked dirt on the fire at dusk, and they went to bed. Lying between the blankets on half of the tarp, with the other half pulled over them for covering, they were soon warm enough. Roberta said her bedtime prayers aloud, then turned over. With his Henry and his Colt close at hand, Litt was asleep quickly.

In Hillsboro, Litt bought blankets and a pillow for his sister while she visited a dry-goods store. When she returned to the buggy, she carried only a coat, shoes, and one change of clothing.

"You need more than that," Litt said, eyeing the one bag.

"No," she said, climbing aboard with no assistance. "That store's expensive. They want two prices for everything, and it's all been out of style for years."

Out of style, Litt repeated to himself. Who the hell decided what was in or out of style? Probably some fat cigar smokers in London or Paris or New York City; people who had never spent a single day away from the paved streets, braving the elements. Style should be whatever kept you warm in the winter or cool in the summer. Nothing more, nothing less. "Humph," he said. He guided the roan out of town and took the road to Waco.

Roberta bought additional clothing five days later in San Antonio. Litt had two quick drinks at a nearby saloon while he was waiting, then returned to the buggy. A short time later, Roberta handed him an armful of packages. "There's more," she said, and returned to the store.

"You did better this time," he said, as they rode out of town.

"They have good merchandise there. Better prices too."

Litt nodded, and whipped the roan to a fast trot. They would have to hurry if they made it to The Spring before dark.

Next day, their journey came to an end two hours before sunset. They had been on Lazy Bee property for quite some time, but Litt had not mentioned it. When they topped the rise, he pointed down the slope to the house and other buildings. "Well, there it is."

"Stop, Litt," she said, putting her hand on his arm.

"Stop right here. Let me just look for a while." She sat wide-eyed with her mouth half open, staring at the house and the river beyond. "Is . . . is all this yours, Litt?"

He nodded. "When I get it paid for."

"And the cattle we've been passing. Are they yours too?"

"Yep."

She squeezed his arm and looked down the slope again. "I'm so glad, Litt, and so proud of you. It's the most beautiful place I've ever seen." She wiped at a tear on her cheek. "If only Uncle Charley could see it."

"Hush," he said, and clucked to the roan.

Roberta adjusted to the ranch life quickly, and was revered by all. Litt could not name a single one of the ranch hands that he had not seen at one time or another staring at his sister admiringly. Two Papas hugged her daily, and treated her like a daughter. Fat Frank never had to set foot in the main house these days, for Roberta had taken over. She not only cleaned the house, she cooked all of the meals for its residents. "Never had a house this good to look after," she once said, after a day of cleaning. "Never even been in one."

Two Papas, who was standing close enough to hear, put his arm around her shoulder. "Some of these things you're working at don't even need doing, girl. Just relax, and take everything a little bit easier."

"Yes, sir," she said, and walked down the hall to her room.

The last week of November turned freezing cold, and the wind blew constantly. Two Papas stayed inside the house for several days, sitting by the fire and complaining about his aching legs and feet. Litt listened attentively, and brought the big man whiskey anytime he asked for it.

The miserable weather blew away the same way it blew in, and by the first day of December it was almost like spring. Litt was sitting on a toolbox at the barn mending a bridle, when Two Papas hobbled from the house on his cane. "I've been thinking that maybe this good weather's gonna hold for a while, Litt. I sure would like to be on the Box M for Christmas."

Blue laid the bridle aside and got to his feet. "All right. We'll leave at sunup tomorrow."

"No, no," the big man said. "You don't have to go yourself, you can just send somebody. You've got your sister to worry about."

"My sister is twenty-one years old, Two Papas, nearly twenty-two. She can look after herself." He stepped closer and put his arm around the big man's shoulder. "You're the only father I ever had. I'll take you home myself."

Two Papas covered Litt's hand with his own, clearly touched by the younger man's words. "You think we should take the buggy, or the wagon?" he asked.

"That's entirely up to you, Two Papas. The buggy would be quicker, 'cause that bay can trot to the Box M in ten days. The covered wagon would be slower, but it'll be a lot drier and warmer if it rains, or the wind starts blowing again."

The big man patted Blue's hand again. "The wagon, I suppose." He turned, and hobbled toward the house.

"I'll grease the wagon this afternoon," Blue called after him. "Get together the things you'll be taking, and I'll load 'em up."

"I guess my crippled ass and some whiskey is about all I'll be taking," Two Papas said over his shoulder.

* * *

The trip to the Box M took twelve days, and was without incident. Two Papas had a good bed in the wagon, and the only things they bought on the way were smoked meat and another case of whiskey. The big man belted down at least a drink an hour for the entire trip. To ease his pain, he said over and over again.

Blue spent a day and night at the Box M, then saddled his chestnut, believing he could make it to the Lazy Bee in seven days. Two Papas had followed him to the barn. "Rope Johnson might be back by the time you get home, Litt. He'll be carrying the money he got for the cattle. Give him a thousand dollars, then put the rest of it in the bank in San Antonio. They'll transfer it on to my bank in Dallas."

Blue gave the cinch a final tug. "Did I hear you right? Give Rope a thousand dollars?"

"A thousand dollars. He's the best there is at what he does, Litt, and there's gonna be a big demand for his services. If we don't pay him, somebody else will. In fact, you'd be wise to send him back to the breaks for another herd in the spring, and let him take 'em straight on to Abilene."

"He might not want to do that, Two Papas. Not after he sees how much money there is to be made. He'll probably want to gather a herd of his own."

"He will go into business for himself eventually, but not yet. I know the man well, Litt, and he's not one to take chances. He'll be perfectly content working for you till he's built up a good stake. Meanwhile, you can get rich while he keeps right on running longhorns to the rails for you."

Blue chuckled, then walked to the water well to fill his canteens. The big man followed. "Sound Rope out on taking another herd up for you before he gets a chance to think on it too much, Litt. If you can get a commitment out of him, you're on your way."

"I will," Litt said, checking to see that his bedroll was tied down tight. He shoved his Henry in the boot, then put his arms around the big man, hugging him tightly. "God, I'm gonna miss you," he said, his voice breaking with emotion. He threw his leg over the saddle, and never looked back.

Three days later, two hours before sunset, Blue stopped at the small town of Gatesville. He stabled his chestnut at the livery and ordered a good feed of oats for the hungry animal. Then, with his saddlebag across his shoulder, and the Henry in the crook of his arm, he walked down the street toward the hotel, passing the double-wall log jail that was said to be escape-proof, with an underground dungeon. He stood close to the famous building for a moment, wondering if indeed there might be prisoners somewhere beneath his feet.

He rented what the desk clerk said was the last vacant room at the hotel, then ate at a restaurant across the street. A few minutes later, he took a seat on a barstool at the Elkhorn Saloon, ordering a pitcher of beer. For the next few minutes he passed pleasant conversation with the bartender, who said his name was Bert. With Litt being his only customer at the moment, the bartender had nothing to do but talk.

A short while later, a man walked through the doorway and took up a position beside Blue. He leaned against the bar. "Is my credit good for another drink, Bert?"

"I guess so," the bartender said. "But there's got to

be a cutting-off place, somewhere. This ain't my whiskey I'm pouring, you know."

Blue pushed money toward the bartender. "Give him a drink on me," he said.

The newcomer seemed to notice Litt for the first time. "Much obliged," he said, lifting the glass to his lips. He was a six-footer who weighed about one-eighty, with brown hair and eyes, and a week-old beard. He smiled broadly, and offered a handshake. "Hank Brady," he said. "Thanks again for the drink. Of course, I can't return the favor, 'cause I ain't got the money."

"Forget it," Litt said, taking the outstretched hand. "My name's Littleton Blue."

"Littleton Blue," Brady repeated softly. Then, speaking even softer, he added, "I've heard that name mentioned in the same breath with the Box M2 Massacre."

Blue sipped his beer, and said nothing. He motioned to the bartender to refill Brady's glass. Brady finally seated himself on the stool, and began to sip the drink slowly. "I guess I'm gonna have to leave Coryell County to find work. Once old man Barber lets a man go, there ain't nobody else around here gonna hire him."

"Barber?" Blue asked, wanting to make conversation.

"Owns the biggest spread in the county, and the other ranchers follow his lead. If he don't want you to work, you don't work."

"Did Barber fire you?"

"Worse than that. He left me to rot in that damn jail across the street. Wouldn't sign my bail bond. I worked for the old bastard for three years, and that's the thanks I get."

Blue sat quietly. He poured himself another mug of beer from his pitcher, and bought a refill for Brady.

"Guess you're wondering how come I was in jail," Brady said after a while.

"None of my business," Blue said, "but it did cross my mind."

"Hell, I don't mind telling you." Brady took a sip from his glass. "Me and my old buddy, Rufus Hinson, were just trying to have a little fun, but the marshal called it disturbing the peace and endangering the lives of innocent bystanders. Hinson had enough money in his pocket to get out of jail right away, but I stayed in there seven days. Finally had to sell my rifle and my six-gun to one of the deputies; only way I could raise enough money to pay my fine." Brady gulped the last of his whiskey, then told the story.

Two Saturdays ago, Brady and Hinson had decided to put one over on the whole town. During the busiest part of the afternoon, Hinson stood at the bar while Brady came through the door and challenged him to a gunfight in the street. Hinson had accepted, and they soon stood in the street facing each other. As soon as a large crowd had gathered on both sides of the street, the two men began to slowly circle each other, thereby putting every single spectator, at one time or another, in the direct line of fire. People began to scramble everywhere, seeking any kind of cover. Brady had heard that one man even jumped through a window. When the men decided that they had carried the joke far enough, they appeared to talk out their differences, and walked back inside the saloon for a drink. The marshal had failed to see any humor in the shenanigan, and promptly threw them both in jail.

Blue agreed with the marshal, but he chuckled at

the story. "Your employer didn't think it was funny either, huh?"

Brady shook his head. "Said somebody should have shot us."

Blue drained his pitcher and sat thinking. He believed that Hank Brady was most likely a good ranch hand, otherwise he would not have been able to hold a job on the county's largest ranch for three years. He appeared to be in his early twenties and in good health. "You say you're looking for a job," Litt said. "Are you willing to relocate?"

"Relocate?" Brady began to smile. "Hell, that's the best thing that could happen to me. I'm broke on my ass, and I've used up all of my credit. Are you saying you've got work for me?"

Blue nodded. "It's the Lazy Bee, in Uvalde County."

"Uvalde County? Ain't that where the Box M2 is?"

"The Lazy Bee is the Box M2. I bought the ranch and changed the name."

"Oh," Brady said, nodding. He sat staring, his hands folded on the bar. "I'd jump at the job, Mister Blue, but I've got one little problem: I ain't got the money to pay off my creditors. Owe six dollars right here at the bar, and a two-week board bill for my horse at the livery."

Blue fished around in his pocket, then slid thirty-five dollars down the bar. "Here's a month's pay in advance. Use it wisely, 'cause it'll be two months before you get paid again." He finished his beer. "Have you got somewhere to sleep?"

"Been sleeping at the livery stable. I rest as good there as anywhere else, and it's free." He sat counting the money in his hand. "Guess you pay thirty-five a month, huh?"

"Thirty-five and found," Blue said, getting to his

feet. "The job will consist of whatever my foreman thinks you ought to be doing at any given time."

Brady nodded. "Thirty-five a month," he repeated. "That's five dollars a month more'n I ever made around here." He signaled to the bartender for another drink. "Old man Barber can kiss my ass."

"Meet me at the restaurant at daybreak," Blue said. "I want to be on the road early." He took two steps, then turned. "Is it true that they have an underground dungeon at the jail, Hank?"

"Hell, yes. I ain't been in it, but I could see down into that hole every time they went to feed somebody by lantern light." He inhaled his drink. "I tell you, it'll make a man think twice before he goes pulling anymore pranks like I did."

"Good," Blue said. "I'll see you at breakfast." He walked to the hotel and went to bed.

21

They reached the Lazy Bee just before noon, five days later. When they topped the rise, Brady stood in his stirrups for a moment, his eyes focused down the hill. He shook his head. "The whole layout looks brand-new."

"We try to keep it looking good," Blue said.

They rode down the hill, and Litt pointed out the cook shack. "After we take care of these horses, you can go in there and introduce yourself. The cook's name is Frank. Tell him you're on the payroll, and he'll feed you."

When Brady headed for the cook shack, Blue walked to the bunkhouse. Litt knew that the long trail drive was over, for he had recognized Rope Johnson's favorite mount in the corral.

Johnson, along with Blackie Elam, was sitting beside the stove, for it was a cold day. He jumped to his feet when the door opened. "Hey! The boss is back," he said, the smile that seldom left his face becoming broader. "Good to see you again, Litt."

Blue stepped forward and grasped Johnson's outstretched hand. "Hello, Rope, you're looking good. How'd the drive go?"

"Had the usual problems, and lost a few head. But I sure didn't have any trouble selling 'em. I could have sold twenty thousand head for top dollar if I'd had 'em." He pointed to the farthest corner. "The money's in that box under my bunk. I'm glad you're back; I'm tired of guarding it."

Blue shook hands with Elam, then turned his attention back to Johnson. "Did you pay the men off, Rope?"

"Paid 'em off in Abilene, and most of 'em scattered to hell and gone. I brought five men back with me, though; paid 'em a dollar a day. I was carrying too much money to be riding alone."

"Good thinking, Rope. We'll put the money in the bank in San Antonio. Two Papas has already instructed them to transfer it on to Dallas."

Blue seated himself at the card table, and Johnson dragged the box containing the heavy money bags over. Litt began to arrange double eagles in neat stacks on the table. "Two Papas said to give you a thousand dollars, Rope." He pushed the money toward the gangling drover. The smile disappeared from Johnson's face, and Litt could see that the man had expected at least as much, probably more. Blue did some quick thinking. "And I'm gonna take it on myself to give you another thousand," he added.

The smile returned to Johnson's face. "I appreciate it, Litt. That's more than fair."

"Got to keep you happy," Blue said. Now was the time, he thought. "Anyway, I've been thinking about asking you to take another herd up for me next spring. You know, drag 'em out of the brakes and drive 'em straight on up to the rails." He sat for a while, waiting for an answer.

Johnson picked up one of the gold coins, tossed it into the air and caught it. "Had something else in mind, Litt." He laid the coin on the table, put another chunk of wood in the stove's firebox, and began to walk around the room. Then he pulled up a chair. "Aw, hell, Litt. For this kind of money, I guess you can count on me." He raised his eyes to meet those of Blue. "It will be the same money, won't it?"

"The same. And a bonus, if all goes well."

The two men shook hands. "You've got a deal," Johnson said. "I'll start draging 'em out about the first of March."

Johnson sacked up his share of the money, then helped Blue carry the remainder to the main house. Blackie Elam had vacated the bunkhouse early on, sensing that the two men wanted to talk business.

Not until he had the money safely under his bed and Johnson had gone to the cook shack, did Litt return Roberta's greeting. "Didn't mean to ignore you," he said, kissing her forehead and hugging her. "I had something on my mind."

"Of course, you did." She squeezed his arm, then hurried to the kitchen. He was soon enjoying beef stew and strong coffee.

His sister joined him for coffee, and sat across the table. "Do you remember a boy who went to school with us named Jack Orr?" she asked.

"Can't say that I do."

"Well, he sure remembers you. Said you threatened to beat him up one time if he tried to talk to me."

"Might have," Litt said, sipping his coffee.

Roberta refilled his cup. "Anyway," she said, "he's living in Uvalde, now. Owns a dry-goods store that he inherited when his aunt died early this year."

Litt refilled his bowl from the pot. "Where'd you learn all this?"

"I had Pete drive me to Uvalde to look at some clothes. I tell you, you could have knocked me over with a feather when I saw Jack standing behind that counter. Almost forgot what I went in the store for.

"Jack used to tend bar at the Buckhorn Saloon. He said he saw you in there last year. He didn't speak to you because he thought maybe you still disliked him."

"I probably never did dislike him," Litt said. "Black-haired fellow about six feet tall?"

"That's him."

"I saw him at the Buckhorn, and I remember thinking that he looked familiar." He pushed his empty bowl aside. "Is all this leading up to something?"

"Well, he offered me a job, wants me to run the store for him starting the first of the year. He says both men and women customers will buy more from a woman." She dropped her eyes to the table. "Especially a pretty one."

"He's probably right." Litt dropped his bowl, cup, and spoon in a pan of water on the cupboard, then stood beside the table. "You're almost as old as me, sis, old enough to make your own decisions. You don't have to work, but if you want the job, take it. I guess this Jack Orr is handsome and single, huh?"

Roberta smiled. "Both."

"Well, I guess it's settled. The first of the year's only

a few days away. I'll drive you down there in your own buggy and help you find a place to live."

"I'll be living at Mrs. Lee's boarding house. It's only a block from the store."

"Oh, you've got it all worked out. All right then, let me know when you want to move out." A few minutes later, he was sitting on the porch with his Henry and a double-barreled ten-gauge leaning against the wall. He had more than fifty thousand dollars under his bed, and lots of people knew it. He would not leave the house until the money was on its way to San Antonio.

They left the ranch at sunup next morning. Joe Getty and Blackie Elam sat in the wagon with Blue, their shotguns hidden under their blankets. Rope Johnson followed on horseback, for he had money of his own to deposit. They camped at The Spring, as usual, and arrived in San Antonio before noon the next day. They drove the wagon straight to the bank, conducted business, then drove to the livery stable, where they turned their animals over to the hostler.

Rope Johnson did not leave his horse at the livery. Saying he had some errands to run, he rode off down the street at a trot.

"I've got some things to do, fellows," Blue said to Elam and Getty. "If I don't run in to you somewhere else, I'll see you at the hotel later."

The men nodded, and Getty spoke to Elam: "Let's go over to Tom's Place, Blackie. Maybe we can get our drinking done before anybody gets drunk enough to pick a fight with us."

Blue leaned against a building, and watching Getty and Elam cross the street. There walked two of the toughest and most highly skilled fistfighters in Texas, he was thinking. Elam was a retired professional, and

Getty ... well, Getty was just "Scrappin' Joe." Litt pitied the drunken cowboy who mistook either man's quiet nature for meekness. He smiled at the thought, then walked down the street.

His first stop was a leather-goods shop, where a Mexican bootmaker measured his feet and accepted a deposit on a new pair of custom-made boots. At another store, he bought a new Stetson, a red flannel shirt, and two pairs of loose-fitting work pants.

He ate two bowlfuls of red beans and rice at a small restaurant, then rented a room at the hotel. He deliberately chose a room with only one bed, for he wanted to be alone for a while. Getty and Elam could fend for themselves.

He lay down on the bed for a nap, for he had not rested well last night. Sleeping on the ground had become difficult for him of late. Maybe living in the big, fancy house had spoiled him, he thought. He pulled the covers up under his chin, for it was cold in the room.

He fluffed up the pillow beneath his head and lay there thinking for a long time. He was already dreading next spring. There had been no fall roundup, and some of the unbranded calves would weigh several hundred pounds by spring. They'd be strong, and difficult to handle. Litt smiled, already knowing that Cecil Hudson would assign the job of wrestling the heavy animals to Elam and Getty. Both were strong men, but the half-grown calves would wear them out long before the day was done. As soon as one of the stout young longhorns was thrown to the ground and branded, Pete Nedd would have another on the end of his rope. Hard work indeed, but Litt would give the men a bonus when the roundup was over.

Which was no more than Two Papas would have

done. Two Papas! In his mind, Litt could clearly see the big man hobbling around on his cane, getting fatter every week. Blue owed him everything, but seriously doubted that he would ever get a chance to repay the big man's generosity. Litt believed that he had seen Two Papas for the last time. He remembered the sallow complexion and inanimate look of the man when he hugged him good-bye at the Box M. His eyes had taken a deeper seat in their sockets, and seemed to look without seeing. He moved about feebly, and his breathing could be heard from several yards away. His coughing had turned into long, loud hacking, and his spittle was the color of charcoal.

At Austin, Waco, and Dallas, Blue had tried to get Two Papas to stop and see a doctor. But the big man would not hear of it. Litt believed the man knew he was slowly dying, and that no doctor could help him. Maybe the whiskey did help, for after each coughing spell he would hit the bottle, then the hacking would stop for a while.

Lying beneath the warm covers, Litt forced his mind to other things, for he loved Two Papas like a father, and the thought of losing the man gave him a sad feeling.

Then Litt began to think of Uncle Caleb. The man was not only a successful farmer, he was an excellent businessman and horse trader. Litt had often heard Uncle Charley say that Caleb had picked himself up by his own bootstraps, that he was a man who could make a living on a flat rock. Litt and Roberta had not known they were poor folks till Uncle Caleb began to visit, always wearing fine clothing and riding in a fancy buggy pulled by a pair of matching dapple-grays. And he always brought gifts for the family. At sometime during each visit he would produce a sackful of cookies and candy for the children. When Litt entered his teens, Uncle Caleb gave him a shotgun to shoot rabbits for the table. Litt learned to use the gun skillfully, and many were the times when the small game he brought home was the only thing Aunt Effie had for the pot.

Litt thought of Uncle Caleb now with reverence. The man had given him a good horse, a mule, and staked him with money, with no mention of repayment. Litt would repay him, all right, and with interest. He expected to return to South Carolina for a visit late next year, and would settle the matter then. And he would offer Aunt Effie a home on the Lazy Bee. Roberta would be long gone by then, probably even married. Having the two women on the ranch at the same time was out of the question. Litt did not believe that Aunt Effie would ever forgive Roberta for riding off with the Yankees, no matter what kind of story she was told. She was a strong-willed woman, and she had made up her mind. Blue chuckled at the thought of having her around the ranch. The cowboys would certainly pick up some new words for their bunkhouse conversations.

When Litt finally dozed off, he slept for more than two hours. He awoke refreshed, and soon began the short walk to Leroy Upton's brickyard. The man sold not only bricks, but all kinds of building material. Blue was interested in some inferior lumber at a cut-rate price to build a chickenhouse; fresh eggs and fried chicken were relatively cheap commodities that were appreciated by almost everybody. Litt also intended to buy a milch cow in the spring, so the men would have fresh milk and butter. He would turn the job of milking the cow and caring for the chickens over to Lanny Henry.

Upton himself answered when Blue knocked at the office door. "Come in," he said. "Haven't seen you in a coon's age. How's Henry?"

"Mister Miles has seen better days," Litt answered. "His health is failing fast, and he's gone back to northeast Texas."

Upton's face showed genuine concern. "I'm sure sorry to hear that, son. Henry's a fine man, and we've been friends for years."

Litt nodded, and accepted the cup of coffee the fat man offered. Upton seated himself on the end of the hardwood counter. "Is there something I can help you with?"

"I want to build a chickenhouse."

Upton thought for a moment, then walked outside. Litt followed. "There's a pile of green slabs out there with the bark still on," Upton said, pointing behind the huge storage building. "I intended to burn 'em as soon as they get dry enough. If you don't want to put your chickens up too fancy, I suppose you can find what you need there."

"I'll take a look," Blue said, beginning to walk away.

"Won't cost you nothing," Upton called after him. "Like I said, I was gonna burn 'em."

Blue looked the large pile of rough, uneven lumber over, each piece a different length and width. He was soon back at the office. "I can get everything I need out there, Mister Upton." He began to chuckle. "Since the price is right, I'll take it all off your hands. I just decided to build a hogpen, too." He inhaled the cup of lukewarm coffee he had left on the counter, then turned toward the door. "I'll send some wagons after the slabs in a few days."

"Get 'em anytime you want," Upton said. "And it was nice seeing you again."

Litt walked to Tom's Place, where he found Elam and Getty sitting on barstools, just inside the door. He took a stool beside Getty and ordered a beer. "I just made arrangements for material to build a hogpen and a chickenhouse," he said. "I'll send Pete and Lanny after it the day after tomorrow."

"Don't care much for the eggs," Getty said, taking a sip from his glass. "I can sure eat my share of the chickens, though."

Blue finished his beer quietly, then got to his feet. "Guess I'll go to bed early," he said. "I want to be rolling toward the Lazy Bee at sunup." Litt smiled when he noticed that both men were drinking tequila. "I'll be leaving now," he said. "I want to have a smaller head than you fellows are gonna have in the morning."

He bought a newspaper from a street vendor, then returned to his hotel room and crawled under the covers.

22

Cecil Hudson was an excellent foreman who knew his business. Sometimes, several weeks would pass without him asking Blue a single question. In the middle of January, he knocked at Blue's door, and he did have a question: "Do you think we could hire a few more men, Litt?"

Blue nodded. "I suppose we can if you say so. Come on in. We'll talk about it." Litt returned to the kitchen and reseated himself at the breakfast table. "Frank just brought me a plate over," he said. "Have a cup of coffee while I finish this off."

Hudson helped himself to some coffee, then took a seat at the table. "Our cows are wandering to hell and gone, Litt, and I just don't have enough men to keep track of 'em. The ones up north are staying in Frio

Canyon, but the others have moved west all the way to the Nueces. Some of 'em might have crossed the river and gone into Kinney County. They won't be easy to find."

Blue sopped the last of his gravy with a biscuit. "We'll have to get some men out there to discourage 'em," he said. "Do you have anybody in particular that you want to hire?"

"No. Blackie Elam knows more cowboys than the rest of us do. I thought maybe we could send him to San Antonio."

Litt got to his feet and dropped his plate in a pan of water. "How many men do we need?"

"At least three. Four would be better."

Blue fished a double eagle from his pocket and laid it in Hudson's hand. "Give this to Blackie. Tell him to get four good cowboys drunk and bring them home with him. By the time they sober up, they'll be on the Lazy Bee payroll."

Hudson nodded, and pocketed the money. "I'll get him on the road this morning." He headed for the door.

"We've got to turn the cattle back at all costs, Cecil," Blue called after the foreman. "I'll saddle a horse myself if you need me."

Hudson stopped in the doorway, and turned to face his boss. "We don't need you, Litt," he said with authority. "A ranch owner is supposed to be at home, where the decisions are made. We're not ever gonna need you." Then he was gone. Blue returned his empty cup to the kitchen. Damn, he thought, chuckling. Can't even ride with my own men.

He poked at the fire for a while, then added more wood to the fireplace. Then he walked to his bedroom and buckled his gunbelt around his waist. He unloaded the Colt, then began to practice his fast draw. "You never get to the point that you don't need to practice," Lon Bills had once said to Blue. "If you get lazy, you'll lose your speed."

Litt had already discovered the truth in that statement. Now, standing behind the closed bedroom door, he began to rip the Colt from his hip, clicking the hammer on the empty cylinder each time he brought the weapon in line with an imaginary target. In less than an hour, his thumb became sore from cocking the weapon, another sign that he was out of practice. A year ago he had a callous on that thumb, and hardly felt the hammer as he went through the cocking motion.

He reloaded the weapon and hung the gunbelt on the bedpost, vowing that he would devote more time to it in the future. These were harsh and lawless times, with all sorts of unpredictable characters running around. A man simply never knew when his very life might depend upon his speed and accuracy with a firearm.

With his heavy coat buttoned up under his chin, Blue began to walk around outside. First to the barn and corral, then through the bunkhouse. With the exception of himself and the cook, the place was deserted. Elam had left for San Antonio, and Hudson had taken the remaining riders west to head off the wandering longhorns.

"Good morning," Fat Frank said, when Blue walked into the cook shack. "It's getting lonesome around here already."

"Likely to be that way for a while," Blue said, helping himself to the coffeepot.

The cook joined him at the table. "Guess you can just tell me what you want to eat," he said. "Nobody to cook for but you and me, till Blackie gets back. The other riders took a wagon with 'em this morning, with tents, bedrolls, and plenty of food. They won't be back for several days."

"I know," Blue said, sipping at his coffee. "Fact is, you're gonna be by yourself in a few minutes. I'm gonna take a ride to Uvalde, see how my sister's making out on her new job."

"She'll be fine," the cook said, rising from the table. "I hope you don't mind me saying so, but Roberta's gonna be fine anywhere she goes. Her looks'll get her by, anywhere in the world."

"Maybe so," Blue said, and left the building.

He rode into Uvalde at midafternoon, and tied the chestnut in front of the dry-goods store. A small bell attached to the top of the door announced his arrival as he entered the building. Expecting to be greeted by his sister, he came to a sudden stop just inside the door. The young woman standing behind the counter smiling was not his sister. Though about the same size as Roberta, with the same type of curvaceous figure, her complexion was much lighter, and her hair was as black as a raven. Her lips were parted on even teeth, and her green eyes seemed to sparkle. "May I help you?" she asked softly.

"Uh . . . I . . . I'm looking for Roberta Blue. I'm her brother."

"Oh," she said, walking from the counter and offering her hand. "You must be Litt. Roberta's told me so much about you."

He grasped the small hand and held it till she pulled it away. "Yes," he said. "I'm Litt."

"I'm Rita Garrison," she said. "You just missed your sister. She walked up to the restaurant with Jack for coffee." She fluttered her long eyelashes and pointed to a chair. "You can have a seat and wait if you like. She won't be gone long."

Litt had never seen a woman who was more beautiful. He had also noticed the absence of a wedding band on her left hand. He looked at the chair, then turned to the young lady, who had moved back behind the counter. He raised his eyebrows. "Maybe you could have some coffee with me after she gets back."

"Maybe," she said, and giggled just right.

Blue seated himself in the chair. During the next half hour, he learned that Rita Garrison lived at Mrs. Lee's boardinghouse for women, where male visitors were never allowed past the living room. She was also Roberta's roommate. She had finished her schooling last year and was now just two weeks shy of her nineteenth birthday. Her job at the dry-goods store was the only one she had ever had. Jack Orr's aunt had hired her right out of school, and Orr kept her on when he inherited the business.

She was an only child; her brother, born two years ahead of her, had died as an infant. Raised on a farm ten miles south of Uvalde, where her parents still lived, she had moved to town for no other reason than to eliminate the daily travel to and from her job. "My father says it's dangerous for a young girl to be traveling alone," she said.

"Your father is right," Litt said. He walked to the counter and stood gazing into her eyes, smiling broadly. "That's why you should never go anywhere from now on, unless I'm there to protect you."

She dropped her eyes, as if embarrassed. "Roberta warned me about you," she said, then giggled again.

The front door opened, and Roberta walked through, followed by Jack Orr. "I told Jack that was your horse at the rail, Litt." She motioned to the man behind her. "I guess you remember Jack Orr, he went to school with us."

Litt grasped the man's outstretched hand. "I don't remember all that much about my school days," he said, "but I saw you at the Buckhorn. Good to meet you."

"Same here," Orr said, giving Blue's hand a firm grip. Litt did not think Orr was a handsome man, even though Roberta had said so. His face was too long, and his ears were not the same size. Litt knew that he himself must be a lousy judge of appearances, however, for the ugliest men always had the prettiest women hanging onto their arms.

Breaking the silence, Roberta motioned toward her roommate. "Have you met Rita, Litt?"

Blue did not answer his sister's question. He looked across the counter to Miss Garrison. "Are you ready?" he asked.

The girl nodded, and grabbed her coat. As they left the building, Litt heard Roberta calling after the young woman: "I told you about him, Rita, better be careful."

At the restaurant, Rita ordered a cup of tea, while Litt settled for strong coffee. "Your folks live south of town?" he asked. "What's your father's name?"

"His name is Pat Garrison, and he's been a farmer all his life. He grows mostly cattle and hog feed now, and keeps about a hundred head of each."

Blue wanted to know more about the girl, but continued to talk about her father. "How does he market his animals?"

"He supplies beef and pork to both of Uvalde's restaurants, and several eating places in San Antonio buy meat from him. Business picked up after the war, and he has about all he can handle now."

Litt nodded, then thought for a few moments. "He hauls meat all the way to San Antonio?"

"Of course not," she said, her tone implying that he had asked a silly question. "He drives the cattle and hauls live hogs in wagons. He has a small slaughterhouse in San Antonio."

"Of course," he said, feeling foolish for only a moment. He covered her hand with his own. "Want something to eat?"

She removed her hand from the table. "Thank you for the offer," she said, "but I couldn't. Mrs. Lee's promised us something special for supper, and she'll be disappointed if I'm not hungry."

He moved a little closer, looking directly into her eyes. She placed her hand in front of her face as if shielding it from a bright light. "Your eyes look like they're on fire," she said. "It's like they could just burn a hole right through somebody."

"I sure wouldn't want to do that," he said, chuckling. "I'll put out the fire." He wiped his eyes with the heels of his hands, continuing to laugh. "Is the fire gone, now?" he asked, raising his eyes to meet hers.

"No."

They talked for another half hour, then the girl said she must be returning to the store. "Just one more thing, Rita," he said, making no effort to get to his feet. "I'd sure like to know you better. Any chance of us going for a buggy ride next Sunday?"

"Yes," she answered quickly. "You think we could ride out to visit my folks?"

"That's what I had in mind," he said, rising from the table.

At the store, he talked with his sister for a while and made arrangements to borrow her horse and buggy on Sunday. "I never knew you to go buggy riding by yourself," she said to Litt, then looked toward her roommate. "So I guess you're gonna have company." Rita smiled, and nodded.

"I'll tell the liveryman to grease the buggy and have it waiting," Roberta continued. "Have fun, you two."

Litt said good-bye to the women, then gave Jack Orr a parting handshake. A short time later, he tied his chestnut to the hitching rail at the Buckhorn Saloon.

Blue was on his second beer, when Jack Orr slid onto the stool beside him. "Just walked down for a beer," he said, signaling to the bartender. "Saw your horse outside."

Litt pushed money forward to pay for the man's beer. "Is Roberta doing all right down at the store?"

"She's doing very well," Orr said, beginning to roll a cigarette. "She's got a knack for dealing with people, and she's learning the merchandise much quicker than I expected. I'll be turning the whole shebang over to her in a month or so."

Blue handed his mug to the bartender for a refill. "I'm glad to hear that, Jack. She seems to be happy with the job."

Orr blew a cloud of smoke toward the ceiling, then changed the subject. "I couldn't help hearing about your ride with Rita next Sunday," he said, taking a drink from his mug. "I'll tell you one thing: You covered more ground with her in just a few minutes, than any of these Uvalde fellows ever have."

"Are you saying she has no suitors?"

Orr chuckled. "Oh, there's a good number of young men around who'd like to think they're suitors. She talks to 'em when they keep hanging around the store, but there sure ain't none of 'em ever managed to get her in a buggy. I'd say that whatever you said to her, you said it just right."

Litt smiled, pleased at what he was hearing. The thought that he might be the only boat on the water gave him a feeling of satisfaction. He had been taken with Rita Garrison, and was looking forward to spending more time with her. As much time as she would allow.

The return ride to the Lazy Bee seemed shorter than usual, for Litt's mind was occupied with thoughts of the beautiful young woman he had met. Rita Garrison was a looker, all right, and had a sense of humor as well. He was looking forward to more laughter with her on Sunday, which was only three days from now. He would let Rita herself set the pace in their friendship, being careful not to do or say something that might scare her away.

He was only halfway home when darkness fell. He relaxed in the saddle and gave his horse its head, for the animal knew the way home as well as its master did. The chestnut quickened its step with each mile, no doubt thinking of the warm stable and bucket of oats that would be its reward for hauling its rider all day.

Litt fed the animal by lantern light, then walked to the house. The absence of a dozen horses in the corral told him that none of the riders had returned to the ranch. Hudson and his crew would probably be gone for a week, maybe longer. The cattle must be halted at the Nueces and driven back east. Any that were allowed to cross the river would be in Kinney County, no more than a day's walk from the Mexican border. Halfway across Kinney County was the town of Brackettville. Any cows that got that far would probably never be seen again by Lazy Bee riders. It was a situation that could not be tolerated. Blackie Elam would probably be back with more riders on Sunday and would immediately head for the Nueces to reinforce

Hudson's six-man crew. With that reassuring thought, Blue doffed his clothing and slid beneath the covers. He was asleep quickly.

On Sunday morning, in Uvalde, Blue unsaddled his mount and released it in the liveryman's corral. Then he stood by while the aging hostler hitched up Roberta's roan. "You say Miss Blue's your sister?" the old man asked, barely missing the buggy wheel with a spurt of tobacco juice.

"Uh-huh."

"Well, I'd say that woman's one of the Lord's great beauties," the man said, adjusting the links of a trace chain and hooking it to the whiffletree. "One of the Lord's great beauties."

"Thank you, sir," Blue said. "That's what some people say."

"It's a fact," the hostler said, spitting another stream of juice. "It's surely a fact."

Ten minutes later, Blue tied the roan to the hitching rail at Mrs. Lee's boarding house. Situated at the corner of intersecting streets, the white, two-story building was on the east side of town. Surrounded by a white picket fence, it had a walkway made of bricks that led to a high porch. He unlatched the gate and made his way up the path, taking the steps two at a time.

A silver-haired woman, her hair piled on top of her head and held there by several combs, answered his knock. "Why, you must be Mister Blue," she said, smiling broadly. "You look so much like Roberta." Before Litt could answer, she added, "And that ain't bad. No sir."

"Yes," Litt said. While he was trying to think of something else to say, Rita Garrison walked into the room, crossing it quickly. "Good morning," she said, offering him the same hand she had refused to let him hold a few days ago.

"Good morning to you," he said, taking the hand. "I'm ready to ride if you are."

She let go of his hand and took his arm. "Lead the way."

As they neared the buggy, Mrs. Lee called from the porch. "Better hang on to that one, Rita. A big ol' purty thang like him ain't s'posed ta be runnin' loose."

The girl hid her face behind her sleeve. "Sometimes she just embarrasses me to death," she said softly.

"Don't let it bother you," he said, helping her aboard the buggy, laughing all the while. "Besides, she just might be right."

He untied the roan, took his seat, and slapped the horse's rump with the reins. The animal settled into its accustomed trot as they took the road south. Litt appreciated the fact that Rita had not gone overboard in dressing for the occasion. She wore a simple dress that covered her ankles, high-top shoes, and a woolen coat with some kind of fur around its collar. Litt was dressed in jeans, flannel shirt, and the same heavy coat he always wore in cold weather. He had a good suit in his closet, but had decided against wearing it. After all, the man he would meet today was a farmer, not a banker.

Pat Garrison's farm consisted of two quarter sections midway between the Frio and the Nueces Rivers, two miles north of the Zavala County line. As Blue rounded a sharp bend in the road, he could see the farmhouse half a mile away. He stopped the buggy and unbuckled his gunbelt, placing it under the blanket with his Henry.

"Thank you," Rita said. "I was hoping you'd do that."

He nodded, and squeezed her hand.

As they rode into the yard, Pat Garrison walked down the steps and took the horse's bridle. Then he helped his daughter to the ground, a big smile on his face. "About time you came home, girl. Your mother's dying to see you."

Rita made the introductions, and Litt jumped from the buggy, taking Garrison's outstretched hand.

The farmer was not a big man, probably six inches shorter than Blue and fifty pounds lighter. He appeared to be in his early forties, and his dark hair was sprinkled with gray. His eyes were the same sparkling green as his daughter's, and his weather-beaten face was the color of leather. "Good to meet you, Mister Blue," he said, pumping Litt's hand. "And I appreciate you bringing Rita home. You the same Littleton Blue that bought the Box M2?"

Litt nodded, and released the man's hand. "I renamed it the Lazy Bee."

"I've heard your name plenty of times," Garrison said, "like everybody else in the county." He took a step backward, looking Blue up and down. "I'll say one thing: You're sure about the healthiest-looking fellow I've seen lately." He motioned toward the house, and began to lead the way. As they neared the steps, he added, "I think renaming your ranch was a very wise decision, Mister Blue."

Litt said nothing, hoping that Garrison would sense that he had no desire to talk about the so-called Box M2 Massacre. The incident was now history, and Blue had every intention of letting it remain so.

Just inside the front door, Litt was introduced to Rita's mother. Ida Garrison's eyes were a pale blue.

Otherwise, she was simply an older and smaller version of Rita herself, with her coal-black hair showing no hint of gray. At the introduction, she hugged Litt's waist, for she could not reach his shoulders. The lady was less than five feet tall. "It's so nice to meet you," she said. "And thank you for bringing Rita home."

"The pleasure was all mine," he said. "She's a beautiful young woman, just like you."

"Aw, go on now," she said, shaking her head. "Anybody with good eyesight can see that I'm not young, anymore."

A short time later, the men were at the feedlot. A Mexican farmhand had just poured the troughs full of grain, and the fat steers were busy feeding. Walking alongside the pen, Blue ran his hand along the broad back of one of the animals. "Being penned up with nothing to do but eat puts weight on 'em in a hurry, huh?"

"Lord, yes," Garrison said quickly. "I'd say they'll average dressing out a hundred pounds more, and the meat's not tough and stringy like grass-fed cattle. People want tasty, tender beef nowadays, and feeding grain is the only way to get it. You can't even give away a damn range steer at the restaurants."

Blue was impressed with Garrison's operation. He had cattle and hog pens of all sizes, connected by an intricate network of gated chutes. Isolating one or a dozen head could be accomplished by simply pulling on a metal lever, which dropped a miniature wall in front of an animal's nose.

And Litt liked Pat Garrison. Through hard work and perseverance the man had carved out his own niche in a harsh area, and had even made most of his tools. He answered questions quickly and directly, and did not ask too many of his own. Maybe Garrison did not ask questions because he already knew the answers, Blue was thinking. After all, he had been here twenty-two years, and seemed to know Uvalde County like the back of his hand. And he would surely know about the Lazy Bee's cattle operation. It was all public information, and easily obtainable.

At the dinner table, Blue stuffed himself with Ida Garrison's cooking: beefsteak, baked ham, hot biscuits, potatoes and gravy, and a large slice of apple pie. The meal was eaten quietly, which pleased him. He had always agreed with Uncle Charley, who insisted that mealtime was for eating, not talking.

An hour later, Rita stood in the yard with one arm around each of her parents, as Blue stood by waiting to help her into the buggy.

"You take care of our little girl, Litt," Ida Garrison said, as Blue lifted Rita up.

"Yes, Litt," her father said. "We've enjoyed having you. I'm looking forward to seeing you again."

Blue liked what he was hearing. All day both parents had called him Mister Blue. Now it was Litt. A good start, he decided. He tapped the roan on its rump and headed toward town, waving good-bye over his shoulder.

"Did you like my folks?" Rita asked when the buggy was underway.

"Sure," he said. "Liked them very much."

"I'm glad." She held on to his arm with both hands. They were half a mile out of Uvalde, when she moved closer to him, squeezing his arm. "If you're gonna be wanting to kiss me, I wish you'd do it now," she said. "We're almost to town."

He stopped the buggy. He brushed her lips lightly with his own, then pulled her to him. She allowed him to put one arm under her coat so that he could feel her body, then clung to him for a long time, returning his wet kisses.

Then she pushed herself away, removing his probing hands and sliding to the end of the seat. "No more, Litt. I'd like to go home now."

He did not argue, just slapped the roan with the reins, confident that his day would come.

At the boardinghouse, he helped Rita to the ground. "Next Sunday?" he asked.

She giggled, and smiled seductively. "Next Sunday."

He walked her inside the house, where she squeezed his hand and headed for her own room.

Mrs. Lee stood by, watching. "Y'all have fun?" she asked.

Blue nodded. "Had an enjoyable day."

"Well, that's good," she said. "I don't know where Roberta got off to. I guess she's off with Jack Orr. I tell you, them two stay together from daylight till dark. I don't know why they don't jist git married, save all this runnin' around."

"I don't either," he said, heading for the door. He truly did wish his sister would marry Jack Orr. Or somebody. Anything to keep her from drifting into the nightlife again.

He returned the horse and buggy to the liveryman, then saddled his chestnut. Half an hour later, he headed north, whistling an old tune as he rode.

23

ou've got as many cattle as this range will support," Cecil Hudson said to Blue, the first week in February. "Maybe more. We drove more than a thousand head back across the Nueces, and I've got four riders keeping them on the east side. At least two hundred head had crossed the West Nueces into Kinney County. They'll swim a river in a minute if the grazing looks better on the other side."

"I know, Cecil." Blue stepped to the stove and re-filled their coffee cups, then returned to his seat at the kitchen table. "As soon as this year's calf crop is weaned, I intend to send every single one of the older cows up the trail to Kansas. We'll keep nothing but heifers and enough breeding bulls to go around."

Hudson thought for a moment. "I'd sure like to head that drive, Litt. I haven't been anywhere in years." He pushed back his chair. "I'm assuming, of course, that the job will pay a little more than foreman's wages."

Blue got to his feet. "Have you talked with Rope? Have the two of you discussed the route?"

"Uh-huh. Johnson has a written record of every day's travel. Even made mention of the best grazing, and the distance between watering holes. I made myself a copy of his log."

Blue stood scratching his head for a moment, then reached for his hat. "Who's gonna be in charge around here while you're gone?"

"Grady Henry can handle it."

"All right," Blue said, patting the foreman's shoulder. "You've got the job." He chuckled, then added, "And it will mean a raise in pay."

Hudson headed for the corral to lay out the day's work for his men. Blue stood on the porch watching as two men rode north toward Frio Canyon. The remaining riders mounted, crossed the river, then headed west at a fast trot.

Blue received the dreaded letter from Sally Miles the next day at noon. He laid it aside and sat down hard after reading only the first paragraph. Two Papas was dead.

Litt sat at the kitchen table for a long time, staring at the wall. He wiped a tear from his cheek with his sleeve. The man who had meant the most to him was gone. The big man would hurt no more. He had been big, all right: physically, mentally, and spiritually.

Blue walked around inside the house for a while, then returned to his seat and finished reading the letter. Two Mamas said that she had found her husband dead in his bed after getting no response to her repeated calls that breakfast was on the table. The condition of the body suggested that he had died early in the night. They had buried Two Papas in the shade of a tall oak near a landmark that the family called Silver Spring. Two Mamas invited Litt to come and visit the grave.

Blue folded the letter and got to his feet. He had already decided that he would never go anywhere near that grave. What the hell did a grave mean? Nothing. Two Papas was not in that hole, anyway. He had already departed for whatever afterlife fate had in store for him. That mound of clay covered nothing except the feeble shell that had once housed the man Litt loved so well. Blue headed for the front door, knowing that he would never visit the Box M again.

A few minutes later, he rode north on the big bay that all the cowboys claimed was the fastest animal on the premises. Litt was not interested in speed today, however. He held the anxious horse to a walking gait. He rode the same trail that he and Two Papas had ridden together on several occasions.

On top of the mountain, beside Frio Canyon, he halted the horse and sat gazing down into the beautiful valley. He remembered that his generous benefactor had called the view a sight for sore eyes. Four rivers ran through Uvalde County, and Litt could see them all from where he was sitting. Although he had sat in this very spot numerous times before, the view never failed to give him a shortness of breath. And the sprawling Lazy Bee landscape was all his own, a literal gift from a dying man. A man he had known less than three years. Blue was convinced that Two Papas had known he was dying. He had given Litt a clear deed to the ranch knowing that he himself would not live to collect the first payment. And even if he had lived, the big man had sold the ranch to Litt at a price that would have been considered ridiculously low by real-estate men. Blue took one last look into the valley, then wiped his eyes. Two Papas had also loved the ranch, he was thinking, and had trusted Littleton Blue to keep it intact. The big man's trust had not been misplaced.

Litt turned the big horse and headed down the hill. As the ground began to level out, he pushed the animal into a hard run. By the time he traveled half a mile, he was agreeing with the cowboys: The bay was the fastest thing on the premises.

He rode down into the canyon and continued south. Cold weather had begun to loosen its grip on the area, and a few green shoots were already beginning to peek through the older grass that had died on the stem. The cows he had seen today were in good shape, all swollen with calves. The few bulls he had encountered had all kept their distance and eyed him curiously, no doubt relishing the thought of thrusting a horn through him or his horse.

He reached the cabin two hours before sunset. Hank Brady and one of the new riders were busy unsaddling their horses. "Don't know how we missed you, Litt," Brady said. "We just rode right through that canyon."

"You missed me the same way I missed you," Blue said. "The only way to see anything in there is to climb above it. I'm already dreading roundup. Don't know how in the hell we're gonna get 'em out of there."

Brady loosed his horse in the corral. "Ain't but one way to do it. You'll have to hire enough riders to make a clean sweep, beat every bush. Gotta get the wild sons of bitches out of there before we can count and brand 'em. Sometimes, the easiest way is to just rope the calves. When you drag their bawling little asses out of there, the mamas'll come running.

"And you've got to always keep another man handy with a rope in case that cow gets out of hand. You know the old saying about bears: 'If you meet a she-bear with cubs, she might attack; if you get between her and her cubs, she will always attack.' Well, a mean old mama longhorn can sometimes be a hell of a lot like that she-bear."

Brady introduced the new rider as Sam Howard. "Good to meet you," Blue said, shaking the man's hand. "I hope you don't let all this talk of hard work scare you off."

The medium-sized man of about twenty-five shook Litt's hand with no hint of a smile. "I'd ruther be workin' than settin' around', anytime," he said.

Blue nodded, and remounted the bay. "I'll be getting along, now. You men take care." He kicked the horse and headed home at a canter.

He arrived home two hours after dark, and cared for the bay by lantern light. Then, seeing that the lamp was still burning in the bunkhouse, he opened the door. "Two Papas is dead, men. He died in his sleep at the Box M." Not waiting for their reaction, he walked to the cook shack and helped himself from Fat Frank's simmering pot.

Blue had sent Pete Nedd to the Graves Ranch with word that Two Papas had expired. Two days later, John Graves himself came calling at the Lazy Bee. Litt was standing on the porch when the man rode down the hill, dismounted, and tied his horse to the rail.

"Just out riding," Graves said, "and thought I'd stop by here. I sure was sorry to hear about Henry."

"He was just worn out, Mister Graves. They buried him three weeks ago. Come on inside and I'll warm up some coffee."

Graves followed Litt to the kitchen. "I won't be needing any coffee," he said. "I would like to trouble you for a glass and a little water, though." He pulled a bottle of whiskey from his coat pocket. "Get two glasses if you'd like to join me."

Litt got two glasses.

They sat at the table for an hour, with Graves doing most of the talking. Finally, the rancher put the cork in the bottle and got to his feet. He stood for a few moments thinking, then sat down again. "Did you ever hear of a man named Preacher Cross, Litt?"

Blue drained his glass. "Uh-huh. Lon Bills used to talk about him."

Graves uncorked his bottle and poured more whiskey in the glasses. "Did Bills tell you that Cross is a man known to sell his gun to the highest bidder? That he'd probably cut his own grandmother's throat if the price was right?"

"I don't guess he did. He just said that Cross was supposed to be fast with a gun, and wasn't very particular about who he pointed it at."

"Preacher Cross is a professional killer!" Graves said, banging his fist on the table. "He's killed at least a dozen men."

Blue drank the last of his whiskey, then pushed the glass aside. "All right," he said. "So he's a paid killer. Does this have something to do with me?"

"It has everything to do with you." Graves scratched at the label on his whiskey bottle. "The word is out around Uvalde that Cross is gonna try to do you in. It probably has something to do with that Thurston Bull shoot-out."

Blue sat thinking for a while. He could easily remember Lon Bills discussing Preacher Cross. "I believe he's plenty fast," Bills had said, "but I know for a fact that he picks his opponents very carefully. It's easy for a man to get a reputation as a fast gunman, Litt, but that don't mean he's ever fought anybody with know-how." Bills had been silent for a moment before adding, "I wonder how brave he'd be if he had to face a man that he knows is at least as good as he is." Bills had sounded as if he was referring to himself.

"Any word on Cross's connection to Bull?" Blue asked.

"Nope. Makes sense that he would be either a friend or kinfolk, though. Come to think of it, I don't know that Thurston Bull had any friends, so he must be kin."

Graves was on his feet, headed for the door. "You just be careful, Litt. I believe that sawed-off son of a bitch is capable of anything, and it ain't written down anywhere that he'll come at you face to face."

Blue followed the man to his horse. "Do you happen to know where Cross is right now?" he asked.

Graves shook his head. "Don't believe he's in the area yet. Word just got out around the saloons in Uvalde that he's been talking. Cross spends most of his time in El Paso, you know." Graves mounted and turned his horse. "Don't get careless, Litt," he said, and left the yard at a canter.

Blue stood watching the rancher ride over the hill, weaving from side to side. Hope he makes it, Litt said to himself.

He took a seat on the corner of the porch. The afternoon sun was warm, and he sat thinking for a long time. He appreciated the warning he had just received, and knew that he could not sit idly by waiting for something to happen. He must find out more about Preacher Cross, and, if possible, learn when to expect the man.

Litt knew that he himself could learn nothing in Uvalde. He would have to send someone else, someone who was not known there. He was still sitting on the porch when the hands rode in. He watched as they cared for their horses. As they headed for the cook shack, Blue called to Brady, motioning him over. "Have you ever been to Uvalde, Hank?"

"Not yet," Brady said, taking a seat on the step. "Been saving my money to buy myself another gun."

"I've got a spare Colt I'll lend you till you can buy your own," Blue said. "But I want to talk to you about something else. Just go on to the cook shack and eat your supper, then join me in the house."

Brady nodded, and got to his feet. As he walked away, Blue called after him, "Keep this under your hat, Hank. Not a word to anybody."

Brady nodded again, and kept walking.

Hank Brady rode into Uvalde next morning at ten o'clock. His first stop was the dry-goods store. He invited Roberta Blue to the restaurant for coffee, saying that he had an urgent message from her brother. Roberta grabbed her shawl, spoke with Rita Garrison for a moment, then joined him on the street.

Brady selected a table at the rear of the restaurant, well out of earshot of the two customers sitting at the counter. "Litt thinks he's got a problem," he said, after their coffee had been served. "And he needs your help."

Roberta said nothing, just cocked her head and raised her eyebrows.

Brady told her the whole story, pausing occasionally to make sure she understood.

"What can I do to help?" she asked when he had finished.

He thought for a moment, then reached for his tobacco sack. "Did you know that your old friend, Dean Dykes, is entertaining down at the County Seat?"

"I knew he was down there, but I haven't seen him."

Brady touched a match to his cigarette and blew a cloud of smoke toward the ceiling. "Well, Litt wants you to get in touch with the man. He thinks Dykes can find out more than all the rest of us put together. The singer knows Litt, all right, but he don't know he's your brother. We want you to tell him that. Back when Litt was scouring the country hunting you, Dykes is the man who told him where to find you."

"Really? Litt didn't tell me about that."

"No," Brady said, shaking his head. "He wouldn't."

They talked for a full hour. Then, convinced that the girl fully understood the role she was being asked to play, Brady walked her back to the dry goods store. Just outside the door, he took her elbow. "Just remember," he said. "If you see me anywhere around town for the next day or so, don't show any sign of recognition. You don't know me from Adam." He untied his horse, threw his leg over the saddle, and rode down the street. He intended to be a paying customer in every watering hole in town before the night was over, and his boss had supplied the money.

He tied his mount in front of the Buckhorn, and took a barstool just inside the door. The young bartender was there quickly, and Brady ordered a beer. Though he usually drank whiskey, there would be none for him this day. And though it was his normal practice to mentally block out every drunken barroom conversation, today he would be listening—and he would remember.

"Haven't seen you around," the bartender said, pushing the mug of foamy brew down the bar. "New in town?"

"Been here about an hour," Brady said, wiping the foam off his chin with the heel of his hand. "Looks like a pretty good place to slow down for a while."

The bartender appeared to be about eighteen years old, with blue eyes and freckles on his nose. He had a thick shock of blond hair that he had trouble keeping out of his eyes. His voice was deep, and sounded several years older. "I've been around here all my life, and I ain't never heard of nobody starving. You looking for work?"

"Don't know, yet. I might decide to light in this area or I might push farther west. Guess it sort of depends." He took a sip from his mug, then began to roll a cigarette. "I don't have to make up my mind right now, anyway. I saved a little money from my last job." Brady pushed his mug forward for a refill. "By the way, my name's Hank."

The bartender offered a handshake. "My name's Chet Bruno." He refilled the mug, wiped at a wet spot on the bar, then added, "I've got to sweep that dance floor and clean up all them tables in back. If you need something, holler." He dropped a cloth into a pan of water, picked up his broom, and headed for the rear of the building.

Brady sat at the bar long enough to finish his beer and smoke two cigarettes, then got to his feet. He had come to Uvalde to listen to the local talk, and so far there had been none. At the Buckhorn, he had been the only customer.

He mounted his horse and rode past the Barn and the County Seat, but no horses were tied at either saloon. It was simply too early in the day for most drinkers, himself included.

He rented a room at the hotel, then delivered his horse to the livery stable. "Want me ta give 'im a bait o' oats?" the hostler asked, stepping from the cubbyhole that was his office. Though stooped at the shoulders, he was nevertheless a tall man, and skinny as a rail. His dirty brown hair hung past his coat collar, and several of his front teeth were missing. One of his cocked eyes was leveled on Brady, while the other seemed to be looking at the corral. He appeared to be about sixty years old.

"Feed and water him," Brady answered. "I'll do the currying myself."

"Jist as ya say," the man said, taking the horse's rein. "Jist as ya say."

The hostler poured the animal a generous portion of oats, then handed Brady a currycomb. "Gonna be in town long?"

"At least a day or two," Brady said. "Looks like a peaceful place to rest for a while."

The hostler chuckled. "Sometimes it is and sometimes it ain't." He trimmed the corner off a plug of chewing tobacco and poked it into his mouth, wallowing it round and round. "Been more'n one man rode a slab off'n that street out there. Hear tell that thangs is likely ta heat up ag'in if Preacher Cross an' Littleton Blue happen ta be in town on th' same day."

"Yeah? Who are they?"

"Blue owns a spread up in the north end o' th' county. Folks say he wuz th' youngest colonel in th' Confederate Army. Well, him an' his crew wiped out Thurston Bull's bunch a while back, killed Bull, too.

"Now, that' ain't settin' too well with Preacher Cross, an' he's shore th' type o' man that can do sump'm about it. He ain't much bigger'n a flea, but he's th' fastest gun Texas has ever seen."

Brady rehung the currycomb on the wall. "What's Cross's stake in the matter?"

"Hell, he's Bull's nephew!" the man answered loudly. "Bull's own sister's boy."

Brady leaned against the wall and began to roll a cigarette. "Is Cross really a preacher?"

"No, no. His ma named him that when he wuz borned. She prob'ly done it hopin' he would be a preacher, though, cain't never tell."

Brady followed the hostler to the office, where the man resumed his work on a bridle. Brady leaned against the doorjamb. "This Preacher Cross is coming here after Blue, huh?"

"Feller rode through here several days ago sayin' so. I know one thang: Ever'bidy Cross has ever said he wuz gonna kill is damn shore dead. I've knowed that boy jist about all his life, an' he'll do jist what he says. I don't know how many men he's killed, but it's a bunch. He's done time in prison twice fer that very thang. That's where he wuz when Blue killed his uncle, ain't been out but about a month."

"I guess Cross grew up around here, then, huh?"

"No, no. He growed up at Van Horn. I used ta own th' livery stable there, that's how come I knowed 'im. His ma wuz named Dovey. She died while he wuz doin' that first stretch in th' pen. I don't guess Preacher ever knowed who his deddy wuz."

Brady stepped outside, ground his cigarette out with his boot, then returned. "This Preacher Cross sounds like a man to leave alone," he said. "I guess he carries enough men around with him to get the job done, huh?"

"He don't carry nobidy with 'im. Don't need nobidy. He's too little ta fight with his han's, but his six-gun makes up th' differ'nce. I hear tell that Blue's good, but I betcha a damn dollar he cain't handle Preacher Cross. Nobidy else damn shore ain't."

Brady stretched his arms above his head and yawned. "Maybe I'll still be around when the show-down comes. Any idea when that'll be?"

"Any old time now, I guess," the hostler said, squirting a mouthful of tobacco juice into a can. "Cross said he'd be here 'fore th' end o' th' month, an' ya can damn shore count on it."

"Well, take good care of my horse," Brady said. "I'll be in town at least until tomorrow. Do I pay you for his keep now?" Brady made a motion toward his pocket.

The old man shook his head and used the can again. "Ya pay when ya leave. Jist don't fergit."

Brady nodded, and left the building.

During the night he visited every saloon in town and listened in on numerous conversations. The talk only confirmed what he had been told at the livery stable. At midnight, he walked to the hotel and got a good night's sleep.

Next morning, he met again with Roberta Blue. She had indeed been in touch with Dean Dykes. The enter-tainer knew Preacher Cross personally, and unhesitat-ingly called him the scum of the earth. Dykes and

Roberta had worked out a system: Preacher Cross could not possibly make his presence known in Uvalde without Littleton Blue knowing about it shortly thereafter.

Feeling that his mission had been accomplished, Brady saddled his horse and headed for the Lazy Bee.

24

Ten days had passed since Hank Brady's trip to Uvalde, and Blue had gone there three times himself since then, paying nighttime visits to Rita Garrison. He had avoided the town on all three occasions, riding straight to the boardinghouse well after dark, and leaving a few hours later by the same route. The local gossip of his impending showdown with a man named Preacher Cross was never far from his mind, and Litt was taking no chances that he himself might be caught in a vulnerable position.

Blue was not afraid of Preacher Cross, even though he was said to be an expert gunman. "There ain't nobody as damn good as folks like to say," Lon Bills had once said. "A man's reputation always exceeds his ability." Litt believed that to be very true. Whatever his own ability, Blue believed it to be greatly improved, for he had been practicing his fast draw for several hours each day. He was faster right now than at any other time in his life.

He had eaten his noon meal in the cook shack, and was now sitting on the rock beside the Frio. He skated a flat stone across the water, then sat for a while, watching the wind-driven ripples. Though he had spent much of his time thinking about Preacher Cross lately, today his mind was on something else: Last night, just before leaving Uvalde, he had held Rita Garrison in his arms and asked her to marry him. She accepted his proposal eagerly and smothered his face with kisses, saying nothing could make her happier. When Litt had been unable to set a wedding date, she assured him that a two-hour notice was as much time as she needed. She clung to him tightly for a long time, and he felt tears on her cheeks as he kissed her good-bye.

The thought that the beautiful Rita might soon be living in his house—and sleeping in his bed—gave him a warm feeling. And before too long there would probably be children. Rita had said that she wanted three sons, each of them as tall as Littleton Blue. Litt smiled at the thought. He would certainly do his part.

Rita had been surprised but not shocked, when Litt told her that Preacher Cross might be coming to town with revenge on his mind. Though she had never actually seen it, she knew all about the vicious game men played with guns—she had grown up in raw country. "My dad says you're a man who can take care of himself," she said, "and I believe it. Do what you must."

Blue was proud of his decision, and glad that Rita had accepted him. Though she appeared dainty and delicate in her store-bought clothing, she had been born to the land, and was by no means as soft as she looked. Even Roberta, who was usually somewhat less than lenient when passing judgment on both men and women, had pronounced Rita Garrison a strong woman, tough enough to make the hard decisions. All of which was pleasing to Litt. He wanted a woman who could think for herself, and was confident that he had chosen well. Rita understood the ranching life. She had been riding horses since the age of six, and had even spent time working in the fields. Litt got to his feet and headed for the cook shack, a look of satisfaction on his face. He had selected the right woman, all right. The thought that he might have married a girl from the big city, who didn't know a wagon shaft from a singletree, was distasteful indeed.

Rope Johnson, accompanied by three men he had hired in San Antonio, had left for southeast Texas three days ago, driving a herd of extra horses and two domestic oxen. Rope would hire more riders from the Beaumont area and begin to drag the longhorns out of the brakes. He expected to have a herd on the trail to Abilene by the first of June, and return to the Lazy Bee sometime in September.

Cecil Hudson intended to put the older Lazy Bee cows on the trail the first week in August, after they had weaned their calves. Blue would keep nothing but heifers, young steers, and a hundred bulls. Even then his grazing range would be taxed heavily, for as a calf grew larger it required more forage. After the roundup, Litt would solve that problem by driving more of the young stuff into Frio Canyon.

"We built two cabins six miles apart on the east side of the Nueces," Hudson said, when he visited Blue after supper. "Not much to 'em, and a fellow'll have to take his water in a jug, but each cabin'll sleep two men and keep 'em dry in wet weather. Next time the big wagon goes to San Antonio we'll pick up a small stove for each shack."

"Any wood around the cabins?" Blue asked.

"Enough. I'm just gonna put one rider in each one for the time being, see how it works out. They can split up the patrolling chores, do whatever it takes to keep the cattle on this side of the river. We built sheds and feeding troughs for the horses. There's plenty of room for their grain inside the shacks."

"How many horses?"

"Each man'll take two. Probably won't be much hard riding, and the riders can mount fresh horses at noon every day."

"Sounds good to me, Cecil. I guess you'll rotate the men often enough to keep anybody from going crazy."

"Every three days," Hudson said, and headed for the bunkhouse.

Blue had heard that Will Christmas, who had been on the Box M2 payroll during the shoot-out with Thurston Bull's crew, was now working for John Graves. Litt remembered Christmas saying that he had grown up at Van Horn, and had spent much of his time in El Paso before making San Antonio his hangout.

Blue lay on his bed, thinking: Since Will Christmas was a gunman himself, and had come from the same area, wouldn't he know Preacher Cross? Or at least know something about the man? It stood to reason that he would. Tomorrow, Litt would have a talk with the man.

Blue rode into the Graves yard at ten o'clock next

morning and helloed the house. John Graves was on the porch a moment later. "Hello yourself," he said in a raspy voice. "Get down and tie up. Got coffee or whiskey, whichever you want."

Blue dismounted and tied the bay. "I'll settle for some coffee. Might warm me up a little." He followed the rancher to the kitchen.

Graves motioned Blue to a chair, then placed a steaming cup on the table before him. He poured his own cup half full of water and finished filling it with whiskey, stirring it round and round with his finger. "Don't drink much coffee anymore," he said. "Takes a little of this to get me going every morning."

Blue nodded. He had heard the same thing from Two Papas many times. "I understand," he said. He took a sip from his cup. "I came over to talk with Will Christmas, just got to thinking that he might know something about Preacher Cross."

Graves took a drink of his whiskey and swallowed hard, making a face as he did so. "He does. He's even mentioned Cross to me before, so I guess he wouldn't mind talking to you about him." The rancher finished off his drink. "Anyway, you can find out right quick by riding up the hill a quarter of a mile. Will took a wagon up there about an hour ago. He's gonna clean out and box up that spring."

Blue got to his feet. "I'll do that, Mister Graves. Thank you for the coffee."

Litt mounted and rode up the hill, waving good-bye to the rancher, who was standing in the doorway with a fresh drink in his hand. Following the wagon tracks was no problem, for the ground was soft and the wheels had bitten deep. Blue turned east at the top of the hill, and had traveled only a short distance when he saw the wagon. He rode forward and tied the bay to a wagon wheel, then walked to the spring. "Hello, Will," he said, a note of familiarity in his voice. "It's been a long time since I've seen you."

Christmas had been busy cleaning out the ditch carved by the spring's runoff. He stepped to the bank and leaned his shovel against a tree. "Yep. It's been a while." He was a man of medium height, with a thick chest and muscular arms and shoulders. His eyes were the same color as his heavy, gray beard. Prematurely gray, Blue thought, for he gauged the man to be no more than thirty years old. Christmas began to roll a cigarette. "What brangs ya all th' way up here?" he asked.

Blue decided to be straightforward with his questions, hoping to receive honest answers. "I've been told that you know a man named Preacher Cross. Is that true?"

Christmas inhaled, then blew a cloud of smoke. "I don't remember no time when I didn't know Preacher Cross. Me'n him's th' same age, ya know, growed up no more'n a mile from each other."

"I see. You two are friends then?"

"Nope. Not since he turnt out like he did. I thank 'at's what killed his ma. Th' Lord never made a better woman, an' it wuz jist pitiful what all Preacher put 'er through. He wuz doin' time in th' penitaincher ag'in when she died."

Blue shook his head. "Seems like a damn shame, Will."

"Guess ya could say me'n him wuz friends when he wuz young," Christmas continued. "Reckin th' year he cheated me outta th' pony wuz when I got off uv 'im. Me'n him shoveled dirt an' dug ditches fer nearly a month jist ta git th' money ta buy 'at little horse; went halvers, ya know. Well, Preacher ups an' sells th' pony th' very next month without eeb'm askin' me. Never give me none o' th' money, neither. Never could git ta feelin' right about 'im after he done 'at. We wuz fifteen 'at year, an' Preacher started killin' people th' next. First feller he killed was more'n sixty years old."

Blue helped Christmas box up three sides of the spring, sharpening the boards on one end with an ax, then driving them into the sandy bottom with a sledge. When the job was done, they stood beside the wagon for a while. Christmas rolled another cigarette and fired it. "I've heerd all th' talk like ever'bidy else. Folks say Preacher's comin' ta pay ya a visit."

"I've heard that myself," Blue said. "But I've been unable to find out when he's coming."

Christmas took a long drag on his cigarette, then coughed out a billow of smoke. "Couldn't say. Preacher's th' type o' feller ta talk about sump'm fer a while 'fore he does it. Prob'ly thanks he's makin' ya sweat." Christmas chuckled, adding, "'At shirt ya got on looks kinda dry ta me."

"Should I be sweating, Will?"

"Don't righteous know. Ain't never seen ya with a six-gun. Jist listenin' ta talk aroun' th' bunkhouse, most o' th' fellers seem ta thank Cross is gonna bite off more'n he c'n chew. Like I say, I don't righteous know.

"I do know 'at Preacher's fast. He wuz fast eeb'm when he wuz a boy. 'At's how I learned, watchin' 'im. I don't reckin he's slowed down none, shore ain't nobidy been able ta put a hole in 'im."

They talked for a while longer, then Blue rode down the opposite side of the hill, taking the shortcut back to the Lazy Bee. He had heard little that was new to him this morning, but at least he now had a complete physical description of Preacher Cross. He would be able to identify the man even at a distance.

Christmas had said that Cross was a selfish little bastard who cared nothing for anybody, including his own mother. Then why would he be so concerned about the death of Thurston Bull? It was Blue's guess that he was not concerned; that he was simply a man who enjoyed the excitement of killing, and was using his uncle's death as an excuse to add another name to his reputation. The fact that Littleton Blue's name was renowned to some degree had fueled Cross's desire for a showdown.

Litt had no fear of riding around alone as he was doing now, for he did not believe Cross would shoot him from ambush. The man would gain no notoriety by killing Blue quietly. He wanted an audience. He had deliberately put out the word ahead of time to create anticipation. After all, what good was fame if there was no one to applaud?

Litt was not afraid to face Preacher Cross—not in the slightest. He had confidence in his own ability. He knew that his draw was as fast as could be expected of anything human, and that his markmanships was second to none. He would kill Preacher Cross if the man came to seek him out. Nor would he allow Cross to choose the time or the place for a showdown. The game would be played according to Littleton Blue.

Litt had no patience whatsoever with a man whose only ambition was to be a feared gunman. Like the bully on the school playground, who would always meet a kid with a stronger arm, the gunfighter would meet a man with a quicker hand—always. There simply were no old gunfighters, a fact that Preacher Cross had obviously never seriously considered. And two stretches in the pen had seemingly taught him nothing. Puzzled, Blue shook his head and kneed the bay toward home. Why a man would continually lay his life on the line to gain a reputation that would surely lead to his own death, was beyond Litt's understanding.

He encountered dozens of his cattle on the ride home, and saw no cow that was not nursing a calf. The calf crop was going to be good this year, and all were fat and sassy. Sighting the rider, most of the cows skedaddled into the brush, their calves scampering along behind. A few old bulls took their ground and snorted, but made no effort to charge, seeming to realize that Litt was just passing through.

At midafternoon, he unsaddled the bay and loosed it into the corral, then headed for the cook shack. "Got any hot coffee, Frank?" he asked, as the cook got to his feet.

"Got some I can get hot mighty quick," Fat Frank said, continuing to talk as he stoked the stove's firebox. "A boy about twelve years old was up here from Uvalde this morning, brought a message from your sister. I couldn't make nothing out of what he said. Maybe you can."

Blue tensed. "What did he say?"

"Just said to tell you that the mare has foaled, then he went loping back down the hill."

The mare has foaled! Roberta's signal that Preacher Cross was in town. The man was finally here, and there was no question about why he had come. Blue sat quietly till the cook served his coffee. "Thank you Frank," he said. "And I do understand my sister's message." The cook smiled and shrugged his shoulder, then went about his work.

A short time later, Blue was in his bedroom practicing his fast draw. Standing in a crouch, with his feet apart and his body leaning slightly forward, he must have emptied the holster a hundred times, until he was convinced that he could do it no quicker.

When the Lazy Bee riders showed up at the corral shortly before sundown, Blue called Hank Brady to the house. Brady took a seat at the kitchen table and accepted the drink of whiskey he was offered. Litt poured a cup of coffee for himself. "Preacher Cross is in Uvalde, Hank. I got the word this morning."

Brady nodded, and sipped at his whiskey. "I never doubted that he'd show up. He's run his mouth too much to back out now."

"Uh-huh." Blue walked to the window and stared at the cook shack for a few moments, then reseated himself at the table. "I'm not gonna rush off down there, Hank. I've got to give my sister time to play her role." As Brady reached for the whiskey bottle to pour himself another drink, Blue shook his head, and put the bottle in the cupboard. "Not tonight, Hank. You can take the day off tomorrow and drink all you want.

"As soon as you eat your supper, I want you to take a message to my sister. Ride straight to Mrs. Lee's boardinghouse, then back here. Don't go into town under any circumstances, and try not to be seen.

"Roberta will be asleep by the time you get there, and Mrs. Lee will complain about the hour. Just tell her that the message is urgent. She'll get Roberta for you.

"Tell my sister that I said to put the plan into action. She knows what to do. Tell her to send me a message by somebody that she can trust to keep it quiet."

Brady got to his feet. "I'll go see what Fat Frank's got in his pot, then be on my way."

"Take the big roan," Blue said. "He's been resting all week."

Two nights later, the drinkers at the saloon called the County Seat were being entertained by Christy Martin and her old friend, Dean Dykes.

Ten tables sat directly in front of the small stage, all occupied by cheering men. Another twenty drinkers lined the horseshoe-shaped bar, and all eyes were on the beautiful songstress. Preacher Cross was among the men at the bar.

As she went into her second song, Miss Martin stepped from the stage and began to move among the men, Dykes strolling one step behind. She stopped at each table long enough to flirt and sing a few words, then moved on.

Then she sauntered to the bar, stopping at the stool occupied by Cross. The gunman was all smiles. In the most flirtatious manner she could muster, she fluttered her long eyelashes and ran her fingers along both sides of his face, singing softly into his ear all the while. Running her tongue over her lips, she pinched his cheek playfully and winked. Then she cut a wide swath back to the stage.

She had scarcely begun the next song, when Cross walked to the table nearest the stage. He bent over the table and spoke to two men who were seated there. Both men got to their feet and disappeared quickly. With a silly grin, Cross waved to the singer and seated himself at the table.

Preacher Cross was neither handsome nor homely. Aside from his being much shorter in stature than the average man, his appearance was quite ordinary. He was clean shaven with close-cropped, brown hair, and probably weighed about a hundred forty pounds. His hands were exceptionally large, with long, tapered fingers that were now busy rolling a cigarette. He continued to smile as he licked the paper, his green eyes glued to Christy Martin's every move. The Colt .44 that hung low on his right leg was hidden from view by the table.

Continuing her dance routine, the songstress wriggled to the edge of the stage, directly in front of the gunman's table. She bent her body forward, singing every word to him and him alone. Cross began to squirm in his seat and pound his fist lightly on the table, clearly spellbound by this fascinating creature named Christy Martin. He reached for her hand, only to have her pull it away coquettishly. She finished her song to thunderous applause, and stood for a few moments waving to the crowd. Then she stepped from the stage.

Preacher Cross was at her side instantly, hat in hand. "Lord, 'at wuz good sangin', girl," he said, motioning toward his table. "Would ya do me th' honor uv lettin' me buy ya a drank?"

"Well," she said, fluttering her eyelashes again, "maybe just one." She allowed him to lead her to the table.

Cross pulled out the chair, and Christy Martin took her seat. "I know who you are," she said, "because I asked somebody. It's not often that I see a man as exciting as you."

Cross looked directly into her eyes, and his silly grin returned. "Wanna see if I'm as excitin' as I look?"

She allowed him to cover her hand with his own. "I can't get away just now," she said. "I'll be free tomorrow night, though." She motioned toward the crowd.

"Look at all these gossipy people staring at us. I'm not gonna do anything that they know about."

"I c'n put a stop ta all 'at starin'," he said, making an effort to get to his feet.

She grabbed his hand. "No, no. All that would do is call more attention to us." She sat quietly for a moment, appearing to do some hard thinking. "I have an idea, Preacher. If you'll meet me inside the livery stable tomorrow afternoon at four o'clock, we'll make a night of it. I know a place where we can go to get away from prying eyes. I'm a very private woman, and I have my reputation to think of."

Cross licked his lips and squeezed her hand. "I'll shore be there purty thang. Ya c'n count on 'at."

"Tomorrow at four, then," she said, getting to her feet and shaking her finger at him playfully. "Not a word to anybody now."

"Not a word ta nobidy." Cross was also on his feet. "Hate ta see ya leave so quick. Ya ain't eeb'm had ya drank, yet."

"I didn't really want a drink, honey. I just wanted to meet the best-looking man in the house." She blew him a kiss, then disappeared behind the curtain, where Jack Orr was waiting. As soon as she changed her clothes, he led her through the back door and escorted her to the boardinghouse. Half an hour later, Orr saddled a fast horse and headed for the Lazy Bee. He had a message for Littleton Blue.

Preacher Cross left the restaurant the following afternoon at twenty minutes to four, and began the two-block walk to the livery stable. His reason for being in Uvalde was by now common knowledge, and many pairs of eyes watched his every move.

Nobody wanted to miss out on the action. Several young boys, each of them in awe of the well-known gunman, tagged along on the opposite side of the street.

At the end of the first block, Cross stopped in his tracks, pointing. "Git ya little asses back wherever ya come from!" he shouted to the youngsters. "If I ketch ya follerin' me ag'in, I'm gonna gitcha all." The boys reversed their direction and disappeared down an alley.

Cross continued his leisurely walk down the street. As he neared the stable, he glanced at his watch, then dropped it back into his pocket. Five minutes to four. Close enough. As always, both front doors stood completely open, creating a certain amount of light in the front portion of the barn.

Cross stepped inside. "Miss Martin?" he called softly. There was no answer. He stood thinking for a few moments. The place looked deserted, but after all, Miss Martin had said that she was a very private woman. He smiled a little, and took another step forward. "Where are you, Miss Martin?"

A tall figure stepped out of the shadows and into the light. "Your business is with me, Cross. I'm Littleton Blue."

Blue made the fastest draw of his life. Even as he fired, however, he felt the wind from Cross's shot rip past his cheek. Cross now lay dead a few feet away, a bullet hole in his forehead. Litt walked forward and toed the body. Then he began to shake his head. Preacher Cross had definitely outdrawn him. Even though Blue had moved first, the little son of a bitch had outdrawn him, and had missed his target by no more than two inches. Why had he missed? Blue turned around and looked back into the barn where he himself had been standing when the shooting started. The shadows were heavy, and the background was completely dark. The little bastard missed because he couldn't see me, Blue said to himself. He walked out of the stable to meet several men who were approaching, feeling luckier with every step he took.

Seth Coleman, the town's mayor, was the first to speak. "Don't reckon there's no use to ask how the shooting turned out."

Litt motioned toward the stable with his thumb. "Preacher Cross's body's in there. I guess the sheriff'll want to see it so he can decide if he wants to bring charges against me."

"The sheriff ain't gonna do a damn thing," Coleman said. "Everybody in this town knows Cross came here to gun you. I can guarantee you that this is over and done. You just go on about your business." Several men echoed Seth Coleman.

"Thank you, Mayor."

Blue headed up the street toward the dry goods store, his strides a little longer than usual. He could see people standing under the store's awning, and knew that Roberta, Rita, and Jack Orr would be waiting there. He quickened his step when he recognized both women running toward him. He scooped the women up one under each arm and headed for the store, their feet dangling at his sides. Inside the building, he sat Rita on the counter, cupping her face in his hand. "Do you want to marry me tomorrow, pretty lady?"

She was off the counter in an instant, her arms around his waist. "Oh yes, Litt. Yes."

Blue kissed her, then turned to Jack Orr, who was

standing with his arm around Roberta. "You want to be my best man, Jack?"

Orr was slow to answer. "Well ... uh ... not exactly." He hugged Roberta tighter. "We were thinking that you might want to make it a double wedding."

"A double wedding?" Litt looked at his sister, who nodded. "A double wedding," he repeated. "It has a nice sound." He kissed Rita Garrison again.